Cirsova®

P. ALEXANDER, Ed.
Xavier L., Copy Ed.
Mark Thompson, Copy Ed.

Fabulous Novels of High Adventure

A Novella of Romantic Danger and Daring

An Exciting Novelette of Suspense in Space

Six Strange and Stunning Short Stories

Review & Poetry

Fall Issue   **Vol.2, No 12**
2022   **$15.00 per copy**

Cover art for The Impossible Footprint by Tessa Sketch, Wild Stars Illo by Jesse White, Fight of the Sandfishers Illo by Raven Monroe, Copyright 2022. The content of this magazine is copyrighted 2022 by Cirsova and the respective authors. Contents may not be reprinted physically or electronically except for purposes of review without prior permission. Wild Stars® is a registered trademark of Michael Tierney. Cirsova® and Cirsova Magazine of Thrilling Adventures and Daring Suspense are trademarks of Cirsova Publishing. Please support independent science fiction: buy copies for your friends, family and Dr's offices!

The Impossible Footprint

By DAVID SKINNER

Daredevil Dylal O'Lal desires the impossible: to put his footprint on the surface of the sun! Though most insist it cannot be done, the existence of a young woman who proves to be wholly impervious to flames suggests his ultimate feat is achievable!

Put out by Esa Nal's blackened mood—and rather literally put out of our house by her dainty, yet rather dense foot—I found harbor with my friend Ron Ti. He, the greatest of our Venhezian scientists, was willing to interrupt his labors for a few restful games of zhekkas, and so he welcomed me in.

Neither of us played very well. We paid more mind to our glasses of warmed poddaya. It was a lackadaisical afternoon.

When Toj Qul arrived unexpectedly, we had thought we might have a third. "Join us!" I exclaimed as Ron Ti rose from his seat to find another glass. But Toj Qul demurred, having come to Ron Ti not as a friend but as the Chief Diplomat of Interplanetary Affairs.

"Do you," he asked Ron Ti, "know a scientist named Jem Toh?"

The wrinkles on Ron Ti's face wrinkled some more as he searched his expansive brain for some mention of Jem Toh. "Ah, yes. He holds a minor chair in Combustionetics. Never met him, though."

"Hm. Has he some remarkable skill in his science?"

"Actually, if memory serves, he has been disciplined for borderline charlatanism."

"Oh?"

"Yes. I recall his latest assertion to be that a sheet of fire, when projected precisely over a grave, acquires a decodable oscillation that carries the idle thoughts of the dead."

"Hm. Well, Dylal O'Lal has asked to meet him."

"What!" cried I. "The Daredevil of Jopitar?"

"The same." Toj Qul spoke impassively, as he often did. He was never one to get excited, no matter how exciting his subject.

"What in the *far-flung* aethir," queried Ron Ti, with not a little befuddlement, "could Jem Toh offer a man such as Dylal O'Lal?"

"My very question to you," said Toj Qul. "My counterpart from Jopitar was not very specific. He has only asked that Dylal O'Lal be allowed to consult with Jem Toh."

"Intriguing," said Ron Ti.

"Indeed. And given Dylal O'Lal's significance, the Council has insisted that I and you—no lesser diplomat and scientist—directly handle this."

"And I shall make the record of it!" I

brightly interjected, the making of historical records being my profession.

Toj Qul blinked. He smiled. Diplomatically. "To be sure."

"All right," said Ron Ti. "Let me don my highest hat of authority and take you to Jem Toh."

"If you please," said Toj Qul.

Venhez is the oldest of the worlds, the most advanced of civilizations, and its cities are the grandest. Stone and crystal, steel and glass, adorn the riverine landscape and exult to the vaporous sky. Our lucent towers absorb every lucid sign—of lamp and star and Sun—and, in dawning excess, return it sevenfold. A Venhezian metropolis is bereft of shadows.

In our imaginations, of course. I would not be an honest chronicler if I did not confess that some curbs are cracked, some windows grimy, and some alleyways unwelcoming.

And yet, imagination is never only a lie, and there is truly an ancient grandeur and crystalline brightness to every city of Venhez. We may be boasting but we are not deluded when we call our capital city not merely Ash-Tar but—as if it were an avatar of Our Lady of Bliss—Ash-Tar the Splendid.

And among its most splendid structures is the Palace of Revelation. Tremendous cubes and pyramids, sturdy spires and suspended spheres, meld in a glorification of geometry, arranged in proportions that defy disarray and instead suggest a consonant order. Thousands of men study and bustle inside.

What wonders they unleash!

And we—Ron Ti, Toj Qul, and I—walked beyond this splendid Palace, across a boulevard, along a path like many paths that the Palace lays forth, to a modest building that, although mimicking the Palace in its appearance, stood at ease between a Poddaya Café and a Kalion Tablet Shop. A plaque said: *Revelation Annex 28, Chairs 345-354, Volitalogy & Combustionetics*. A list of the resident scientists included the name of Jem Toh.

Ron Ti had indeed donned his highest hat, its brim descending to a mid-shoulder tassel, its peak emblazoned with the Looped Cross. Much as his rank was thereby declared, there was in it as well a kind of humility; for by declaring himself via conventional garb, Ron Ti could pretend that he himself, his well-known visage, was not enough to open every door. As it is, every Venhezian scientist—every scientist among the planets!—instantly recognizes and defers to Ron Ti. The high hat was superfluous.

The director of the Annex was called for, and came scurrying. Ron Ti politely demanded to see Jem Toh. The director was nonplussed—for Jem Toh, it appeared, was not well regarded; but when Ron Ti repeated himself, the director jumped and scurried down the hall, saying, "This way, sir."

Jem Toh's office was no more cluttered than that of any scientist (scientists being neat only in their laboratories). We found him huddled at his desk, flanked by stacks of books and unfiled papers. He was young, almost boyish. When he glanced up at the noise from his door, he beheld Ron Ti and bolted to attention, toppling tomes left and right.

"Ron Ti!" he yelped. "Welcome!"

"Jem Toh," acknowledged Ron Ti. "This is Toj Qul, Chief Diplomat of Venhez, and this is Hak Iri, part-time chronicler."

"And poet!" I added.

"And poet, yes." To the director, Ron Ti said, "You may leave," and the director, with an ill-humored glare at Jem Toh, departed.

Toj Qul began, "I have received word from Mynon O'Non, Chief Diplomat of Jopitar. He tells me that a certain Jem Toh has been corresponding with Dylal O'Lal. Are you that Jem Toh?"

"Yes, I am."

"I am also told that Dylal O'Lal wants to meet with you."

"This is true."

"Why?"

"Well…" Jem Toh brought a thumb to his teeth and nibbled the nail. "O'Lal wrote in confidence."

Softly Toj Qul said, "We ask on behalf of the Council."

"Will you tell them my answer?"

"Would we not?"

Jem Toh said only *tch*.

Toj Qul inquired, "Is it scandalous?"

Jem Toh's eyes went wide. "No, no, no. He's just… planning something."

I asked, "Some daredeviltry?"

Jem Toh raised his fingers excitedly and nodded. "Yes, yes, yes. But we're not ready."

"What," wondered Ron Ti, "has it to do with combustionetics?"

"Everything!" Jem Toh cried, then paused, reluctant to say more.

"Jem Toh," said Toj Qul, "you know that the Interplanetary Law bids we stay to our own worlds, and only by conciliar permission may men travel upon the aethir. I know that neither you nor Dylal O'Lal would ever travel by some outlaw path. Tell me his purpose, and we will lawfully work with the Council to welcome Dylal O'Lal."

Jem Toh frowned. "O'Lal tells me that Mynon O'Non has not been so… *inquisitional*."

Toj Qul might have been annoyed by Jem Toh's impertinence, but Toj Qul never displays annoyance. "The Jopitarians," he replied, "are indulgent of Dylal O'Lal, who is undoubtedly a remarkable man. They approve his every request without question. Are we Jopitarians?"

Jem Toh grunted.

Toj Qul smiled lightly. "Jem Toh, I suspect that your reticence comes from a certain pride. Your studies are off the beaten track, are they not? You are uncovering things unimagined. And the remarkable Dylal O'Lal has sought *your* expertise, *your* assistance, *your* revelation. I do understand. Amazing plans are not casually divulged! I, too, would never want to expose my work prematurely."

Jem Toh's suspicious squint was softening!

"Gentlemen." Toj Qul turned to me and Ron Ti. "Can we not promise to join in Jem Toh's confidence, and withhold any report to the Council? For now, at least? Frankly,

I think I would like to be amazed."

Appreciating the ploy, I and Ron Ti agreed.

"Then we four are bound! What, Jem Toh, does Dylal O'Lal ask of you?"

Relieved that he could share his peculiar science, Jem Toh confided, "He needs my help to put a footprint on the Sun."

It was the signature of Dylal O'Lal to survive an exotic and hazardous place and, at the deepest or highest or farthest point of the hazard, impose a print of his foot. Not of his *boot*, mind you, but of his bare appendage, toes and sole and heel. The print need not always be literal, as into the snow of a tallest mountain or into the mud of a most poisonous hollow. He had also stamped his foot in the beating torrent of a precarious waterfall, in the searing roil of a lava plateau, and in the frigid churn of a comet's tail. Whatever the conditions, his foot was nude, and his stamp, however transient, was made.

Needless to say, his foot—and it was always his left foot—had been battered and ravaged over the years. The financing of his escapades always included a good portion for podiatrists, surgeons, and balms. Yet his foot persisted, and his endurance of its degradation became another sort of challenge.

Do you think this insane? Of course you do! So do I. But then, you and I are not *he*.

The man was compelled! Compelled to confront the Cosmos!

And confrontation does bring injury. To be sure, with every bare footfall, Dylal O'Lal seemed to encourage *gratuitous* injury; but consider another perspective, as written in his autobiography:

I step like an uncovered and uncivilized babe; I make an offering to the Cosmos that allowed me to prevail.

"The Sun!" I blurted.

Jem Toh nodded vigorously. "O'Lal intends a descent to the radiative shoreline, a descent which is doable, if only for the bold; but his real trouble will be that footprint. Remember, the fires of the Sun are not precisely *fires*. Sunfire is not any amalgam of fire, water, earth, or air but is its *own* element. An eruption of the aethir! And most relevantly, it doesn't *burn* what it touches. It *disintegrates*. O'Lal's foot would instantly cease!"

I scoffed. "And what of his leg? His torso? His head? One cannot dip only a toe in the Sun! One would be engulfed from the start!"

"Well, yes," interposed Ron Ti, "but even sunfire can be countered, if only for a while. There are hyper-berulion sunsuits in storage at the Palace of Practicality. I'm sure Jopitar has its own store." He sniffed. "In fact, Jem Toh, I should think this is more a task for the engineers. Protecting Dylal O'Lal's foot without actually *covering* it—although admittedly quite a trick—is a practical matter. You, Jem Toh, are a man of *research*. Are you saying *theory* has changed? Don't tell me you have discovered something *new* about sunfire." He said "new" with a bit of a sneer, as if to remind Jem Toh of his career-stifling enthusiasm for crankery.

"Oh, no, Ron Ti, no, no. I have discovered something about *commonplace* fire. But I expect it has implications for sunfire—for all of the elements, in fact."

"Really?" Ron Ti's skepticism was thick; yet so also was his curiosity. "Do tell."

Jem Toh, in some agitation, came from behind his desk and, leaning in amongst us, said *sotto voce*, "I have evidence that fire can be *ignored*."

Ron Ti raised an eyebrow. "Ignored?"

Toj Qul and I exchanged a wince.

Jem Toh affirmed his own statement with a jiggle of his head. "If we do this right, the sunfire will not disintegrate—nor even *harm!*—O'Lal's foot, because O'Lal will simply *ignore* the sunfire."

"Ignore."

"Yes, yes, yes!"

Ron Ti huffed. "And your evidence that this can be done?"

"I... Wait." Jem Toh tugged at his cuff and consulted his timepiece. "Brilliant! There's a show in half an hour. You can *see*. Let's go!"

We watched him bound out the door.

Though startled, we followed.

And that's how the four of us—a genius, a diplomat, a poet, and a crank—ended up downtown in the nightlife district, enjoying the evening show at Wik Obu's Dazzling Theatre of the Absurd & the Impossible.

Wik Obu has established his theatres in all the great cities of Venhez. The one in Ash-Tar, to which we went, was, perhaps, the most splendid; but it was not essentially different from the others. It had the air of a club, a place of glamour and social display. Jem Toh and I were underdressed; but we two slovens were provided ties. Ron Ti left his obtrusive hat with the cloak-girl and adequately combed his hair with his fingers. Toj Qul, of course, was already finely attired, being ever an impeccable representative of Our Lady's world.

Past the bar—where the ranks of bottles glimmered and the ranks of people clamored—lay the broad pit of the theatre. Arc-shaped tables rose in steps, in the round, from the central squat cylinder of the stage. No vantage was denied to the audience. No deceptions are in Wik Obu's theatres, no backstage, no drapes, no hidden doors. What the audience witnesses might be absurd, might seem impossible, but everyone can clearly see that nothing is faked.

Or so Wik Obu contends.

The marquee had told us that our evening would be graced by The Pin-Cushion Man, The Glass-Eating Woman, The High-Wire Toddler—and the subject of our visit, The Girl Who Cannot Burn. Ron Ti complained that science was surely scarce in such a place. As Jem Toh blanched, I admonished Ron Ti that *all* things are susceptible of reasoned inquiry, even the antics of sideshows. He conceded my point with a chuckle. In any event, none of us had an objection to dawdling in the decadence, to groaning at the dozens of inserted pins, to cringing at the masticated shards, to giggling at the acrobatic three-year-old; but with all that, it was rather a while before The Girl was on. Ron Ti and I met much poddaya and many deep-fried mushrooms.

Toj Qul allowed himself enough Markhurian whiskey to become excitable and yell out more than once. Jem Toh sipped some icy soda water but refrained from joining much of our chatter, rather anxiously awaiting the first presentation of his Evidence and never unaware that the venerable and incisive Ron Ti was sitting beside him.

As the Toddler neared the end of his act and dangled with some panache, Toj Qul whiskily yelled, "The tyke's amazing!"; and though his yell was no worse than the similar exclamations of the crowd, it prompted someone to yell in turn, "You noisy reprobate!"

It was Mor Ag, our friend!

Mor Ag approached us along the riser, his arms wide, his smile big. We acknowledged him with a hearty "Mor!" Several patrons shushed us indignantly. His Love-Girl Lue Jes followed him, tap-tapping in her heels to keep pace with his strides. Her face was merry as ever.

Mor Ag bulked before us, blocking our view of the stage, as if he were a fair substitute for any entertainment. "Imagine meeting you all!" he said, as he plucked some of our mushrooms and started chewing. "And who," he chewed, "is this anxious fellow?"

I answered, "Jem Toh. A colleague of Ron Ti."

"And what brings him among you? Is it his birthday? I hope it's his birthday and we're here to celebrate!"

Remembering our bond of confidence with Jem Toh, Ron Ti replied inaccurately, "No, he just recommended tonight's performance, and we decided to make an evening of it."

"Always good to make an evening of anything!"

"Sit, sit!" invited Toj Qul.

"Yes, dear," put in Lue Jes, her voice politely lowered, "let's sit. We're blocking everything."

As they sat, the crowd started clapping. Not for Mor Ag, but for the Toddler, who had made his conclusive landing. We had missed it. Toj Qul groaned in disappointment. But then the conviviality at our table carried us forward, as stagehands tore down the high-wire and began setting the stage for The Girl.

"You'll enjoy this one," noted Mor Ag. "She truly doesn't burn."

Jem Toh piped up. "It's marvelous, isn't it?"

"Yes. I've seen her performance several times. Always a marvel!"

Ron Ti gave a noncommittal *hmm*.

Soon the stage was set. The lights were dimmed. People who had gone to the bar or the lobby to stretch their legs, now scampered back to their tables. Even Mor Ag turned and quieted.

The spotlight brightened on a walkway, serpentine like a garden path, trimmed not with orchids but with pipes, pipes that opened on the path, some high, some low, like two facing choruses. An alluring young woman—not The Girl, but a barker—appeared. She wore a pompous coat, its buttons large, upon on a low-cut, pinstriped vest, her snug trousers pinned to pointed shoes. Her tilted cap called out with a tremendous feather. Some steps past the end of the path, she gathered our attention by posing, legs apart, profile to the sky, and of a sudden snatched her cap, the feather whipping, and flung the cap behind herself. The pipes whistled and roared. Fire leapt at the cap. The audience squawked. Another instant and the pipes silenced, the conflagration vanished, and the cap descended in ashes.

"Fire!" the woman hollered. "The element of destruction! Of undoing! The *violent* element. The *angry* element. *Devastation!*— if we neglect it. *Ruination!*—if we allow it. The *fearsome* element that must be tamed!"

She drew forward, clasping her hands, and spoke with a theatrical intimacy. "Yet what if fire were powerless? Not defeatable—as by water—nor conquerable—as by earth—but *powerless*. As harmless as the stillest air! What if your flesh were such that the burning cannot *touch* you? Your soul such that the spark cannot *see* you? My flesh, your flesh, may be prey to the flame, and our souls may be obvious to the blaze, but there is one who walks unsuspected by the ingling heat!" She stepped to leave the stage, arms out in presentation, and proclaimed, "I give you—The Girl Who Cannot Burn!"

The Girl entered the light without swagger or flourish. Her rich yellow hair tumbled to her back, crowned by a ring of twigs and flowers. Her neckline opened tentatively to her bosom; her gown wrapped her in petal pastels. Despite her appellation, she was amply settled into womanhood. Yet, in her next movements, her youth was affirmed; for she made no theatrical gestures, but smiled with a child's sweetness and waved at us all with a timid, gentle hand.

On slippered feet she started walking.

Past the first few pipes, nothing happened. I disbelieved that any fire would come. Only a *trick* was in the offing! Then some of the lowest pipes hissed. Fire grasped at her slippers. Fabric began to darken and curl. Her hem caught the bounding flames. Gasps went up. A *trick*, for certain! She hadn't hesitated. Through a garden she wandered. Now pipes belched at her knees—and petals trembled with ignition! The crowd rumbled in astonishment. "Stop it!" some cried. Some rose from their seats. I myself rose with a cry. I was impelled to rush the stage—to knock her away!—to blanket her as I must, and suffocate the burgeoning fire! Mor Ag grabbed my sleeve and snapped, "Wait, wait;" and I beheld The Girl unperturbed, her face brightly serene, her smile held forth for us all, so that none of us need fret. Dumbfounded, heart pounding, I reluctantly sat. Her gown fluttered in burning winds. Sparks ferried patches of cloth. Her hair wafted in the growing cyclone. *Great Guardian Powers, protect her!* Her crown now crackled; the flowers ignited. *Let it be a trick! Else she will die!* The highest pipes now spewed the bluest fires. Still in disbelief, the audience shrieked. The Girl was lost in the furious swirl! Yet she walked serenely. The pipes went silent. Her gown and her slippers unraveled behind her in a feast of combustion.

She left the path and displayed herself, unsinged, unbaked, unburnt, unharmed.

The only flush was in the rose of her undulant nudity, which, to be frank, given the recent inferno, one hardly noticed. Or, to be more frank, one gladly noticed; but we Venhezians, unlike some folk in the Planetary Chain, are not surprised by the absence of clothing, nor, more to the point, scandalized by it. Our Lady Herself is often barely adorned. We are an amorous world.

That said, we are not incapable of modesty. Having made her point about hair and hide emerging unconsumed, The Girl crossed her hands with a downward V of her arms; and as stagehands scurried behind her, extinguishing what fires remained, she awkwardly curtsied.

The audience thundered its awed delight.

Her name was Kol Een. Jem Toh gained us access to the dressing rooms. The bouncers already knew him. He had met Kol Een a while before. When she opened her door, she was entirely clothed, in blue dress and white tights and simple laced shoes. Her hair was drawn back by a perky bow. She hugged Jem Toh with surprising affection. Jem Toh, though smiling, seemed to wriggle away.

We were too many to enter the tiny room and so we packed the hall outside. Jem Toh introduced us each, and we shuffled around to offer Kol Een our nods and handshakes. Mor Ag burst forward and bear-hugged her, exclaiming, "You're a marvel, my dear!" She squeaked and thanked him.

A young woman manifested behind Kol Een, with lips thin and straight—and eyes as narrow as Kol Een's were wide. "Oh!"

said Kol Een. "This is my sister Ah Neet. She's also my—manager, I guess."

Ah Neet asked flatly, "What are you up to, Jem Toh?"

"Nothing! It's Dylal O'Lal. He's ready to visit, and the Council—well—they're involved now."

"The Council *always* gets involved."

Jem Toh shrugged. "Sooner or later, yes."

"Dylal O'Lal is coming?" asked Kol Een, brightly.

Jem Toh nodded. "Yes. Yes, yes." He glanced at Toj Qul. "If he may."

Toj Qul, tamping down his whiskiness, inquired slowly of Kol Een, "Know you of Dylal O'Lal's plans?"

"Oh, yes."

That intrigued us all. I was about to suggest that we perhaps find a place more suited to conversation, when a voice like an avalanche suffused every wall. "Toj Qul! Ron Ti! Give your location!" There was no mistaking the bellow of Hul Jok, the War Prince of Venhez, Supreme Commander of the Forces for Planetary Defense—and best friend to me for twenty-five years, ere the two of us were in our knickers.

I shouted, "Dressing rooms, Hul Jok!"

"Is that Hak Iri?" came the roar.

"Yes!" Upon this, my second shout, faces appeared in opened doors, to cast reproachful stares.

"Are you with Toj Qul or Ron Ti?"

"Both!"

"Stay put!" bellowed Hul Jok.

The ground foretold his titanic approach. Unseen by us he slighted the bouncers—

"Imbeciles, I am Hul Jok!"—and a moment later he arrived. He planted his plinthian boots and, thumbs hooked in his barrel-hoop belt, surveyed our waiting gaggle of eight—crammed there in the hall—and scoffed, "A pen of piglets!"

"You were looking for me?" asked Ron Ti, mildly.

"Did I not call out for you? Yes. And Toj Qul."

"Is something amiss?" asked Toj Qul, soberly.

"No... This reed, is it Jem Toh? And this—oh!" He softened at the sight of Kol Een. "This imperishable rosebud must be she! For *she*," as he squinted at Ah Neet, "seems more a thorn."

Ah Neet scowled. Kol Een flushed on behalf of her sister.

Ignoring Hul Jok's typical tactlessness, I asked, "You know of Jem Toh? And Kol Een? How?"

"Dylal O'Lal is here!"

Toj Qul frowned and levelly declared, "*Most* irregular. The Council has not yet given him permission to journey here."

"He has not landed, Toj Qul. He awaits in orbit. He presumed Venhez would not begrudge him a visit. And whyever would we? He is Dylal O'Lal!"

"Nonetheless—"

"Besides, he's not landing. We're going to him."

"We are?" asked I.

"We are! Come, all of you, even the Thorn. The *Victuri* awaits!"

I snickered. The *Victuri*—greatest aethir-torp in all the Fleet—the death-bringing warship of the War Prince himself!—seemed a bit *inapt* to taxi us up to Dylal O'Lal. I teased Hul Jok, "The *Victuri*? Expecting trouble in orbit?"

"In orbit? Bah. At the Sun—mayhaps!"

"The Sun!" Jem Toh gulped. "I'm not ready!"

Ron Ti grumbled, "Going there *now* does seem premature."

"And it's getting rather late," muttered Toj Qul. "Surely in the daytime..."

Hul Jok guffawed. "It's always daytime where we're headed! Gather yourselves, piglets! We have devils to dare!"

Although no planet has attacked another in untold centuries—the folly of war having been acknowledged throughout the Planetary Chain—no planet is without its War Prince, nor has any abandoned the wisdom of vigilance. No aethir-craft, however small, however innocent its cargo, flies unnoticed by the War Castle of Venhez; and unusual flights are flagged for assessment by the Prince. Because Dylal O'Lal's private sloop, though flying without deception or belligerence, bore only Jopitar's half of the necessary conciliar permission, Hul Jok was duly alerted. When he learned that the pilot was Dylal O'Lal, he kalioned directly. The two conversed. Wisely, Dylal O'Lal was open with the inquisitive Supreme Commander, though he did request discretion. Hul Jok, already a fan of The Daredevil, insinuated himself into Dylal O'Lal's plans, and, rather than prod the Council to permit, made the Council moot by princely declaring Dylal O'Lal a temporary charge of the

Castle.

Thus did Hul Jok take command of the whole affair. But then, taking command is his mode.

Toj Qul truly was disinclined to join us. His fine-tuned schedule did not allow a diversion to the Sun, "much as," he joked, "a diplomat might be useful, should you encounter the Lords and Ladies." He also had to report *something* to the Council—and no doubt unruffle some feathers after Hul Jok's intervention. Finally, he was planning to have a hangover. He offered to inform our respective offices and Love-Girls of our coming absence from Venhez. He assured Jem Toh of our bond of confidence and, with apologies, left.

I imagined Esa Nal's reaction to the news from Toj Qul. Steaming kettles came to mind. Did Esa Nal, of that tempestuous morning, expect her tempestuous kick to launch me off the planet? Of course not! Ah, my short-sighted Esa Nal. Forever launching me off on *some* orbit.

Meanwhile, Mor Ag and Lue Jes, having been told what we were up to (in confidence, of course), eagerly came along. Though Ah Neet fussed about the suddenness of this voyage, Kol Een was giddy to meet Dylal O'Lal. Besides, neither girl wanted to resist Hul Jok. Nor did Jem Toh. Ron Ti was willing to go, prematurely or not, and I was as eager as Mor Ag and Lue Jes.

We rode to the Castle in Hul Jok's chariot, a monstrous limousine that longed to be towing ocean liners. Its interior was more capacious than our recent hallway. Despite my low appointment in life, I am regularly elevated from the common by my ancient friendship with Hul Jok; and so, unlike Jem Toh, Kol Een, and Ah Neet, I did not boggle at the leathered luxury which received us, but only smirked, like one jaded, at their awe. Said I with a chuckle, "Wait till you see the *Victuri*."

For the limousine was an ashman's cart beside that glorious projecticle of Heaven; and just as I had expected, the awe of our three neophytes swelled once, twice, thrice and again, as, in the expansive courtyard of the Castle, they beheld the silver-sheened *Victuri* on the landing pad, and rose in the tower beside it, and crossed the gangplank toward it, and entered its oval hatch. They, like anyone, had seen many an aethir-torp in schoolbooks, newsrolls, and kalion plays—but never in proximity.

Behold!

The fins of sweeping and tapering grace; the mighty berulion hull, not even smudged by cosmic detritus; the intimidating panoply of copper ak-blastors; the five colossal engines akin to bottled volcanoes.

And within!

Within the ship, the trio gawked. Bulkheads and railings sang of white and gold; screens and dials spoke of lightning and light. Let us, though, without further description, stipulate that the *Victuri* was astounding throughout and proceed with our chronicle.

Even the tiniest and oddest of stories and images make their way through the chain of all our planets, and so, by the by, Dylal O'Lal learned about The Girl Who Cannot Burn. He had already been planning his solar descent but was stuck on the matter of his final footfall. He hoped that Kol Een might teach him the *spin of will* that kept herself from burning. He wrote her a letter.

By then she was already cooperating with Jem Toh, who believed that her resistance to fire—although unnatural—was not *magical* but a clue to undiscovered definitional properties of the fiery essence. He was studying her reaction to controlled combustions. She, being a helpful girl, was amenable to his experiments.

So when she welcomed Dylal O'Lal to meet with her, she also suggested that he meet first with Jem Toh, who was (so she thought) nearer an understanding of what, for her, was mostly an unthinking talent. Accordingly, Dylal O'Lal contacted Jem Toh, who, though jealous of his research, recognized that the participation of the respected Dylal O'Lal would give that freakish research an imprimatur of legitimacy.

Thus were three souls aimed to intersect—as it turned out, far above the clouds of Venhez.

Barely troubled by the petty orbital hop, the *Victuri* sailed through the unmoderated pressure of the naked aethir and came aside Dylal O'Lal's sloop. *The Lifted Wing*, as the sloop was known, tapped itself with bursts of gas into an open bay, where it was secured by clambering mecha-men. The bay door was closed, and a gangplank extended.

Dylal O'Lal did not have a limp but there was a small skew to his gait, as if he walked perfectly well but not as you or I walked. He was tall, nearly as tall as Hul Jok, though thinner, his strength not a fortress wall but an anchor's cable. Age and adventure had scraped him a fair bit. Gray touched his hair; yet blue lit his eyes.

We were waiting on the landing. Hul Jok marched out and greeted Dylal O'Lal as if they were established friends, with a clap on the shoulder and a pump of the hand. Dylal O'Lal accepted the familiarity. He twitched in surprise when he recognized Ron Ti. "I hadn't expected *you*, sir," he said with a respectful nod, which Ron Ti returned. Hul Jok laughed. "Worry not, O'Lal, we brought *your* noodler, too. Forward, Jem Toh!" Dylal O'Lal eyed the rest of us—to see which of us men would present himself as Jem Toh—when he saw the only other face he knew. Kol Een's eyes captured his. Her lips amiably turned. She took the hand of the hesitant Jem Toh and, with a tug, encouraged him foward. "This is Jem Toh," she announced, cheerily. Jem Toh sputtered a sort of hello. Dylal O'Lal firmly shook his hand, in a way that lofted the anxious young man. Then he proclaimed, "Miss Kol Een," using that feminine prefix popular on the outer planets, and speaking with a politeness that seemed, to this poet at least, a bit warmed by unplanned pleasure. And toss my every poem out the window, if Kol Een did not respond with a deep and agile curtsy.

Then the rest of us were introduced, not quite as afterthoughts.

Hul Jok is not, himself, a scholar or scientist; yet he can discern excellence in a man of any field. He did not need the prior approbation of all the worlds to judge Ron Ti worthy of admiration; and during his ascension to Princehood, he had sought out the eminent genius and quickly made him a friend.

By the way, and to be honest, just as I would never have experienced periodic luxury, I would never have personally known Ron Ti—nor, for that matter, Toj Qul and Mor Ag, nor the two others of our brotherly circle, Vir Dax and Lan Apo—if not for the vector of Hul Jok, which had drawn me among the Venhezian Elites.

Out of admiration for his friend Ron Ti, long before the events herein, Hul Jok had set aside a laboratory in the *Victuri*, one more elaborate than a warship's usual science nook. And while we had been dallying at Wik Obu's, Hul Jok appropriated pieces of hyper-berulion from the Palace of Practicality—Dylal O'Lal had brought one of Jopitar's sunsuits, but Hul Jok correctly presumed that Ron Ti would need some h-b for experiments—and, at the same time, Hul Jok's adjutant went to Annex 28 to gather Jem Toh's research. Such research would normally be maintained in the Annex's dynamic archive, but Jem Toh's debacle with a so-called Recursively Ignited Unceasing Impetus had shamed the Annex sufficiently that he was instructed to keep his research privately in his office—an office so disorganized that the adjutant, unable to unearth the data pertaining to Kol Een, simply scooped up every paper, scrap-book, and memory pod and deposited the mass in a corner of the *Victuri*'s lab.

To further help the investigation, Hul Jok had thought to invite Vir Dax, whose matchless intimacy with the mechanisms of life might have made sense of the peculiar Kol Een; but Hul Jok ultimately decided against the invitation, believing that Vir Dax's heedless enthusiasm for zoetic inquiry, ever amplified by an unprecedented subject, might result in Kol Een's dissection—a gruesome turn you might think unthinkable, but then you haven't spent time with Vir Dax.

And if you have read my chronicles of other events in which all seven of our circle were participants, you may be curious about the absence, in *this* chronicle, of the precocious Lan Apo. The boy was simply away, in a forest or on a mountain, we knew not which, distancing his mind from the minds of the crowd, whose lies, big and small, pricked at his consciousness. For it is Lan Apo's rare gift to read the true thoughts of men, and it wears on him, at times. He might, indeed, have been able to elucidate some unconscious aspects of Kol Een's brain, relevant to her unflammability; but even if we had simply wanted his company, we already knew, from his Love-Girl Kia Min, that he would be out of touch for a while; and so he, too, like Toj Qul and Vir Dax, did not come with us to the Sun, nor witness what we witnessed.

Hul Jok set our uncomplicated trajectory and left mecha-men to maintain it. We would sail sunward in several lessening orbits, because (so I am told) one cannot sail sunward directly; for the pull of the Sun—enormous enough to corral the planets!—accelerates an aethir-torp, until course control becomes a strain; and therefore a pilot, mecha or not, moderates that pull by approaching the Sun askance. The benefit for us was that Ron Ti and Jem Toh were not rushed in their work.

Fortunately none of the spatial movements affected us within, as we were steadied by the *Victuri*'s gravity imitators.

Once we were on our way from Venhez, it was, per the standard clock in Ash-Tar, only an hour or so before midnight. None of us had thoughts of bed, however. The air was of a dinner party, the sort that would find its peak in the smallest hours. In fact, Mor Ag and Lue Jes, neither averse to any festivity, became our host and hostess, rapidly assembling platters of meats and breads from the mess and mixing what drinks the martial stores permitted (including, of course, not a little of the nectarous pod-daya).

The two scientists and Kol Een were in the lab itself. The rest of us were above, spectating from the observation deck along the lab's perimeter. We were behind reinforced glass and surrounded by devices and monitors, but there were chairs as well and room to mingle. An intercom allowed us to hear and be heard.

"Everyone," Ron Ti called. He stood, arms to his sides, hands in his pockets, narrow to the top of his thinly etched face, like a data spike on one of his jittering graphs. We were his students, called to order. "Earlier today, I was happily playing zhekkas. I

was already neglecting fruitful chores. Now I am bound for the Sun, drafted into investigating an unlikely and ludicrous phenomenon." He coughed. "*Ludicrous*, indeed. I have eyes, however. Evidence is evidence. Jem Toh has confirmed that the pipes and fires at Wik Obu's are genuine. Have you not?"

Jem Toh nodded rapidly. "Yes, yes, yes."

"And he has done his own tests. But trickery *must* be ruled out."

Jem Toh raised a finger. "We do know Kol Een is not a liar."

"Well..." Ron Ti glanced at Kol Een, who blinked under his scrutiny.

Jem Toh insisted, "She has given no evidence of mendacity."

"She seems without guile," Ron Ti conceded.

"She is!"

"Hmph. Granted."

By rationally noting Kol Een's integrity, Jem Toh had only interjected a further fact—or so it could be said. His defense, however, had been *quick*, and firm. Not rational so much as—sentimental. I don't think he realized this. And while he was enjoying his superior's concession, he overlooked Kol Een's gratified gaze.

Ron Ti directed Jem Toh to present his specific findings. Jem Toh scurried to the pile in the corner and rummaged for his notes on Kol Een, which he, unlike Hul Jok's adjutant, easily unearthed. He stuck pods in his pockets; he embraced stacks of paper. He arose encumbered—then hesitated, like a hoarder with no place to settle. He looked on his work. He said *tch* and bit his lip. "I don't expect you to agree with all this." Ron Ti was dismissive of Jem Toh's hesitation, scolding, "Are you a scientist, Jem Toh? Are those your findings? Bring them, then, and let us proceed in our study together."

Was it *ecstasy* I saw in Jem Toh's expression? I believe it was! For the peerless Ron Ti had contradicted Annex and Palace, and accepted Jem Toh as a peer.

So together the scientists reviewed the data theretofore. Certain outcomes Ron Ti selected to see for himself. It was the case, for example, that Kol Een's nail clippings and clipped strands of hair burned quite typically. Her spit boiled as expected, when apart from her. In drawing some blood to likewise boil, Jem Toh pricked one of Kol Een's fingers. She yelped as if hurt. Jem Toh was startled into a spill of apologies. Lightly she suggested he kiss the wound. Obliviously he offered her a small bandage.

Ron Ti also targeted Kol Een's flesh with calibrated jets and wafts of flame. It was far less dramatic than the event at Wik Obu's. No clothes were erased. In its clinical progress it even *bored* us, somewhat—except for Hul Jok, who had not before seen a demonstration of Kol Een's gift, and in delight shouted at Ron Ti to damn the fussy science. "Make it bigger! Hotter!" Ron Ti demurred.

Ron Ti soon concurred with Jem Toh, that there was nothing about Kol Een's *parts* that resisted burning. Rather, something *holistic* protected her. Her wholeness—her form—her *substance*—entailed an immunity to fire. Or, this holistic immunity had been a *potential* within her, brought forth by some condition of her life...

Agitatedly, hands aflutter, Jem Toh cried out, "Yes, yes. Kol Een was not this way as a child. I have considered one very possibly relevant condition! There are many records and oral histories regarding *peculiar* girls. Even girls who walked untroubled through fires. Testimonies go back millennia. And all of these girls, to a one, were past menarche—and they were maidens. Maidens like Kol Een! Kol Een's not a Love-Girl. No man has touched her."

"So *she* says," scoffed Ah Neet.

Kol Een gasped. "Ah Neet! You know I... never... I'm still. I *am*."

"A virgin?" asked Ron Ti, drily.

Kol Een blushed.

Ah Neet snorted. "And what if she is? So am *I*. And trust me, I'm *quite* flammable." She spoke with surprising force and disdain. "Jem Toh gets so *silly* sometimes."

Jem Toh winced. "I've told you, Ah Neet. Maidenhood seems indicated as a factor. There's been patterns, Ah Neet. I've done the research."

Ron Ti responded dispassionately, "While there might be unusual effects of an individual's coital condition, if *such* is the ultimate matter with Kol Een's immunity, then all is for naught if Dylal O'Lal is not the same." He addressed Dylal O'Lal: "Are you a virgin?"

The question was unfortunate. Delivered bluntly, it caused all our stares to strike Dylal O'Lal. He stiffened. His chin rose. His long inhalation was terrible. His eyes widened, but with an angered constraint, a slow swelling of indignation. His face went dark and he gave no answer.

Now, a Venhezian doesn't think much of such a question. Though some, like Kol Een, might be a trifle self-conscious, Venhezians wallow loudly in the mechanisms of love. But, of course, Dylal O'Lal was Jopitarian—and Jopitar is a place different indeed. Their cloud-islands are too small to foster our sort of urban decadence. Jopitarians are, in a word, *rural*, and inclined to the discretion of small communities. And that is no doubt to the benefit of Jopitar. Who am I to say? The Lord of Jopitar had his designs, as did Our Lady of Venhez. We just live in their worlds.

As it was, we were not to learn of Dylal O'Lal's *condition*. Mor Ag wisely intervened. "Come, come," he exclaimed. "We have ogled our men of science enough. They need to work without the weight of our eyes." He stood up energetically. "Besides, my friends, I hate to say it, but this ain't no show of wonders. Ron Ti's no Wik Obu. Ha ha! And *confidentially*, I've had my fill of combustion." He clapped once. "Lue Jes, my Cake, did we not see a deck of cards?"

"We did, my Cookie, we did. Shall I get it?"

"Please do. My boys, some pokah!" Gesturing to a nearby conference table, Mor Ag gently set his hand on Dylal O'Lal's shoulder. Dylal O'Lal grunted and accepted the diversion. Before I followed them and Hul Jok, I glanced down into the lab. Ron Ti was shrugging. I barely heard him mutter, "I think I should check her brain emanations." Jem Toh trembled in frustration,

then joined Ron Ti beside Kol Een, whose cheeks were flush.

Ah Neet stayed where she was and scowled.

Out of deference to our guest, a stranger to Venhez, we played a Jopitarian version of pokah, called Six-of-the-Wind. It was Mor Ag's choice. He, of course, knew perfectly how to play, for his appetites have impelled him to know the customs, languages, histories, beliefs—and games—of every race; and he knows more than any man. Hul Jok played well, having socialized with Jopitarians at interplanetary councils. As for me, I understood Six-of-the-Wind solely in its metaphorical aspects, as manifested in the poesy of Jopitar. That is, I played badly.

Lue Jes kept us in snacks. Our bets were made using various nuts. The conversation rambled; and the one subject, women, that might have been expected among gaming men, was carefully avoided. At one point Dylal O'Lal thanked Hul Jok for providing the *Victuri*. "I suppose I'm taking advantage of you," said Dylal O'Lal, wryly; for otherwise he would have had to engage an aethir-torp robust enough to skirt the Sun. He had been spared a lot of bother— and had saved a lot of money. I remarked that his endeavors must often be logistically and financially complicated. "They usually are," he acknowledged. Then a wistfulness touched him. "But not always." And in the comfortable air of our table, he told us about an early endeavor, one not so elaborate.

"You know that the islands of my world follow the winds. Those winds last for centuries. They create ruts in the sky, and our homes glide through those ruts. Islands congregate on the currents. But air is not earth, it's not even water, and the winds eventually, eternally, separate our islands. For a long time we can connect islands with tubes and trolleys, but one day the strain is too great. When it is clear that two islands are taking different winds, the tubes and trolleys are withdrawn.

"I grew up on Donnelay. All my life we were joined to Carrary. When I was eighteen, the break had come. The tubes were folded up, and the trolleys packed away. All that remained were the colossal cables, which would be halved and drawn in during the Fare Thee Well.

"The night before, I went to Obbin Station. No one was there, not even the workers. No one would see me or stop me. I climbed the barbed fence. I realized later that the barbs had cut me. I hadn't noticed.

"Now, of course, I was not the first to walk across a cable. Blowhards and madmen, fugitives and suicides, and many a daredevil had crossed. But they weren't *me*. I was the first among myself.

"And no, a contented boy doesn't do such a thing. Not a boy with an inheritance, an apprenticeship, an academy path, or..." He stopped. "Or an unbroken betrothal." He stared at the surface of the table, at the heaps of nuts, at the arrays of cards, at nothing and no one. He inhaled deeply. "But a scrapper and thief? He does such a thing.

"I didn't hesitate. I had decided already. There was only the climb. And the walk. The darkness may have steeled me, as if there weren't an abyss below but only an unlit bed of grass. I followed the running lights. My skin strobed with a garish blue. I was safe from passing aero-torps and thopters. Then the grass reminded me of what it was not, as the lightning argued between the clouds—and cascaded deep, where the thunder was forgotten. Above me auroras, red and purple, smeared the downpour from the aethir. Between all I was marked as utterly small.

"Think of it! You spend your time in the streets. You conclude that oblivion is the only promise. Then you stand in the maw of the Cosmos. You *fathom* it. Death no longer toys with you. You toy with Death.

"I was exuberant.

"And, Mr. Iri, it took no money, and my only plan was to put my feet where no one's feet should be." He chuckled grimly. "Perhaps my acts have become overblown. But I will act until the Cosmos tires of me."

Dylal O'Lal's reminiscence would one day be in his autobiography. Prior to our early-morning game, he had publicized the tale only briefly, in one interview or another; and never with the intimacy he vouchsafed us. We were all of us contemplative for a while, even as we ante'd and called. Then, a few crafty bluffs and outrageous hands—and the raucous cries therefrom—and our pointless amusement resurged.

Soon after, Lue Jes leaned in at my side

and whispered, "Hak Iri, could you help?"

"With what?"

"It's Ah Neet."

Hul Jok overheard. "The Thorn? Bah. She complaining about something?"

"Hush, you. She's just... gloomy." Lue Jes kept her voice quiet. "I've been trying to brighten her. Maybe Hak Iri could help."

I shrugged. "I suppose. This game certainly doesn't need me."

Mor Ag snickered. "It does so! You're helping us win."

"Uh-huh. Deal me out. Let's go, Lue Jes."

Ah Neet was watching the work in the lab. I would have let her be in her solitary seat, but Lue Jes, ever the busy hostess, could not bear an unhappy guest—nor, indeed, an unhappy *anyone*. And there *was* something gloomy about Ah Neet.

"Dear," said Lue Jes, "did you know Hak Iri is a chronicler?"

Ah Neet turned slightly. "Yes. He was introduced to me, you know."

Lue Jes giggled. "To be sure. But I mean he will chronicle *this*, our adventure." She slipped to the other side of Ah Neet and sat close beside her, lightly placing a hand on her forearm. "You should tell him how you came to be here."

"By limousine."

Lue Jes merrily laughed. "I meant more *fundamentally*. As the girl who made her sister famous!"

I sat down, too, though I put my chair at a *wee* distance. Helpfully I said, "I *am* curious."

"Are you?" replied Ah Neet. She turned her doubtful face to me. I assured her I was. She muttered, "I already told *her*," jerking her head at poor Lue Jes. I tell you, I was less and less inclined to worry about Ah Neet's festiveness. But Lue Jes's encouraging eyes kept me in place. I declared, "I prefer things firsthand," and raised my palms, invitingly.

Ah Neet sighed. "There's not much to say. Our brothers do jackass stunts on kalio-share. They use 'sister' as an insult to taunt each other. I *repeatedly* knocked them for that. They finally dared me to match them. I told them even Kol Een could do their stupid things. They cruelly chose to hold their arms over a can of burning trash. They endured their usual self-damage. My arm... It hurt for a long time. Kol Een didn't want to do it. I forced her to. You can guess what *didn't* happen to *her* arm..."

It was, of course, a bit of a journey from the amateur wallows of Ah Neet's reckless brothers to the sensational pinnacle of the wonderful Wik Obu. I presumed that Ah Neet had lucidly seen her sister's theatrical potential and exploited Kol Een more adroitly than might her brothers. However, before I could elicit the details from Ah Neet—and, in the process, *somehow* ungloom her and thereby satisfy Lue Jes—we were interrupted by Ron Ti.

"Everyone!" He paused while we all gathered at the glass. "It is clear to me that Kol Een is, as Jem Toh has put it, *ignoring* the fire. Her body—her zoetic matter—is absolutely unremarkable. Despite her conscious uncertainty about the mechanism, there is a definite core of willness in the unwavering specificity of her immunity. Her brain emanations are unusually altered in the presence of the fiery essence, even in the peripheral sorts of burning, as from acid. Things *willful* and *elemental* are implicated. Jem Toh was on the right track. Kol Een uses her mind to suppress the Principle of Excitation."

None of us listening was especially stunned by the claim of willness in Kol Een. (Even I, the lowly Hak Iri, have a middling willness, in that I can project messages with my mind. Very few people on all the planets are as powerful as Lan Apo, but of course nearly everyone can operate will-waftic devices.) What stunned us, rather, was the utterance of the word *Principle*.

We—all of us, you and I—may speak every day of the Elements, of Earth, Air, Fire, and Water—and, when we are pedantic, of Sunfire and Aethir as well—but we naturally neglect that these are the terms of our imprecise, if not incorrect, ancestors. It is not Earth that we discern, but the Principle of Permanence; not Air, but the Principle of Dispersion; not Fire, but the Principle of Excitation; not Water, but the Principle of Flow; not Sunfire, but the Principle of Renewal; not Aethir, but the paired Principles of Ideation and Existence. We have deepened our primitive knowledge—for water is not in fact a pure example of Water the Element, but a subtle amalgam of Principles in which the Principle of Flow predominates.

And to think that Kol Een could willfully reach into the lowest of the Cosmic Strata and directly nullify the effects of a Principle!

Such a claim—based on the data of a known crank and after but a single night of further research—would, from any other man, have been ridiculous; but this man, after all, was the inimitable Ron Ti. His instincts and insights, in the realm of revelation, are incontestable!

"Now," continued Ron Ti, "you might be thinking that if I am correct, as I am, then we are finished here, and Kol Een can offer nothing to Dylal O'Lal. Fire and Sunfire—Excitation and Renewal—are obviously distinct. We have not discovered that Kol Een can suppress the Principle of Renewal. But I wonder. Could she, if she willed it? Perhaps she already has this potential. It may even be a dormant actuality. Fire and Sunfire are as twins, after all.

"So our next step is clear," he proclaimed, in that odd tone of flat indifference that always signaled, from Ron Ti, an excess of internal excitement.

"We must expose Kol Een to sunfire."

Our hubbub of doubt and protest had barely started when Ron Ti, his hands and voice raised to stop us, said, "This should not be unexpected. Whatever she might impart to Dylal O'Lal is not worth imparting if we have not established that it suppresses sunfire. Do you fear I am going to *immerse* the girl? Nonsense. That might wholly disintegrate her and prevent any further tests. We will gather some sunfire—I have the h-b to build a bottle—and I will start with the smallest singe—on the tip of her pinky, I should think."

"Fire spreads!" yelled I. "You'll be inviting the sunfire to rage up her arm and banish her every particle!"

"If the sunfire begins to 'rage,' as you overstate it, I will starve it instantly. There will be a failsafe to convert Kol Een to h-b."

"With the Mineralizer?" asked Mor Ag. "Indeed."

If you have read my chronicle *The Oath of Hul Jok*, you know that the Last Lunarion—whom we, the seven, had defeated and caged in the Museum of Strange Things—eventually, in its bitter fury, will-witched our Love-Girls to free it, and, having willed Hala Fau, Hul Jok's Love-Girl, to steal the *Victuri*, took all our women—our loves!—to the devastated Aerth, the star once green, where it meant to renew the malignant Mounish dominion and, in further salacious revenge, befoul our bewitched women as its Queens. In our pursuit of this despicable Lunarion, we learned that the remaining rulers of Aerth—the grotesque spawn of human Aerthons and demon Lunarions—disposed of their foes by converting them to selenion, the metal peculiar to the Moun. Vir Dax, using his unpalatable but persuasive methods on the Wise Ones of the spawn, obtained for Ron Ti the secret of this mineralization, and indeed, after we had rescued our Love-Girls and liberated Aerth, Ron Ti used his newly built Mineralizer to neutralize the Last Lunarion, reforming that devil into a statue that even now stands in a public square of Ash-Tar, as an assurance to the Planetary Chain that the Lunarion Pollution could never more menace us all.

Hul Jok roared, "Will Kol Een be any less dead? What good exchange could it be, to become stone rather than dust? Bah! That Lunarion may retain its life of awareness, but it, like its kind, is all but immortal. Our Rosebud is only a girl!"

"Who cannot burn," quipped Mor Ag. "Not only a girl, eh?"

Ron Ti retorted to Hul Jok, "I have enhanced my Mineralizer. I can reverse its function. It shall not fail, nor harm."

Then she who faced fatality made the conflict moot. "I am willing," said Kol Een, plainly.

Dylal O'Lal looked at her with admiration. With portent he averred, "None may disregard such a will. Continue with the tests."

Thus we all acceded to Ron Ti's confidence.

There was no Mineralizer on board, but the design for it was whole in Ron Ti's wondrous brain and the material stores of the *Victuri* were immodest. As for how one contrapts a bottle out of hyper-berulion, using the tools in one's own hands, I can hardly say. Even could I, I would not, lest my chronicle become a dismal tract on engineering. I prefer the ignorant astonishment of the poet.

As Ron Ti—with the wide-eyed assistance of Jem Toh—got to his intricate constructions, Kol Een was no longer needed and so departed the lab. She joined us above, settling naturally with her sister.

Kol Een was tired. And hungry. Ron Ti had kept her in sustaining morsels and sips of water (and allowed her breaks to rest), but her time in the lab had been long. Lue Jes caressed Kol Een's cheek in sympathy, lamenting "Poor girl," and, vowing to replenish the child, scampered off to collect something of a meal.

There then were Kol Een, Ah Neet, and I. The other men had drifted back to their table, their game abandoned as they slouched and idly drank. The swell of the dinner party had been pricked and was deflating, as happens when the clock heads dawnward.

We were granted a final flash. Ah Neet glared at her sister, her face wrinkling in anger. She spat at Kol Een, "You idiot. You're being used." Then she stomped off, out of the room, leaving for someplace away from us. Lue Jes was returning with a plate and a glass. She gave both to Kol Een, gently commanding, "Now eat, dear," and hastily followed Ah Neet, energized to dispel an unhappiness.

In the awkward event, I considered leaving myself, but that would have left Kol Een alone, and that seemed unkind. The quiet between us, however, as she wearily ate, offered another sort of awkwardness, and so I asked her, apropos of Ah Neet's outburst, "Why did you agree to be touched by sunfire?"

She hummed thoughtfully. "Because there's more to learn. It's another step in Jem Toh's work. He works so hard. Have you seen how pleased he's been tonight? And Dylal O'Lal still needs to make his footprint. I'm his key. Won't it be wonderful when he steps on the Sun? And if I lose a pinky—or worse, I guess—then, I don't know. We go home."

"I suspect you'll resist the sunfire."

"So do I," she serenely replied. "But to be honest, I don't see what I can teach Dylal O'Lal. Ron Ti says I *will* my resistance. If I do, I don't know how. And *knowing how* is what matters. *How to will it.* If we could make a potion from what I am, I know Dylal O'Lal wouldn't take it. He doesn't want a potion. He endures things *deliberately.* I... don't. I'm not a daredevil. I'm just an impervious girl."

"You seem daring enough. Perhaps *you* could step on the Sun."

"Oh, no, no, no. Ah Neet says the same thing. Put me in a sunsuit and drop me barefoot on the Sun. 'Be the one who actually does it!' She insists I could do anything *he* might. But I don't even want to. He *desires* it. It's what makes him the man he is. Why would I take that from him? It's not my place. He'd be bereft. Ah Neet doesn't see that. And that's why she's angry. You heard her. I'm being 'used.' Fine talk, coming from her. When I was younger, I didn't exactly dream of daily immolations. She's the one who made me The Girl Who Cannot Burn. But even then I don't feel *used* by her. I could always quit. Though why would I? It's a lark!"

"She might also just be scared for you."

"I'm sure she is. I *am* her sister." A tranquility overcame her. "Anyhow, I'm not being used. I'm helping others succeed. That is my success."

Our proper solar orbit was still half a day away. Although Ron Ti and Jem Toh were fervently crafting, to us their work was obscure and soporific. In general our enthusiasm was spent. Hul Jok ended the overlong evening and ordered us to nap—especially Dylal O'Lal, who had volunteered to gather the sunfire and needed to be sharp. Barked Hul Jok, "Get unconscious. Get refreshed. We have battles on the morrow!"

Because Hul Jok, in his princely duties, sometimes literally goes into battle (not against other planets, of course, but against the lawless, such as the Syndicate of Aethir Pirates), and because the neutered mechamen are hardly men-at-arms, the *Victuri* can have an actual crew. And its officers have their cabins. Though Mor Ag and Lue Jes cozily took a single cabin, the rest of us took a cabin each. In mine, on my bunk, I immediately fell asleep.

I dreamt of the Sun.

Not the energetic orb that scientists measure and define; not the furious globe that explorers encircle and savor; not the sphere of roiling Renewal that gathers to itself every other Principle and, in its self-expulsion, infuses the dormant aethir with Light—Precious Light! the Amalgam of All, the Instigator of Matter and Vitality—nay, not *that* Sun.

The Sun I dreamt of was that remembered by our stories, the abode of purity and perfection, the Hearth of the Nobles.

I was a visitor—uninvited and unnoticed. Each of the Lords and Ladies was acting *domestically*, in a setting of luminescent floors and walls, washing garments, baking bread, tending plants, playing zhekkas,

reading in chairs, lounging on couches, planning the worlds, chatting and laughing. I knew, even in my dream, that these busy folk were not human. The Nobles are not a race. None was born; none sire nor bear. Each was as a person *instantiated*, millions of years agone, by the Will of the Great Wisdom; and though they really embody the natures of male and female, they are not precisely men and women. Yet in the Sun they make a home and live warmly as brothers and sisters. My dream affirmed this story.

Then my dream, disturbed and bewildered, leaned into my ear and asked, *Why is nothing disintegrated?* For the rage of the sunfire was in every window; it traversed the floors and walls. Still the domestic objects persisted. Imbued by the recent surfeit of science, I replied to my dream, "Everything is made of hyper-berulion." My dream found that doubtful. *Even the Nobles?* "No, not them. They're simply..." *Ignoring the sunfire?* "Exactly! Just like..." *Kol Een.*

I awoke unsoothed by premonitions.

We had napped well into the next day. We arose, made our morning ablutions, shared in a pot of kofayf, and, after Hul Jok confirmed the *Victuri* was decelerating for final orbit, went as a group to the lab.

I will note that the sisters were mutually civil. Perhaps, when I hadn't been looking, Lue Jes had reconciled them; or, more likely, done was done, Kol Een was resolute, Ah Neet was resigned, and a fresh day was no time for discord.

Ron Ti and Jem Toh, obsessed with their goals, had driven on while we slept. They had finished the Bottle. The Mineralizer still needed quite a few screws and wires. The two men were only a bit twitchy and red-eyed.

Hearing that we had reached the Sun, Ron Ti entrusted the completion of the Mineralizer to Jem Toh, picked up the Bottle, and led us to the bay. We followed as ducklings. He had earlier directed mecha-men to withdraw the sunsuit from *The Lifted Wing*. The sunsuit now hung in the prep area of an airlock, beside a bank of aethir-suits.

Ron Ti displayed the Bottle to Dylal O'Lal. It was a tad larger than a fooskitball. "As I said, it's a simple mechanism. This is the opening for the wispule. As soon as you catch one, release this lever to seal it in. Then signal us, and we will pull you back."

Perhaps you have heard—if not, hear now—that wispules are knotted nodes of sunfire, arising briefly in the sunny chaos; that a wispule, when trapped in h-b, lasts for many hours; that a sharp-eyed man in a sunsuit can snatch a wispule, as he might snatch a fish from a lagoon; that a mecha-man cannot, for its meager mecha-brain is scrambled by the noise of the Sun, nor can a dumb machine remotely controlled, for the response is too delayed.

To be sure, it takes an adroit and patient, keen and swift sort of man to capture an evasive wispule; a man not unlike—a dare-devil. One of which we had on hand.

Dylal O'Lal had been training to wear a sunsuit. He had intended a few dry runs of his descent, none all the way to the radiative shoreline, nor any climaxed by a bared foot. This current task, though having an unanticipated objective, was in most ways merely his first dry run.

He would control his motion in freefall—and even accelerate his swipe at the wispule—using an internal array of will-waftic thrusters. The thrusters employed magnetic bursts instead of gas (which would require ports—fatal holes!—in the h-b suit). Magnetism engages well with sunfire, being a species of Light, one graced with a pinch more Permanence and Flow. Indeed, Dylal O'Lal would be tethered to the *Victuri* by a coiled strand of magnetism, generated by the *Victuri*'s prodigious power plant.

While the rest of us cluttered the edges of the area, Hul Jok assisted Dylal O'Lal. It amused me to watch the giant War Chief, normally a loud and charging boar, tugging on sleeves and pressing on seals, wordlessly and methodically, as if he were wrapping a child for a romp in the snow. But then, prepping a man for the Sun was, even for Hul Jok, a time for calm and care.

The sunsuit was thicker and stiffer than an aethir-suit. Whatever was normally external (such as the air-maker) was stream-lined and completely internal. There was no faceplate, but across the eyes the h-b faded to transparency. On the breast there was a small depression, just enough to catch a shadow, depicting the Curled Cross of Jopi-tar.

Once dressed, Dylal O'Lal stretched a bit to test his limbs. Since the suit ensealed him, he could only converse by kalion; but strung against his neck was a small kali-obox, which, while he was aboard, served as his mouth and ears.

A mecha-man blandly announced through the intercom that we were in stationary orbit. Ron Ti stayed at the airlock station—along with Mor Ag, who would help—to monitor Dylal O'Lal and manage the tether. Hul Jok went to the bridge to steer the *Victuri* himself. The rest of us, being only spectators, decided the bridge was better for spectating and so accompanied Hul Jok.

The *Victuri*'s conning tower, which houses the bridge, is squat, barely a swelling on the hull. Though the towers of most aethir-torps are sensibly windowless and the view outside piped in through feeds, the *Victuri* offers a windowed panorama, port to starboard and round the bow. Hul Jok exacts the unmediated sight of whatever is facing his ship.

And as the *Victuri* was oriented with its decks perpendicular to the radius of the Sun, we beheld the great Solar Disc as our colossal horizon. Turbulent forests of leaping flame crashed upon whirling lakes of fire, repeated over thousands of planets-wide burning plains. And lo! *The glare!* Aggressive illumination all but disregarded the calibrated darkening of the windows, and erased every glow of screen and skin. We flinched and shaded our eyes.

Hul Jok stood before us, arms akimbo, blackened by his own shadow. "A sensible Captain," he said mirthfully, "would orient his ship *away from* the terrible light." He spun and faced the inferno. "But who among us would forgo this magnificence!"

"None," I replied. "But it *is* rather bright."

"Aye! And I have befriended the only poet who prefers comfort to grandeur!"

"Not so!" said I.

And I thought to explain to my friend, by way of correction, that I was not lamenting my lack of comfort but only acknowledging its inevitability in this realm of imperfection. I was nigh tempted to quote my own verse: *So in singularity / Are we by beauty burned / By gaining our serenity / We are in tempest turned.* However, my narcissistic allusion was forestalled when a dozen impacts rang the hull, the *Victuri* lurched and shuddered, and the battle klaxons blared.

We were ambushed!

The ships pummeled us as they hove into view, port to starboard and round the bow, nigh a score of monstrous spheres. Sunfire cloaked each in swirling glare. One might think them peculiar ejecta of the Sun, were it not for the deliberate array before us and the missiles being thrown.

Hul Jok silenced the klaxons. "Hak Iri! Weapons station!"

I had fought alongside Hul Jok and my friends before. Being no warrior, I had been propelled by a formless belligerence. Afterwards, I dabbled in some proper training at the War University. Which is to say that Hak Iri was one poet who could indeed man a weapons station.

Over the intercom Ron Ti called, "What in the *far-flung* aethir is going on?"

"We're at war!" shouted Hul Jok.

Ron Ti scolded, "What did you do?"

"'Tis not my doing! Hak Iri, all batteries! Fire!"

I had aimed the ak-blastors to blanket the enemy. I fired them all. The kick was enough to overcome the *Victuri*'s dampeners. It staggered us. The vibratory pulse rushed to the spheres. Missiles wobbled in the passing pulse. Some few exploded. Others reasserted their vectors. The cloaks of sunfire wavered slightly. We glimpsed metal beneath. The spheres were unmoved.

"Ak-useless," growled Hul Jok.

Our near-point repulsors, which had been active from the start, were not ineffective; but the missiles were remarkably evasive. Survivors struck us with savage bursts of sunfire. The hail should have neatly eliminated us, were our hull not pure berulion. The sunfire struggled. Our unhyper'd hull was thinly cratering, to be sure, and gaining a sheen of lava, but that stalwart berulion scoffed at elimination and reprieved us.

Hul Jok ignored the alarms about the hull. "Torpedoes! Fire!"

Furiously flew our torpedoes. Into the cloaks they disintegrated.

"What I expected," grumbled Hul Jok. "Set all firing to automatic. Blastors steady on the ships. Torpedoes among the missiles. Saturate the field. Let us harry the enemy, at least." As I made the settings, he stepped back from the view of the fiery bedlam. Already the outer layer of the transparent berulion was smearing.

We were alerted to an incoming kalion message. Hul Jok accepted it. We heard a single peremptory utterance. "Surrender."

Hul Jok snorted. His response was as concise. "No." He closed the conversation.

He asked, "Is Dylal O'Lal still on board?"

"Yes," answered Dylal O'Lal, calmly. "We hadn't started yet."

"Good." Hul Jok paused. In the thrumming bombardment he was quiet. Thinking. "Jem Toh!"

Jem Toh was startled by hearing his name. "Uh! Yes? What?"

"Time for some combustionetics. Make me a tiny bomb."

"A bomb?"

"Aye! The shattering sort!"

"Um. What yield?"

"Enough to kill more of them than us!"

"Oh. How many of them are there?"

"Lots! Get to it! Ron Ti!"

"Yes?"

"Join Jem Toh. The enemy are cloaked in sunfire. You put that bomb in the h-b bottle and fix it so it explodes when it's past a cloak."

"Ah! Will do."

"Mor Ag! You will join Hak Iri in torpedo bay six. You and he will jam that bomb into a torpedo."

Mor Ag cried, "On my way."

"Load up at an armory. All of you. And O'Lal?"

"Listening."

"If the enemy doesn't destroy us outright, they will surely board us. They clearly have sunfire weapons. Only you are invulnerable. Keep that suit on. Think you can fight in it?"

Solemnly he replied, "I can fight in anything."

"Correct response! Go with Ron Ti. You will take the bottled bomb to bay six."

"On it."

Hul Jok faced those of us on the bridge. "Hak Iri! Why are you still here? Move!"

I moved.

"And ladies! There's blastors, vests, and helms in that cabinet. Grab one of each, find a nice nook, and aim at that door. We hold this bridge till victory! *Hue hoh!*"

Dire was the moment. Combat was poised to consume us! Hul Jok was all the more elated.

Because we were dispersed in the *Victuri* and our actions were often simultaneous, I was not myself witness to every event. What I know, of course, I know only because we veterans later traded stories. For the sake of this chronicle, however, I will narrate as if, during that hectic half hour, I was omnipresent.

Having assigned us to our missions, Hul Jok took the reins of the *Victuri* and tried to escape. He was in no way fleeing the fight. Our position, however, was rotten. We were melting. We were solely at mercy. We lacked even a prudent path of retreat. The *Victuri* could not stay.

Neither could it escape. Our every maneuver was countered by the spheres, which had englobed us. We remained at their center, however we juked or dashed.

I hurried to the torpedo bay.

I was not unfamiliar with the *Victuri*'s layout but I accosted a mecha-man and bid it guide me. We armed at an armory. We scuttered down ladders and through passages. Several armed mecha-men met us at the bay. Hul Jok had ordered such squads to the bay, the lab, and the bridge. Mecha-men fight poorly—for their imaginations are deficient—but, while serving as fodder, they can shoot in the proper direction.

Had we the time, we could have fabricated an h-b torpedo from our raw h-b. Ideally, had the Mineralizer been operational, we could have simply converted a normal casing to h-b. As it was, we had the Bottle. This limited the size of our explosive, of course, and nothing on hand was sufficiently small and powerful. For many minutes after Hul Jok's directive, Jem Toh fussed over recipes of combustion; until he realized that a small container, unable to deliver a tremendous explosion, could yet trigger an explosive *cascade*.

"Yes, yes, yes!"

Jem Toh exploded with joy; for he had finally remembered his own reckless artistry, and forthwith started recreating his Recursively Ignited Unceasing Impetus.

Ironically Ron Ti, the greater genius, had the duller task of devising a package to seat Jem Toh's Impetus within the Bottle, sense the Bottle's passage through sunfire, and activate the Impetus on the other side. He used data from the *Victuri*'s sensors on the thickness and intensity of the enemy cloaks. Ron Ti's task was *so* straightforward that, inadequately engaged and sagely inclined, he repeatedly offered advice to the busy Jem Toh, who was much too engrossed to be annoyed.

Panting a little, Mor Ag arrived at the

bay.

Our task, as you will recall, was to jam the Bottle Bomb (once we had it) into a torpedo. Before they had separated, Ron Ti had rapidly primed Mor Ag about the panel to open and the internals to push aside. So long as the Bottle was secured, our work needn't be pretty—although, given the potential for an unplanned detonation of the torpedo's existing warhead, we had to work cautiously. We chose a torpedo and gently extracted it from its rack.

The thrum of the assault had never ended, ever swelling, as the hull was shaved and the heat invaded.

On the bridge, the women had tucked in, left, right, middle, behind three different consoles, not in hiding but defensively, their blastors ready to flood the entrance. Lue Jes was the coolest. When the Last Lunarion's will-witching had been suffocated by Hul Jok, our liberated Love-Girls, Lue Jes among them, had set upon the Lyon-Kats, slaying those foul beast-men in a spasm of vengeance. Lue Jes, that is, that happy soul, had been baptized already in blood. Ah Neet was barely anxious, since her thorniness disposed her to a cathartic blasting. As for Kol Een, she who traipsed through holocausts worried more about her sister and us all. Her thoughts, founted by a coalescing sense of loss, notably poured over Jem Toh: *Our Lady of Love, preserve my boy!*

That young scientist and his elder peer were tinkering and hammering. We waited on them. Time aheating!

Under the thrum I was able to pause to consider our enemy. Only one army was known to wield the animus of the Sun. But in what wise should we, of all, be struck by the Guardians of the Hearth? Many an aethir-torp had grazed the Sun; many an explorer had bathed in solar currents. Yet the ire of the Guardians had never arisen. The Guardians had never appeared. However could they? They resided in stories! In the hopes of the Planetary Chain! Agone, agone, these thousands of years! What was it about our expedition—a bare foot on a shoreline!—that should so enwrath the Nobles, that myths were manifest?

An unexplained wrath is no less fulsome. Though we had harried the enemy sufficiently to frustrate any *coherent* assault, our ak-blastors and sensors were being eliminated by random strikes of sunfire. Two of the five engine nozzles had been spirited away. More to the point, we were losing the doors on our torpedo tubes.

At last, in two locations, the hull was penetrated. The bombardment ended. But the respite was false. The spheres fired stingerships at the holes. The stingerships, being manned, were even more evasive than the missiles. We couldn't stop them.

And we were boarded.

The breached areas had been sealed off automatically, lest we lose our air to the aethir; and the seals were decidedly robust, since breaches on a warship are presumed to originate in hostility. Thus were the boarders instantly trapped. Of course, nothing inside the *Victuri* was either type of berulion, and the boarders—armed (as Hul Jok had feared) with sunfire guns—casually disintegrated every obstacle.

Jem Toh and Ron Ti, alerted by Hul Jok to the boardings, all but melded their brains to hastily finish the Bottle Bomb, which, with bold trepidation, they soon handed to Dylal O'Lal, who cradled it in his arm and, joined by two mecha-men, hastened to the bay. Then, neither hunkering down nor taking up arms, the ragged scientists tirelessly turned to completing the Mineralizer, so that, should the fight continue long, we might easily generate h-b.

The mecha-men guided Dylal O'Lal.

The two teams of boarders, having breached the *Victuri* in random locations, had to snake towards their objectives, one team to the bridge and the other, no doubt, to the engine room. It was the latter team that Dylal O'Lal ran across.

The boarders were plated in bronze, their segmented armor floating on shimmering mail, their pauldrons embossed with the Circled Dot of the Sun, and their helms fronted by silver masks, the expressions stern, each sculpted eye glaring without pupil or iris. These were the Guardians not of Solace but of Rebuke. The stories had remembered this well.

Dylal O'Lal had not expected an onslaught of angels. The radiant team of three entered his hallway with a tactical grouping that was disconcertingly *human*, rifles low and spacing mindful; and, as Dylal O'Lal hesitated in awe, the Guardian on point smartly opened fire.

One mecha-man spasmed and clattered to the floor, a good portion of its chest having vanished. The other—before its head had joined the air—managed to blast one of the Guardians, which was thrown by the pulse (its shoulder splintered) and dropped against a bulkhead.

Dylal O'Lal's sunsuit dissipated the darts of sunfire meant for him, and having thereby surprised the two remaining Guardians, he willed his magnetic thrusters towards his foes and swatted both into confusion. With a leap he swung the Bottle as a flail and downed a Guardian, cracking its mask. The last was hit again with willed magnetic thrusts and, as it staggered, angrily spewing pointless sunfire, Dylal O'Lal drew his own blastor and, barrel high at the Guardian's face, pulsed the angelic creature out of this life.

Disbelieve me, if you like. You have heard the Guardians are immortal? Your stories are inaccurate.

The blood of Dylal O'Lal was not so cold that he would top off the unconscious Guardians. He let those two lay defeated. He had nothing to bind them with, nor the time to bind them; but he shouldered their rifles. The rifle of the dead Guardian and all of their sidearms he blasted to uselessness. Collecting himself with a lengthy breath, the Daredevil of Jopitar clutched the Bottle, deduced the path begun by his defuncted guides, and continued to the bay.

Our torpedo waited, a patch of its guts exposed. Between us and the door stood a wall of four mecha-men. Mor Ag and I heard the thud of two more stingerships arriving. Agitated by these fresh violations, I was impelled to escape our little fort and commence a bloody hunt. In me churned the distempering spirit of my ancient ancestor, the thoroughly unpoetic and barely literate scourge of the wilderness, Hak Iri the Vicious. Only Dylal O'Lal's arrival gave my dispassion a foothold, and the *other* Hak Iri was again tamped down.

By then the bridge was besieged. Hul Jok had gone silent. His last order had been to launch when ready. Dylal O'Lal handed me the Bottle. "'Tis Guardians we're fighting," he declared. When he heard about the bridge, he gave us one of the sunfire rifles and left to support the defenders.

Like frontline surgeons, Mor Ag and I crudely sutured the novel organ into the torpedo, and then resealed its skin. We lifted it into a loading rack. Since only one of us was needed for the final steps, Mor Ag hurried to the bridge, vowing most especially to protect Lue Jes.

Hul Jok had excluded bay six from the harrying volleys, hoping that its inactivity would conceal it, and indeed, its tubes were unharmed. Perhaps mere luck had aided us. We had a clear path out of the ship. The diminished sensor data was enough to aim at a sphere. Using the launching station, I dispatched our modified torpedo.

At that point I am sure the enemy were marveling at our futile tantrum. *Surely* we had nearly depleted our torpedoes and vibratory charges. In fact we had! Why did we persist so foolishly? Little could we harm!

And in their complacency, the enemy made no move against yet another racing torpedo. The cloak of its target would, after all, erase it. And so the cloak did. Through

the sunfire the torpedo ceased to be. Meanwhile the Bottle, unceasing in its momentum, kept on; and before the enemy noticed, the Bottle was beneath the cloak and above the bare metal of the sphere.

Or so I presume. The torpedo was hard to monitor, and I was not beside it. All must have happened as we expected, however, for the Impetus surely woke.

The mecha-men outside the bridge, had they any souls, could be said to have *nobly* delayed the enemy. In any event, they had been effective obstructions, even delivering a few good injuries until they were scattered as scrap.

The door to the bridge was densely armored. Though its surface yielded wholly to any touch of sunfire, those touches, landing as they did in dartish bursts, could only erode the thickness. Indeed, the pace of the boarders had been restrained, as if they sought to break the door without inundating those behind it.

Another team had joined the first. The Guardians, primed to enter, now numbered six.

Hul Jok had retrieved a personal armor from a cabinet, an aethir-suit tiled with iron slabs, that, when donned, made him a quarter again as huge. He was an articulated boulder, ready aside the sizzling door. Too he grasped his gigantic warhammer, a thing of utter mass; and when the boarders pushed through the failed door's falling fragments, Hul Jok's hammer fell upon them as a meteor to the land. Of a sudden and to their shock, they were brutally melee'd. Sunfire darts pierced and sliced him, but Hul Jok whirled and pounded.

"*Hue hoh!*"

Three Guardians clambered on him. Wolves to the bear! He staggered; they struck. The other three, previously downed by the hammer, advanced into the bridge. Their heads jerked, left, right, as of insects, their hidden eyes scanning, seeking *something*. One emphatically pointed at Lue Jes's position.

The women barraged them.

The chest of a Guardian was crushed. The other two Guardians dodged. Their sunfire peppered the bulwarking consoles of Kol Een and Ah Neet.

And here the savvy reader—who tidily recalls the issue of this chronicle and sits, book in hand and poddaya in glass, comfortably removed from the mayhem I am recounting—this savvy reader, I suspect, is smirking in anticipation, thinking, "O ho! Now we see, does sunfire do naught to Kol Een?"

For sunfire surely did aught to Ah Neet, who in four places bled from dart-drilled removals of her flesh, and who in pain—none could blame her!—huddled more deeply behind the metal.

But Kol Een?

Naught.

Save for the new holes in her vest and dress.

She was only momentarily surprised. She had been expecting this immunity, after all. Then, hearing the cries of Ah Neet, Kol Een abandoned her safety, and emboldened by her own undamaged body, she scampered openly through the skirmish to aid her wounded sister.

Dylal O'Lal appeared at the door and, without hesitation, began hurling his own sunfire at Hul Jok's assailants. Their bronze plating (apparently akin to h-b) dissipated most of his shots. However, the Guardians were outfitted for rapid assault and so were not *sealed* in their bronze. Agile armor has its gaps. One assailant stumbled aside, bleeding too much from too many places.

Meanwhile Guardians were firing at Lue Jes, but only to suppress her action. None aimed to hit her. Still she flinched. She got off only a few more wild blasts before she was tackled.

Then the Impetus had its say.

The recursive ignition eviscerated the initial sphere. Within moments the engines exploded. A shockwave hurled the cloak, whirling it, tangling it in cloaks nearby— sunfire shredding sunfire—as cloaks were torn open and hulls exposed to hails of igniting shrapnel.

Again: so I presume. None of us directly saw anything. Sensors indicated the fury of flaring energies and the lessening number of spheres. Starkest light filled the bridge, pulsing to the births of multiple minor suns.

The *Victuri* shook in the quaking aethir.

Fortunately, as Ron Ti had calculated, the sunfire maelstrom confined the reach of the Impetus. We were not struck. Soon the Impetus was spent, the remaining shrapnel unignited; for much as Jem Toh had always *meant* an Impetus to be "unceasing"—to be, that is, a perpetual nucleus of motive combustion—the design lacked not only stability but longevity. This Impetus, however, had lasted long enough. Half a dozen enemy ships were killed—and who knew how many Guardians.

We had made our point.

Hul Jok shook off his battered assailants, stomped backwards, and, raising his warhammer in one bloodied gauntlet, thundered, "Your ships are shattered!" He uttered in a voice *abraded*, through some wound of throat or lung. "Of all your thoughts, there's one I surmise. *Why now? Why* did we not use our terrible weapon *immediately*? Because, you fools, we didn't *have* it." He coughed; then snarled. "Not half an hour into this battle, and we devised a way to *decimate* you. We will use it again," he bluffed. "Nay! Give us another half hour, and we will do *worse*." His eyes promised hell. "None of *my* army are dead. I offer truce. Stand down." He struck the deck once with his hammer. The bridge trembled. "*Stand. Down.*"

The Guardians were no doubt receiving kalioned reports from their Command outside. Were they ordered to cease fire? Were they—as would be any breathing creature—cowed by Hul Jok's thunder? Either way, they did stand down, retreating to one side of the bridge.

They did not, however, release Lue Jes.

"Our truce," growled Hul Jok, "makes no provision for prisoners."

A Guardian stepped forward, presumably the leader, or one to whom, in all the combat, leadership had passed. For a radiant being, it spoke rather gruffly. "So much

trouble. You should have surrendered."

"Why do that, when one can prevail?"

"You have not prevailed. You have only... surprised us."

"Know you my name?"

"Yes."

"Then how were you surprised? Release the woman."

"I cannot. She must be contained."

"Contained?"

"She has ferried corruption to the Hearth."

"Corruption? *Lue Jes?* Ha!" He laughed in disbelief; then coughed heavily. "You really don't know us."

Just then Mor Ag had reached the bridge. As he beheld his Love-Girl on the other side of a standoff, unhurt but restrained by the enemy, his bile rose; when he heard talk of containment and corruption, he seethed. But he recognized the delicacy of the confrontation and did not intervene, even with an angered exclamation. He caught Lue Jes's eyes and, in one intense look, conveyed all his resolute love. Then he slung his rifle and slowly—*unprovocatively*—walked over to Kol Een and Dylal O'Lal, who, with some supplies from the bridge's med cabinet, were tending to Ah Neet.

The Guardian retorted, "We know enough. This woman was will-witched by a Lunarion. We sense it. She was not merely captive nor merely enslaved. Her soul was adopted by the soulless, and her will directed by the wicked. She was an extension of evil."

Hul Jok scoffed. "So she was bewitched. *Temporarily*. We freed her!"

"From a Lunarion! An avatar of depravity. Were Lunarions just another nation? A tribe? A race? You beheld them. You know! They were hatred embodied. And *she* was hatred embodied. For however long! Such corruption never fades. Should it near the Sun anymore, it would taint the Hearth."

"I am not corrupted," protested Lue Jes, plainly and sadly.

Moved by his Love-Girl, Mor Ag spoke up. His anger, though in check, was clear. "If we must leave, we'll leave."

"You are already within the jurisdiction of the Hearth. There is only one outcome for evil."

Hul Jok tensed. Truce or not, his warhammer lifted. "You would kill her!"

"Of course not. That would smash the jar. The corruption would fly. Out of our reach! Into the Sun! Had she died in all this nonsense..."

"Yet you threw missiles in her direction."

"We knew of your berulion hull. *You* needed to know of our resolve. By the Nobles, you risked too much defying us! You should have surrendered. The more time we waste..."

Kol Een demanded, "Are the Nobles just?" She stood with fists at her sides.

The Guardian drew back. "You doubt it?"

"Let me speak to them."

"What! You cannot—"

Kol Een dropped her vest. She plucked at the holes in her dress. "See these? Sunfire made them. See behind them? Nothing. No wounds. I can stand in the Sun. I can walk on the Hearth. Take me to the Nobles. I would hear their own voices condemn this generous woman."

"How can you possibly..." It stared. She *had* been shot. She *had* no wounds. It hesitated in confusion. "We... We cannot take you."

"Why not? Ah. Yes," bitterly. "You aren't wearing sunsuits—and sunfire hurts you all as much as it hurt my poor sister. A bit removed from your masters, are you? Maybe *too* removed." She looked off into the *Victuri*, contemplating a path. "Should I just walk out an airlock? Fall toward the fire? Will a Noble catch me? Should I hope Our Lady's hands would bear me up?"

For all her bitter impudence, Kol Een was very afraid. She knew she was tempting the Nobles. Yet her sister was dying, and justice seemed distant.

The Guardian snapped, "You must—" Then it stopped. It tilted its head. It seemed to be receiving a kalion call. Its voice was low and hard to understand, but it was soon clearly caught in an agitated exchange.

Perhaps the Nobles were shamed by Kol Een. Perhaps her evident will had impressed them. Perhaps they had been reminded of greater obligations, as endowed by the eternal Great Wisdom. Perhaps they were simply embarrassed by the overzealous and bad decisions of their underlings, who had become maladroit in their idleness.

Mercy held sway, in any event, and the command went down.

The Guardian relented and turned to its fellows. "Release her." They did. Warily, then hastily, Lue Jes parted from them, flying to Mor Ag's embrace.

Addressing Hul Jok, the Guardian droned, "Take her away. Immediately. Bring none like her again. We will now withdraw." Then all of them, carrying their wounded, vacated the bridge; and having gathered those downed by Dylal O'Lal—as well as those yet skulking aboard (for one other team had encountered none of us)—the Guardians took to their stingerships and rejoined their hobbled fleet.

Everyone on the bridge wearily abided until Hul Jok confirmed that the *Victuri* contained only us. "Ends that," he said, without much exultation. "Now the rest of you get me and Ah Neet to the infirmary."

Down in bay six, after the Impetus had finished and everything went rather quiet, I wanted to check in with Hul Jok; but as I had no idea what was going on, I reckoned it was best to be silent and await any orders.

Likewise reckoned Ron Ti and Jem Toh, who laid low in the lab, continuing their work on the Mineralizer.

When we received word of our victory—or *escape*, if you prefer—we joined everyone else in the infirmary.

Mor Ag and Kol Een were doing their best for the fading Ah Neet. Ron Ti, though he is not *per se* a medical doctor, brusquely intervened and employed his broad knowledge and broader hubris to keep Ah Neet in this world.

As the weeping Kol Een stepped back from Ron Ti's urgent efforts, she realized Jem Toh was near. She burst and threw her arms around him. "Oh, Jem, you're alive,

you're alive!" Her tears of joy concealed those of sorrow. She unabashedly kissed his lips. He did not entirely resist.

Lue Jes was tending to Hul Jok. Much of him had been bruised, including his throat, and here and there his blood had got out, but nothing inside his bulk had been ruptured or broken. The scars would arrive and simply join the others.

Looking to Ah Neet, Hul Jok rumbled, "Let her not die, Ron Ti. She has bled on behalf of us. I saw her fell a Guardian. I will see her given the Order of the Looped Cross. She shall be known as the Thorn of Venhez!"

Ron Ti replied, "Well she should. Let me work."

Dylal O'Lal, yet uninjured, was no less exhausted. In every movement he had defied the constraints of his h-b garb. While Hul Jok and especially Ah Neet were cared for, he had leaned himself weakly against a wall. Worried for him, I unsealed the sunsuit and helped him out of it. Without drama he collapsed into a bed.

Mor Ag, having helped Ron Ti all he could, tugged Lue Jes away from Hul Jok. "The brute is fine," he told her. Hul Jok grunted in agreement. She let Mor Ag hustle her to a corner, where he fussed over *her* well-being. They fell to intimate whispers.

After methodically bringing Ah Neet to a painless sleep, Ron Ti declared, unnecessarily, that we should really return to Venhez.

So we did.

Not on the *Victuri*, though. Staying aboard was imprudent. Though the *Victuri* was not internally ruined, its shell was not whole and its engines were a mess.

We transferred ourselves and some extra supplies to *The Lifted Wing*. Then we shut down the more volatile components of the *Victuri*'s power plant, alerted Venhez to the situation, and set the *Victuri* on a ballistic path beyond Markhuri's orbit, for later retrieval by the War Castle.

As we watched the *Victuri*'s functioning thrusters twinkle in calculated choreography, propelling the otherwise dormant aethir-torp into the cold, Hul Jok vowed that his ravaged ship, which had borne so much, would be a beauty again.

And so it was.

Although our path home was more direct than had been our path to the Sun, *The Lifted Wing*—a simple sloop—was in nowise as fast as a healthy warship. For several days we sailed.

Those days were muted. We rested in the aftermath of battle and pondered Whom we had fought.

Every hamlet of the Planetary Chain has its memories of the Nobles. Mor Ag the cultural gourmand had gorged on the variations and contradictions, till even the consistent assertions left him unsatisfied and with amusement he would only affirm that someone, somewhere, sometime, had somehow heard something about some existent somebody. Never did he expect his skepticism to be ended; and never did he expect his amusement to become resentment.

The Nobles are real enough. They threatened my girl!

Lue Jes, in her way, tried to rouse his more natural cheer. She was not unsuccessful. Mor Ag is not of an inimical disposition. And his girl still breathed beside him. She soothed, "You can't be angry about what didn't happen." Insofar as he dwelt on the threat, he neglected the mercy.

Also in her way, Lue Jes did not fret over her supposed corruption. She didn't *feel* corrupted; no more so than any creature. And should arise in her an impulse to depravity, did it matter if it originated in the residue of a monster? She would resist it regardless. "Besides, you heard the Guardian. None of the Lunarion's evil will shadow me in death. I will meet the Great Wisdom unstained."

Unlike Mor Ag, Hul Jok had never been a skeptic. His every particle adores Our Lady of Joy. His hardened breast is sacrally tattoo'd with the Looped Cross. His fealty to World, Chain, and Hearth is whole. He didn't even feel betrayed by the assault on him and his ship. The Guardians had only been doing their duty. Hul Jok would have massacred them—all and every one!—had they tried to "contain" Lue Jes, but he didn't begrudge his foes the defense of their realm. Indeed he was *grateful* to them. By their assault, they had granted him a singular victory. Hul Jok had defeated the Army of the Sun! What greater claim for any War Prince?

I suspect the claim will be unique for a while. The Hearth has not stirred since our encounter. Our clash with the Guardians was not a sign that the Long Seclusion is done. The ancient stories, whatever their divergences, concur that the Lords and Ladies did not *frivolously* retreat into the

Hearth. Something profound compelled them to abandon their blatant commerce with us and adopt an aloof and selective providence. Not even proximity of the Lunarion Pollution could reverse such a fateful choice.

Think in this way of our clash:

The dogs of the household barked madly at the midnight fox, and the farmer, disturbed from his slumber, put the dogs to leash and shoo'd the fox, and impassively recurred to his pillow.

I believe that's all it was.

*T*he Lifted Wing was not uncomfortably small; but sit too long in any one spot, and you'd quickly feel *confined*. At least I did. On the second day I had to go for a walk.

Any room I passed I entered—partly out of curiosity, partly to lengthen my path. I soon entered what turned out to be a cozy den. There were shelves of books and a writing desk. A reclining chair and floorlamp took a corner. There was even a rug. The room was inviting.

Which probably explained why Kol Een and Jem Toh were so at home on the floor.

In the moments before they noticed me, my thoughts rushed to Esa Nal. That was only natural, I suppose. Esa Nal is not as fruitly rounded as Kol Een, but the sight of Kol Een's all-out made me fairly homesick for my dainty tart. I hadn't been kicked in days.

When they did notice me, Kol Een squeaked, and Jem Toh lifted his hands, as if he wasn't sure where they should go.

When I didn't exit immediately—I was a bit lost in Esa Nal—they shuffled on the rug and plopped against the chair. A couple thus surprised, had they been folk from Jopitar, Satorn, or Mharz, would likely have scrambled for clothing, or reproached the intruder, or spun up some fuss or another. But after all, we three were Venhezians.

Eros be!

Kol Een was not even as self-conscious as once she might have been. Her glow was sublime. Jem Toh, though mostly relaxed, was still a trifle *himself*, proclaiming to me with a pinch of agitation:

"It's okay! Kol Een's my Love-Girl now."

"Obviously."

"No, no, no. I mean we made the vows."

She snuggled happily against him. "Life is too short."

I chuckled. "Worry not, Jem Toh. I know what you meant. This is good. Truly." I smirked. "But have you properly considered it? Kol Een is no longer a maiden."

She scrunched her face and purred. "No, I am certainly *not*."

Jem Toh was nonplussed. "*Tch*. Well. Of course she isn't. What else would she... Oh, *no!*" He grabbed Kol Een's shoulders and shouted, "I terminated your maidenhood!"

She playfully poked his chest. "Yes. You. *Did*."

"No, no. No! I mean—your immunity, Kol Een!"

"My—?" She gasped. She shook her head. "No. Don't be silly."

"Kol Een! I've told you! *Maidenhood is indicated as a factor.*"

Her face paled.

Now they scrambled for their clothing.

There was no lab on *The Lifted Wing*. We hurried to the mess. Jem Toh lit a burner on the stove. Nagged by a sense of novel absence, Kol Een carelessly pressed two fingers on the reddening coil. She yelped and yanked her hand away, and having half-forgotten what one should do when burned, she stood unmoving while her fingers tingled terribly, before leaping to the sink and chilling her pain under a cold running tap.

I had only been teasing when I had noted Kol Een's loss of maidenhood. Now I felt darkly *responsible* for this second and far less joyful loss, as if my joke had been an invitation to diabolical mischief.

Kol Een withdrew her fingers from the water and stared at them. She said flatly, "It's gone."

"It's just one experiment, Kol! We should confirm—"

"No. I can tell."

"Don't give up—"

"It's not that. I can *tell*."

His face sank. "I'm so sorry."

"It's not your fault." She sighed. "Well. Maybe it is. It's *our* fault. This was always going to happen, I guess... Oh. Oh!" Her eyes went wide. "Dylal O'Lal! I can't help him now! And poor Ah Neet! When she wakes up she'll be *furious*. Wik Obu won't have much use for The Girl Who Burns Like Anyone Else. What do I do?"

Jem Toh—trained, perhaps, by his recent intimacy—had the lover's good sense to draw in Kol Een and enfold her with his arms. Kol Een, cheek against his shoulder,

SHANE PLAYS GEEK TALK
is a journey into
the things we love!

D&D | RPGs | OSR
Tabletop Games | Video Games
Comic Books | Indie Comics
Star Trek | Star Wars | Doctor Who
Movies | TV Shows | Fan Films
Fantasy | Sci-Fi | Pulp Fiction
Retrogaming | Retrocomputing

...AND MORE!

SHANE PLAYS GEEK TALK

D&D & RPGS, GAMES, COMIC BOOKS, MOVIES, TV, SCI-FI, FANTASY, RETROGAMING, RETROCOMPUTING, WEIRD STUFF, GEEK NEWS... AND MORE!

A JOURNEY INTO THE THINGS WE LOVE

stared off sadly into the mess, and was reduced to a dumbfounded "Huh."

Kol Een later confided, "You know why Ah Neet is a virgin? Because she *rejects* being otherwise. She turns it away. I was never like that. I was holding my virginity for that *moment of giving*. It would be my gift. And I always knew I would be transformed; but... I gave *so* much, didn't I?" She paused. I had no helpful response. She smiled wistfully. "But I really don't mind. My gift was all the greater. I do love Jem Toh."

Dylal O'Lal was less disappointed than any of us expected.

Kol Een approached him abjectly, explaining what had happened, and even cradling his hand in both of hers to offer her commiseration.

He answered with equanimity, "That's how the Cosmos is. I'll find another way." And then, with some gravity, he stated that he was happy for the new couple, and that no need of his would ever have obstructed the consummation of any betrothal—although, not being Venhezian, he was a bit dazzled by how *rapid* this betrothal and consummation had been.

So Dylal O'Lal ended our adventure with his solar plans uncertain. He might yet step on that shore. The Nobles had forbidden only the return of Lue Jes or her like. The Sun, although under guard, was presumably yet open to exploration, study, and a dash of daredeviltry. And it was a fact that sun-fire could be ignored. If, in the end, Dylal O'Lal never learned how to will his foot to survive the fires of the Sun, "well," he mused, "then I expect I'll try something else impossible."

David Skinner loves science fiction. He has been writing steadily since he was twelve. Notable novels are "The Wrecker" and "The Giant's Walk." He has stories in StoryHack and Cirsova Magazine. He blogs infrequently at www.davidskinner.biz.

Out October 1 From Cirsova Publishing!

An Atlas of Bad Roads
Misha Burnett

Orphan of the Shadowy Moons (Part 3)

By MICHAEL TIERNEY

Having escaped enslavement at Arendahj and returned to the Teluchi Islands, Strazis has before him the momentous task of leading a war of liberation! Many rally to Strazis' cause but his old foe Eirlik has other plans—as does Eirlik's father!

Chapter Thirty-two
The Art of Sticks

Ell Cee Baron marched with a stiff military stride past the guards at the lower gates of the Worldlord's tower and into a hallway filled with fine crafts and ornate arts that represented all of the Teluchi Islands. The Worldlord's official residence felt disconcerting to someone who had usually seen Eagal Ir Radin riding a skier into battle with his cannons firing and shakara flashing.

The twin doors of the private stateroom were opened without asking when he approached, and inside was a bustle of activity from seamstresses working to combine weave and leather with the new riding armor of Strazis. The Worldlord's son stood in the middle of the room's chaos, trying to find gloves with the right fit, while his body was fitted with the dark blue and crimson colors of the Issandran banners.

The two men exchanged greetings.

"I've been given permission by the Worldlord to accompany you now that the call has gone out and your pledges are gathering here at Issandra," said Baron.

"I welcome your company and advice," Strazis replied. "Thank you, Ell Cee. I'll need the help."

"You have it."

"Thanks again." Strazis then motioned for the seamstresses to take a break. As soon as they left, he crossed the room to face Baron directly. "You've had a look of concern on your face ever since I returned. What's bothering you? Have I done something you disapprove of?"

Baron shook his head emphatically.

"No, Lord Strazis. I disapprove of nothing."

"Well, what then? You've known me since I was a child and are willing to ride with me into battle. I need to know what it is that's bothering you."

"Lord, you know that I have served the Worldlord faithfully my entire life. But if you must know, my admiration for you, what you've survived and accomplished, your skill with a blade, these are the deeds of the greatest man I've ever known, excepting only the Worldlord himself."

Strazis made no reply, taking a chair and waiting for Baron to continue.

"As you said, I've known you since you were a child, and have always known that you were… unique. You were a dream come true for the Worldlord—the heir he had always wished for. And your skier flies higher off the water's edge than any I've ever seen, proving the strength of your spirit."

"Why are you flattering me?" Strazis asked.

"I see in you the next Worldlord. On the sad day he leaves us, I am confident that you should be the next to wear that mantle and keep the Teluchi Islands united."

"And it worries you because you can see that I don't want the title?" Strazis jumped to the conclusion that Baron was dancing around. "Even if my father can't."

"But why?"

"I love and respect these islands. This was my home, but my heart changed when I ran wild in nature, and even more so when I was taught the humility of being a slave. Now, to me, the thought of the mantle of Worldlord is no different from putting the chains of Arendahj back on my wrists."

"But the contests?" Baron was shocked to hear the confirmation of his fears. "You're proven yourself to be the best swordsman in the islands in so short a period of time."

"I don't think that I'm the best. I've never really fought against my father, and there are still others who consider themselves better swordsmen than me," Strazis

countered.

"None that have actually met you in a duel. And you keep accepting their challenges. Why would you do all this if you don't want to be the Worldlord? And what about this army you're raising to purge the world of your enemies? Once you're victorious, the islands will need your leadership."

"Arendahj." Strazis answered. "That's the reason for everything I'm doing. I made a vow to return and free the slaves, and I'll do it or die trying. But once that's done, all I want is the freedom to explore and see the world—not just beyond Arendahj and the western reaches; I want to see what lies on the whole other side of the world."

"How can the world have another side?"

"Believe me, it's there." Strazis stood. "Look at me. I've been an outsider here from the start. Now I've learned that there's so much more beyond the islands and feel I need to keep searching to find where I really belong."

"But what about the love you have here?" Baron countered. "The Worldlord went to war to avenge you, and now the islands are willing to follow you into the unknown. How can you walk away from that kind of devotion?"

"You know," Strazis picked up a pair of short metal rods connected by a stout chain, "I thought you came here to pledge yourself to the war on Arendahj, and give me another lesson in Sticks."

"You're so good with a sword," said Baron, "why would you even need to know the art of Sticks?

"My left hand isn't always controlling a

skier," Strazis smiled.

Chapter Thirty-three
A Vision of Perfection

The brilliant gloss of the polished marble walls and columns reflected Phaedra's exquisite white gown and flowing golden locks that hung to the middle of her back as she glided without a sound down the hallways and past ancient artifacts, relics crafted by artisans long since turned to dust, and magnificent suits of armor. These suits not only shielded most of a wearer's body, but also carried weapons that were an integral part of their build. The sleeves on the forearms had three long shafts each, which extended to the wrist and could be aimed like miniature cannons. There were many other strange parts formed from the same metals as the island skiers that baffled modern day viewers who tried to guess their function. Every suit was different and would normally enthrall most onlookers with their strangeness, but she only saw them as bars on a cage.

The hallway opened up to a balcony, where she slid her hands across the railing and gazed out over the wooded hills that rolled into a misty horizon, from which cool streams and waterfalls traced their way downward through the valleys that looked to have been scooped by the hand of some colossal being. There were other artifacts lining the hills that towered over the valleys, strange pylons covered with mystical carvings that stood like lines of fingers pointing toward the sky. These pylons were everywhere around the fortress called Blackmaste, which was built into the side of a mountain deep within the lands of the Shezendoa.

Phaedra had heard tales about how Blackmaste had once been a home to the Moon Gods, but she found it a place of nightmare. There were few guards and no defensive garrison of soldiers; they were not needed. Lizard-like nightmares with longs necks and heads that were all jaws flew the skies on huge wings and would perch on the pylon tops, scanning the ground for their next meal.

Gaebel called them gatakmo and always assured Phaedra they would never harm her, claiming that they would be her protectors for as long as she remained in Blackmaste.

Otherwise, the land she looked out over was a calm one, and she found gazing upon it soothed her anguish at her long imprisonment in a gilded cage so far from Promessus. She had been well-treated and never threatened by Gaebel but found his explanations for her supposed rescue implausible, although she did not know why.

The brown-skinned Shezendoa worshipped Gaebel in much the same way that some islanders worshipped the Moon Gods. Her skin was gold, like his, though a darker shade, and the Shezendoa treated her with a similar respect, serving her every command, except requests to leave. Gaebel steadfastly denied her this, claiming that war raged across all the islands of Teluchi and that any passage would be profoundly unsafe. He claimed to be, like the gatakmo, her dutiful protector.

As the solar cycles passed, Gaebel never made demands of her, but still she saw hunger in his eyes and was certain that he was trying to beguile her.

She turned her attention back inside Blackmaste and toward a massive aquarium built inside the walls. It was completely enclosed and connected by shafts with motors that circulated the waters through a self-sufficient and incredibly massive system of aquariums that wound throughout the entire fortress. Certain fishes ate the plants, and other fish ate their spawn, while scavengers endlessly patrolled the coral-filled bottoms, looking for anything dead or soon to die.

Legends said that the system had been designed by the Moon Gods to house a diminutive water people called the Vylmirian Dancers, which they had found at the bottom of the great ocean. Supposedly the entire race had been imprisoned in these walls, only to go extinct long ago; the system now supported only varieties of fishes and plants.

But Phaedra knew this was incorrect.

She had watched the water over long intervals, standing motionless as a stone, barely breathing, nearly falling into a meditative state. Only then did the water people first show themselves, and they had since become both familiar and comfortable with her.

Several tiny manlike figures popped out from a connecting shaft, webbed hands and feet furiously working to send them streaking through the water. They returned Phaedra's inquisitive gaze with their own, their large oval eyes reflecting the lights. When they stopped to float, they resembled stars of flesh as they drifted past with their arms and legs outstretched, the webbing connecting them gathering the currents that pulled them along.

Although these creatures appeared to be made of flesh and bone that was jointed like a man or woman, Phaedra had initially considered the legend that they were a race of people to be mere conjecture based on their appearance. But after watching these Vylmirian Dancers that were her only friends during her long cycles of solitude in Blackmaste, she had become convinced that they were indeed intelligent creatures.

The sound of boots echoing down the hall signaled that Gaebel had returned from another of his many absences that grew longer every time. The Vylmirian Dancers saw the consternation on her face, and with a single flex of their bodies, instantly vanished back into the connecting tubes.

As the footfalls drew ever closer, she soon heard voices.

"This is not good," said Tracus. "The Shezendoa have grown weary of your unfulfilled promise to restore the ancient devices to a usable condition. We've sent men scouring every inch of this continent, into nightmare hells where many lost their lives. All with no results. Now I'm hearing rumors that Arendahj has found a power source on their own and, even as we speak, are learning how to use it. This will split Shezendoa loyalties more than they already are."

Faintly, Phaedra heard the delicate sounds from the medallion Gaebel always wore, the one that seemed to her to be almost identical to the one worn by the golden youth, Strazis, back during her time on Kalikantari.

"That can't be possible," Gaebel snorted. "Arendahj is supposed to be working with us. Everything I'm doing is to keep them and all the Shezendoa safe. I won't tolerate talk of a split."

Then he called out to Phaedra.

"Hello, I didn't know you were out and about. As always, you are a vision of perfection."

"I didn't hear you coming," she lied as she turned away from the aquarium and saw the lines of concern around Gaebel's eyes.

"I have news for you." He reached for his medallion and clicked something that stopped the music when he and Tracus moved to stand with their backs to the aquarium. "I know you've been unhappy here."

"I've been well-treated." Phaedra forced herself not to smile when the Vylmirian Dancers reappeared at Gaebel's back, emulating his stance and movements in mock water dances. "But this is not my home. I feel like a prisoner."

Gaebel sighed in exasperation, every motion of his body instantly repeated by the delighted Vylmirian Dancers.

"Phaedra," he said, "I've never imprisoned you. There are trails in the forests and caverns in the mountains that you were welcome to explore but never did. There, you would have found clear pools of water the same color as your eyes. This may not be your island home, but it is exquisite here. You're the one who made it into a prison."

"I might have thought of Blackmaste differently if I'd come here of my own choice," she replied. "In all this time, you've told me nothing about any event concerning my home or family. What news do you finally have?"

"The wars plaguing your islands have finally stopped." Gaebel and the Vylmirian Dancers nodded. "The Worldlord once again controls the Teluchi Islands, with your father at his side. So, if you wish, I'll send you home."

"I thought you were worried about the islands moving against you?"

"I am, and they are. I'm hoping that your return will stop their invasion. I will miss you when you leave. I'd prefer you to stay, regardless of the cost."

Phaedra did not hesitate. "Send me home."

"I'll start the arrangements." Gaebel nodded again with a weariness she had not seen before and turned to walk away—catching a glimpse out of the corner of his eye when all the Vylmirian Dances streaked into hiding. "Did you just see something moving in there? Where did it go?"

But he received no answer. Shrugging, he and Tracus walked away as his medallion began to play music once more.

Phaedra pressed her face to the glass of the aquarium.

"Goodbye, my friends. You're the only thing I'll miss about this place."

Chapter Thirty-four
Fated to Die

With its wings spread wide, the raptor circled high in the air, searching for prey in the emerald waters below. But the hunting was poor, as the schools of fish had been chased to deep water by the armies of skiers churning around the island of Issandra.

Sweeping low, the raptor glided over those armies as they slowly moved through the sea gates and out onto open water, the lead section arranged in the formation of a spearhead.

One impressive figure rode at the forward tip of the spear, resplendent in his black and scarlet gear, wearing a bestial mask with horns rising on either side.

With a flap of its wings, the raptor caught another upward draft and angled away, soaring past the loftiest tower of the Issandran capital and directly over the head of Eagal Ir Radin.

"That's not a good sign," the Worldlord said as his cloak billowed about his shoulders. He turned his attention back to the army setting out for Arendahj. "But someone is always fated to die whenever armies go to war."

"My Lord," his new wife from Vanessa said as she walked naked out onto the balcony and twined her body around his. "Can I not distract you?"

Eagal Ir Radin made no reply, his eyes intently watching the skier riding at the front slowly fade into the distance of the ocean horizon. Just the night before, the Worldlord had offered his last counsel to Strazis, giving him every bit of advice that he could think of that would be required to maintain an army that massive. The young man had listened and responded well to his every instruction, but still the Worldlord was filled with a foreboding.

"So it's come to this," he said softly to himself.

"Come to what, my Lord?" his new wife asked.

"Something that I don't know if I should even tell you... Vanessa." He was so distracted that he could not even recall his new bride's name, but she did not seem to mind, apparently thinking it to be a pet name based on her home island.

"Tell me," she prodded, "please. It will be our first bonding of the minds."

Eagal Ir Radin pointed at the sea in the direction where the leading edge of the army that continued to pour forth had disappeared.

"I've had a dream that I believe was sent to me by the Moon Gods," he shook his finger, "and now that dream has come to pass."

"What dream?"

"I saw the moment that I just now watched, where my son rode out at the head of an army. This was the dream that woke me on the morning I rode out to Kalikantari, the day I found him waiting for me on the waters."

"That's quite a story, my Lord."

"I've never told it before to anyone."

"Why would that bother you? It sounds like a good dream."

"Because, my dear Vanessa, I've never

had a dream of him at an age beyond this point."

"Come inside," she purred. "You're being silly. Let me distract you with more pleasant things to think about."

The Worldlord paused a moment to watch the last riders passing through the sea gate, flowing in a wave of shining metal. They all moved as one in a uniform fashion, except one who broke away and turned back to Issandra. The skier and rider were instantly recognizable.

"Dextran."

Chapter Thirty-five
The Sinking

Despite having triangulated the area where he had arrived in the western expanses with the location of Kalikantari, Strazis still knew that he was only guessing what direction would lead him to Arendahj. With so many men at his back, a guess wasn't good enough.

Faced with his first major decision, Strazis confounded his war council by ordering his army to stop for an early rest at Kalikantari while he sent scouts out ahead. That they should take a last chance to fortify themselves before the long crossing was not what concerned them. It was his instructions to the scouts—for them each to ride out to a predetermined spot on their compass, then stop and toss float balls normally used for baited fishing lines, and watch what happened.

When he explained his reasoning, and how he was searching for currents that would carry them where they needed to go,

his council was beyond confounded, with some beginning to worry that they had trusted their fates to a madman. But Ell Cee Baron would tolerate no such talk, and soon Strazis' madness was confirmed as wisdom when one scout returned to tell of the fast-moving water he had encountered. What made the discovery more significant was that it moved in the same direction that Strazis had calculated in his triangulation.

Once more, the army of Strazis set forth.

The stormy season had only recently passed, and the threat of unexpected turbulence was on everyone's mind during the long and hard ride that followed. There was no place to stop and rest, to stretch their legs to keep them from cramping. No one talked; each man's only company was the sound of water until night fell. Then they would tie their skiers together in small groups for stability against the waves and strap themselves into their seats while they slept.

On the morning of the third day, an advance scout brought the first report of land ahead, but he had also seen something else that he had difficulty describing.

A council was quickly convened.

As always, Ell Cee Baron served as Strazis' second in command, with leaders from each of the other islands in direct charge of their men. Some faces he did not recognize. A significant force had pledged themselves from Promessus, but when Dextran had dropped out the moment after they sailed, Rhank and Stansar had refused command and deferred to another who pledged at the last minute: Eirlik.

So far the councils had been short and Eirlik silent, offering no advice. But, thanks to his bad blood with Strazis, his presence cast a pall of distrust and foreboding. Still, Strazis made no complaint and respectfully accepted the presence of his former tormentor.

The council formed their skiers into a wedge, with Strazis at the center.

"Are you sure it was an island?" Strazis asked the scout. "The land didn't stretch to both ends of the horizon?"

"I'm sure."

"Did it have an easily accessible beach, surrounded by forest on land that rose high in the center?"

"Yes."

"That sounds like the Isle of View. That's what we're looking for. It will make the perfect staging area for our assault. What was it you couldn't describe?"

"Sir," the scout looked at Baron for help, "the biggest thing I've ever seen on the water were the barges of Vanessa when they attacked us outside the waters of Tyle."

"You saw a barge?" Baron asked.

"No," the scout shook his head. "I saw a black vessel near the island, built with twin pontoons like our skiers, but it was huge, big enough to carry thousands."

"I know what that is," Strazis quickly calmed the murmurings of concern. "It's a ship of Arendahj, and it only carries a hundred, at best." He looked around at each council member. "I told you about them," he said—and looked at Eirlik, who had no idea what he was talking about—"before we

set out. I'd seen that they've been active on the Isle after I escaped Arendahj. None of this is a surprise."

"What interest would the Shezendoa have in this place?" Eirlik finally spoke.

"I'm not really certain," Strazis replied while still focusing on the others, "but there is a black city at the Isle's center, ancient and abandoned, made out of basaltic rock and obsidian. Inside there is some kind of machinery powered by moonlight."

Suddenly everyone broke into laughter, certain that he was jesting.

"It's not a joke," Strazis asserted. "I'm not certain, but that could be what the Shezendoa are interested in. But none of that matters. We need to take that island, which means we need to destroy that ship."

"It could be that they know we're coming," said Nevil Daa Nara of Keton, "and they're trying to deny us access to land."

"Even more reason to take the Isle," said Baron.

"Maybe we should just pass it and go straight to launching our attack on Arendahj," Eirlik suggested, but received mostly strong disagreement.

"No," Strazis asserted. "First, we take the Isle of View, and then we move on Arendahj."

"What's your logic in that?" asked Calarn of Andera, who had been the only one not to scoff at Eirlik's plan.

"Two things," Strazis answered. "First, we gain the experience of learning how the Arendahj ships fight. That will give us information we'll need to plan our main attack."

"And what about the element of surprise?" Calarn asked.

"That's my second point. If we try to go around that ship, we might find out it's faster than we are. They could warn the city that we're coming."

Strazis sat back and let the others argue for some time before speaking again.

"Who will ride with me?" he finally asked. He expected a moment of silent reflection, not the instant response that he received.

"Attack!" Ell Cee Baron let the chant. Only Eirlik and Calarn declined to join in, but gave grudging nods of consent.

"Then we go immediately. Be aware that they have weapons that we're not yet familiar with and have the advantage of height and probably speed. We can't board them, trap them, or face them head-on."

"Then how are we supposed to fight them?" Eirlik scoffed.

"We fire our cannons at the support structures that connect the main body of the ship to their flotation pontoons. No one tries to go toe to toe with them. We arrange our skiers to strike in single file waves from every direction; that way they can't concentrate their fire. Each skier takes a turn looping in and hitting them with everything our cannons have."

"Keton accepts your plan," Nevil Daa Nara stated proudly. "Let's begin assembling attack formations immediately!"

"He's a fine ally," Baron nodded in Nara's direction after the council split up to relay their orders, then cast a questioning look at Eirlik, who had hesitated to leave.

"It's a foolish plan," Eirlik asserted. "You're already dividing us and wasting manpower on a secondary target. I should be in command here, not a naked-faced bastard that looks like a little boy. We should concentrate on Arendahj, and the rest of the world can wait its turn."

"We have a plan," Strazis stated flatly. "I'm not going to repeat it. If you don't agree with me, then you and your men stay out of it."

"Fine," Eirlik taunted as he moved away, "we'll stay in reserve for when you need rescuing."

Strazis exchanged a shake of the head with Baron.

The army from Keton led the first wave in.

The massive vessel waiting at anchor on the waves was caught by surprise when they first spotted their approach. They cut their anchor and immediately angled to face their attackers head-on. When they did, the line of Ketonian skiers split into two, heading off in opposite directions until both wings looped back in to fire at the vessel's struts.

When they did, every cannon aboard the vessel erupted simultaneously, spraying the water with liquid death. But their aim was spotty and scattered, while most of the Ketonian cannons hit their mark, their liquid fire instantly eating through metal.

"Their weapons are basically the same as ours," Baron called out as he rode next to Strazis with the next wave. "They just have greater range because they're firing from a higher elevation."

Strazis led the split that attacked one side and Baron the other, giving Nara's men an opportunity to clear the area.

An Issandran who had impatiently pushed to the forefront exploded right in front of Strazis, who roared past to fire a volley at the struts.

The waters around the Arendahj vessel began to fill with the smoke from liquid fire and burning metal that grew so thick that no skier could approach close enough to shoot.

The black vessel then began backing up, trying to withdraw to the safety of the shore, but Baron had already blocked that avenue of escape and was unintentionally given a fresh opportunity to attack.

The metal pontoons and struts of the vessel sizzled and billowed with even greater clouds of smoke. Then the astonishing happened. When the struts collapsed, the main vessel dropped and crashed into the water with a force that caused a huge upsurge of liquid fire-filled water to splash into the air, falling back down on the heads of the crew as their ship was dragged down under.

Liquid fire devoured every man on contact.

There were no survivors.

"I didn't expect this," Strazis remarked when Baron and Nara rejoined him.

"This was an overwhelming victory," Nara proudly proclaimed. "Were you expecting defeat?"

"No," Strazis replied. "I was referring to how fast that ship sank. It must have been tremendously heavy to go under the way it did. But you're right. It is a great victory."

When Strazis turned to order everyone to the Isle of View, he was shocked to discover that the skiers left in reserve had become a thin and scattered line.

Strazis raced to the remaining men and the skier who was positioned in command, and demanded an answer.

"Eirlik and Calarn called their men to arms." He pointed to where a dark mass of skiers disappeared over the horizon. "They said your attack was a diversionary tactic. It was a lie, wasn't it?"

"It was," Strazis seethed.

"I never trusted that man from Promessus."

As filled with rage as he was, Strazis smiled at that last remark.

"Where are you from?"

"Velhi! I know you did not recruit us because our island is so small, but we came anyway."

"What's your name?"

"Farsun."

"Farsun. No more?"

"I've yet to earn my titles."

"Then you and your men from Velhi ride with me, and maybe this is the day you'll earn them."

Chapter Thirty-six
The Assault on Arendahj

The first thing Strazis saw as he drew near to Arendahj was that it had already fallen. He had shown Eirlik how to defeat the Shezendoa ships, and burning slicks on the water marked where each one had been destroyed.

The sea gates on every tributary had also

been destroyed from skier cannon fire, and flames were gutting the nearest towers.

Eirlik and Calarn were already well inside the city.

Farsun and the riders from Velhi lined up behind Strazis and followed him up the river delta and into Arendahj. The bodies of Arendahj soldiers and slave guards were everywhere, having been no match for islander fury.

Strazis ignored the burning city and headed straight for the slave complex, past the island with the giant carved door and the panicked worshippers who crowded the bridges so quickly that one had collapsed, spilling them to flounder in the river.

When he reached the entrance to the slave pens, Strazis found the doors were already flung wide by crowds struggling to escape. Behind them roiled a strangely colored mist, and wherever the mist gathered—soon there were only the dead. In moments there was no one left to rescue as mists filled the processing center.

He gave quick orders to Farsun, Ell Cee Baron, and Nevil Daa Nara to keep clear. The mists and Eirlik's men were to be avoided.

Strazis changed objectives and used the waterways to head deep into the city and directly for the tallest building, where he saw countless numbers of finely dressed Arendahj citizenry filling the elevated bridges. A cacophony of screaming, shouting, and wailing filled the air as everyone ran for the river delta.

"Baron!" Strazis pointed as he tried to shout over the noise. "Take down those

bridges! Cut off their routes of escape! Nara, round those people up and lock them in chains!" When Nara gave him a questioning look with empty palms held out to each side, Strazis added, "Trust me, you'll find plenty of chains. Bring them to me."

Then he heard another voice shouting orders nearby.

"Rhank, herd those slaves between us and the guards! We'll use them for shields when we come in from the other side."

Eirlik immediately left down a parallel waterway with most of his men.

"Farsun!" Strazis called. "Dock my skier with yours!"

Before Farsun had even managed to produce a tether, Strazis had already leaped up on the path next to the waterway. A cluster of buildings stood on the opposite side of the next waterway over, where warriors from Andera and Promessus choked the canals. Rhank, Eirlik's second in command, was busily directing cannon fire at the entrances of those buildings. The skiers were so closely packed that they jostled with each other for position, and debris flew from errant shots that struck the upper parts of the buildings.

"Aim at their feet!" Rhank commanded with irritation, and cannon fire blasted all around the figures trying to flee the now burning buildings. But through the doors came slaves, not citizens. All of them clean, well dressed, and wearing golden collars. And behind them followed the mists. "Flush them around the building to where Eirlik has the guards trapped!"

The slaves milled at the doorways when

the cannon fire stopped those at the front, who blocked those to the rear frantically trying to escape the mists.

One figure that Strazis recognized slipped free when the mists struck the doors, but took only a few steps before falling to the ground as the whispery ever-reaching tendrils of the mists began to roll over her. Sanina!

"Farsun!" he called out. "You and your men circle around and clear out Eirlik's men! Now!"

With a smile, Farsun handed the tether to another and raced away down the waterway that looped around an upscale park area and would bring the skiers from Velhi full circle and behind Eirlik's force.

But Strazis knew that this maneuver would take too long. He sprinted to the other side of the pathway and dived into the water. He pulled himself up onto a skier, right behind the rider, continuing to climb until he was on top of the engine, and then jumped onto the cannon barrels of the next skier over. He repeated this jump from the cannons of one skier to another, again and again, until he was able to leap onto the path on the other side.

Running to the buildings being targeted, Strazis put himself directly between the fallen Sanina and the men of Promessus, just as he had tried to do for Tanith Woanan on Kalikantari and. He commanded Rhank to stop the attack.

Rhank ignored Strazis. He ordered his men not only to continue firing, but to aim at those still escaping through doorways that the mists had not yet reached. He then drew his sword.

"I've heard you're good in a duel," Rhank snarled as he charged. "But how good are you in a real fight instead of a dance?"

Strazis drew his blade and wasted no time. After a single deft movement of his sword, Rhank dropped his weapon and fell lifeless to the blood-soaked stones.

A roar lifted from the men of Velhi when they rounded the bend to realize that all of Eirlik's men aimed their cannons at Strazis. But their fire was held momentarily by the surprise Farsun's men had created.

Strazis did not wait to see what happened next. He took a deep breath, turned, and plunged into the mists of death that now obscured his view. It took some time, but eventually he emerged, carrying Sanina's lifeless body.

"I'm sorry," he whispered into her ear as her head lolled from side to side as he walked. It looked to him like she was shaking her head, but her unblinking eyes told him otherwise. For the first time, he realized just how out of place she had always appeared to be in the slave pens, better fed and with skin never blemished by a whip. He had thought this was because she was a newcomer, but now he came to the realization that she had been one of Ameron's prize pets all along.

He began to wonder if she had been clouding his mind by drugging the food she saved for him every night. Every form of persuasion was used in Arendahj, and the Sanina he thought he knew was not the woman in his arms. He had been manipulated in so many ways by a master manipulator.

"Delusions of grandeur, you said," he whispered. "No simple island girl talks like that."

He laid her down well clear of the mists, then looked up to see both the men of Velhi and Promessus were watching him with expressions of astonishment.

"You walked through the mists of death," called Farsun, "and came out untouched?"

Strazis shrugged.

"I held my breath," he said in a matter-of-fact voice, not caring to explain how he could do it for so long. With a cold glare, his attention turned to the men from Promessus.

One warrior looked at the fallen body of Rhank, then let out a cry of defiance and fired his cannons wildly at Strazis. Before the others could take aim, Farsun and his men charged into the middle of the Promessian ranks, destroying their formation and engaging them in hand-to-hand combat with their swords.

Disorganized and without a leader, the Promessians quickly surrendered.

"We have your skier!" Farsun called out and pointed at the warrior bringing up the rear and pulling it in tow.

"Join up with Nara's men," he ordered as he remounted, "and we'll regroup with Baron."

"What about our Promessian prisoners?"

"Let them go. The city has fallen. I don't want this fight to turn into islander against islander."

By the time dusk had begun to fall, they found Baron with his forces positioned on the island with a carved door.

"This place makes me uneasy," Strazis confided as he glanced at the remaining citizens gathered on their knees and bellies in front of the graven door, pleading for help from beyond. The prisoners Nevil Daa Nara had dragged to the island by barge were quick to join them. "But it is strategic. We control all traffic from the sea and out."

"What are they doing?" Nara asked about the citizens as they chanted in a language strange to him.

"Praying for salvation." Strazis looked through faces of the citizens for Ameron and Philandreas.

"From an image of a door carved in a rock?" Nara seemed astonished.

"They think it will protect them. They're begging for it to open like a real door."

"The madness of Neth and Nean." Nara spat on the ground.

"Strazis, the battle is over," said Farsun. "Look!"

Lines of victorious skiers began streaming from the burning city that had fallen silent and dark, its lights extinguished, the only illumination coming from buildings left to burn unimpeded.

"Aarondodge is ours! Aarondodge is ours!" the men from Andera and Promessus shouted in unison, neither understanding the correct pronunciation of the city's name, nor caring. With Eirlik at their lead, they headed straight for the island where Strazis waited.

"I'm sorry, Strazis," said Baron. "Your

dream of liberation turned into a slaughter."

"The city may have fallen," said Strazis, "but this fight isn't won yet. Not until we capture the city's leaders."

"I doubt Eirlik will recognize that fact," said Farsun. "His men are celebrating like it's all over."

Strazis had taken a single step in the direction of the beach, when an explosion of light erupted into the air above the river, blinding Eirlik and his men, who floundered about as the light remained steady and bright.

Shielding his eyes, Strazis was shocked to turn and follow the beam of light back to its source. It came from the rock image of the door, flowing from a crack in the center with a brilliancy that rivaled the sun.

Something seemed to be moving in that crack.

Chapter Thirty-seven
Amnesty

"I'll be blunt," Dextran Taa Constous said to Eagal Ir Radin on the other side of a parchment-filled table. "As we sit here, my son is leading an army from Promessus across the western waters to take revenge against those who made your son into a slave."

The Worldlord seemed uninterested in the Warlord's words.

"And I took Vanessa after they broke the treaty, all in your name. How did you like the new treaty wife they sent?"

The Worldlord gave a conciliatory nod.

"Surely all this has erased any old prejudices that you should've forgotten by now?"

"What are you asking, Dextran?"

"I want you to cancel your decree that forbids Eirlik to ever again walk Issandran soil. He had to wait outside the sea gates just to ride off at your son's side."

"He was not at Strazis' side," said the Worldlord. "I appreciate that he went, but let's be honest with each other. There is bad blood between our sons. Neither Strazis nor I trust Eirlik. I doubt even you do."

Dextran's back stiffened at the accusation, but he kept his emotions in check.

"Whenever they return and report on how the war transpired, if I learn your son has changed, then I may change my mind about the decree."

"You put all the blame on my son." Dextran placed both hands on the table and leaned across. "I've made this request as a courtesy. Perhaps I should make it a demand, so that I'll know if you truly value the loyalty and support I've always given you? But I will not beg."

When the Worldlord sat back, seemingly deep in thought, so did Dextran, but a hand surreptitiously fingered his hidden knife.

"They're both men now," the Worldlord said at length. "And your son did answer Strazis' call. They should settle things between themselves as men. Very well, Dextran. I'll cancel the decree."

Dextran pushed a blank piece of parchment in Eagal Ir Radin's direction, who reached for an inkwell and fresh quill. Moments later, he pushed the parchment back to Dextran, who nodded after a quick look and added it to the other declarations on the table.

"Thank you," he said. "There's another concern that we need to discuss."

"Another?" the Worldlord asked incredulously. "What else is bothering you?"

"It concerns Phaedra," Dextran looked around the room at the scribes recording the minutes of their meeting. "This needs to be discussed in private. Take a ride with me?"

The Worldlord nodded, officially concluded the meeting, and grabbed his cloak. As they exited the tower and passed through repeated guard stations, their conversation became casual, discussing their triumphs and history like old friends.

"I heard a story," said Dextran, "that during the rebellion, Told Maton complained about how your tower fortress could never be taken. That no one could storm those stone doors."

"I heard that," Eagal Ir Radin replied. "Maton thought the tower would be easier to topple."

Dextran laughed.

"If an army could get the kind of access needed to do that," he said, "then the war would already be over because he would have had to have killed every fighting man on Issandra before that."

"True," said the Worldlord, looking about to see that no one could hear as they climbed down the stone steps leading to the docks. "It's been a long time since you mentioned Phaedra's name. I've been thinking about her, too, since Strazis returned."

"Then you're probably thinking the same thing I am: What if Phaedra also survived, but never had a chance to escape?"

When their boots hit the docks, their footfalls echoed across the lagoon. Dextran paused a moment and looked at his reflection in the still water that reflected the light from several moons.

"If that were true," the Worldlord said when he reached his skier, "where could she be? Strazis never saw her after the fall of Kalikantari, so we know she wasn't fed to the terhali, and there was the headless body of a young girl that was burned at your estate."

"That had to be Phaedra's slave," Dextran replied. "They should have found two young girls. What if the Black Assassins took Phaedra, too?"

"Then they would have executed her like they did all the other children, and tried to do to Strazis. But don't give up hope."

"What are you talking about?" Dextran asked.

"Our sons are sailing to the home of the Black Assassins. Who knows what they might discover?"

"Arendahj is not their home."

"Now what are you talking about?" The Worldlord looked stunned.

"The Black Assassins have contacted me." Dextran looked across the lagoon to the sea gate, seeing that they were closed, but knew a smaller side gate that could fit a single skier was always kept open during times of peace.

"About Phaedra? Now I see why you wanted to talk alone!"

"Exactly!" Dextran struck his knife into Eagal Ir Radin's unarmored chest. "They offered her life for your death."

Mortally wounded, Eagal Ir Radin staggered backwards but did not fall. Ignoring the protruding blade, he pulled his shakara and swung at Dextran's head in the same motion.

Barely dodging in time, Dextran drew his blade and desperately defended himself from a dazzling attack that employed the reckless daring of a man who realized that he was already dead.

The only sounds over the lagoon were the clash of their blades and the drumming of their boots on the dock. The Worldlord furiously pressed his attack and slipped his blade beneath Dextran's guard, piercing his stomach. By then, all the blood had drained from his face, and he sagged to his knees.

"You betrayed me," the Worldlord said between gasps for air. "I never realized that Eirlik was only a reflection of you."

He collapsed across the wooden planking.

"Why didn't you call for help?" Dextran tried to staunch the blood pouring from his wound as he watched the Worldlord's eyes turn completely black and then haze over.

Then, from out of nowhere, a flash of light blinded Dextran, but it passed quickly, leaving him looking around, mystified by what had just happened. He attributed it to delusion caused by his injury.

Swaying side to side, Dextran stumbled over Eagal Ir Radin's body and staggered onto his skier at the far end of the dock. Barely able to pull the moorings free, he fell into the skier's seat and headed for the sea gate.

Chapter Thirty-eight
The Chiming and the Challenge

Strazis paused in his climb up the hill and looked back at those gathered below. Both the islanders and citizens of Arendahj were crumpled to their knees and averting their eyes from the intense light emanating from the center crack of the door carved into the island rock.

It was odd that this light caused Strazis only mild discomfort and did not prevent him from seeing the source. As he drew nearer, he realized that the illumination came from a large but indistinct figure that emanated power and was molded from light.

The figure stood at the heart of the crack in the middle of the door, a gulf of night sky and dim stars beyond.

"Who are you?" Strazis noticed when he shielded his eyes how his golden skin became nearly invisible in the brilliant light. "What do you want?"

There was no response other than a perfectly formed hand reaching forth and grasping at the medallion hidden beneath his body armor.

Then the hand withdrew, and a faint chiming filled the air like nothing Strazis had heard before, but it enthralled him and stirred memories of things he never knew.

As abruptly as it had appeared, the light vanished.

When everyone below raised their eyes to where the light had been, all they saw was Strazis standing alone at the base of the rock door.

As he descended, he noticed how the previously smoke-tinged air had become strangely fresh. Even the grass of the island seemed greener.

"What just happened?" Ell Cee Baron asked as he, Nevil Daa Mara and Farsun gathered around.

"Tell the men to ready themselves," Strazis replied when a Promessian skier began racing toward them.

"Eirlik, the conqueror of Aarondodge, demands that Strazis choose a representative to discuss the charges against him," the rider declared.

"Charges?" Baron demanded.

"I personally witnessed Strazis murder a commander, Rhank, and the warriors from Velhi attacked Promessian skiers by his command. Eirlik specifically wanted me to tell you that Rhank was his friend."

"You can tell Eirlik this," said Nevil Daa Nara. "He is responsible for the butchery of the slaves we came to liberate. His attack on Arendahj was premature and accomplished nothing more than razing the city. No one has been conquered here."

"Well said," said Strazis. "Are you volunteering to represent me?"

"Certainly," said Nara.

"You haven't done anything that needs defending," said Baron.

Despite protests from Baron and Farsun, Strazis agreed to Eirlik's demand, and Nara left alone to meet with Eirlik and eight of his commanders.

"I want to see what he wants," Strazis explained.

Standing on the beach, barely able to see the group by the lights on their skiers, he was certain it was Nara's voice he heard raised in a heated argument. Meanwhile, Baron and Farsun surreptitiously instructed their warriors and those from Keton to prepare for combat.

"What did he want?" Strazis asked when Nara returned, never taking his eyes off Eirlik's skier.

"He says that this is between you and him, and suggests settling it by direct combat, one on one, on skiers."

"What else? I heard you arguing."

"He demands you withdraw all your men to the far side of the delta. Then you and he will meet further up the river, where there is plenty of room to maneuver, and resolve your dispute there. I don't like it and don't trust him. I don't think you should do it."

"Tell him I accept."

Chapter Thirty-nine
Ameron's Escape

Phaedra had traveled past so many crossing rivers and varieties of landscape that she knew she could never retrace her course, which she was certain was by design. The day before, she had watched the sun rise on her left. This day's dawn was on her right. She knew they had circled many times. The night before, she had overheard an argument between members of her escort about how the trip to the ocean had already taken too long. Since then, they stayed on the same river.

The Shezendoa working the craft were all from Blackmaste. The ship itself was large enough to carry a dozen passengers and crew, and the vessel was like no other watercraft she had ever seen. With a completely black exterior, it rode low to the water with twin pontoons like a skier; it was not built for economy of space but for luxury and leisure. There was something else that made this craft unique: it had an invisible bubble screen. When activated, it was as solid as aquarium glass, but whenever her Shezendoa guard wanted, it simply disappeared, and she enjoyed the cool breezes that washed over her.

She saw the guards suddenly focus their eyes downriver and their demeanor stiffen, so she listened closer. When they kept their voices too low for her to hear and tried discreetly to pick up spears and check the swords at their sides, it made her sit up and look around.

Directly ahead, there was another vessel similar to the one she rode in, except it was decorated with bright colors and drifting with its nose circling about as if trying to decide what direction to go.

Several Shezendoa leaped from the colorful watercraft and splashed frantically for the shore, leaving a lone passenger behind. The abandoned man leaned over the edge, weighing options. Finally, he sat back down and waved, but looked very nervous when Phaedra's skier approached.

"So, Ameron," said one of Phaedra's guards who leapt aboard the other skier, "coming to visit Gaebel? Where is Philandreas?"

"Please," Ameron begged. "Don't hurt me! Gaebel doesn't have to worry about Arendahj anymore. Islanders stormed the city, and those butchers killed anyone who didn't

escape."

"You're lying."

"I swear in Neth and Nean's name! An escaped slave named Strazis returned with an army. Philandreas and I tried to escape, but he gave me a skier with no power! I got lucky enough to find some other escapees to push us away, but as you can see, they were no fighters. I don't know where Philandreas went."

"Why are you so generous with this information?"

"Because I want to live!"

Phaedra saw Ameron gasp at the sternness in the eyes of her guards. She had seen how much Gaebel hated those who lived in Arendahj, and the Shezendoa who served him shared that hatred. It seemed that many of their relatives had ended up in the slave pens.

"Tasson," said Sentar, who had taught the Shezendoa language to Phaedra, "let's take him ashore and kill him. I'll deliver the island woman, and you take his skier back to Blackmaste and tell Gaebel. He'll be glad to hear that Arendahj has fallen."

Ameron began to beg.

"I agree." Tasson pulled Ameron to his feet and tied his hands behind his back. Then he pulled his knife.

"Please! You're making a mistake!"

Phaedra looked away when Ameron tried to make eye contact with her.

"You don't want to do this," Ameron continued to rant. "Gaebel can use me! I've found what he's been looking for."

Tasson had forced Ameron half over the side and was prepared to slit his throat but hesitated.

"What are you talking about?" he asked. "Tell me what you know."

"Then you'll kill me," Ameron's panic seemed to calm after discovering something with which to barter. "I'll only tell Gaebel. I can tell him so many things that he wants to know. He and Arendahj were stout allies in the past. We've learned things since then. I'll tell him everything."

Tasson sheathed his blade and forced Ameron back into his seat. After Sentar and the others had returned to Phaedra's craft, Tasson picked up a long pole dropped by those who fled and began pushing the powerless skier back upstream.

"Excuse me," Phaedra called out as the vessels passed in opposite directions. "Did you say that your city was conquered by an escaped slave named Strazis?"

"Yes?" Ameron replied with some concern after Tasson nodded for him to answer.

"Did he have skin like mine?" She pulled up a sleeve and displayed her bare forearm.

"Yes!"

"And you let him escape?"

"Yes ..." Ameron's voice became remorseful.

"Then it's no wonder your city fell. Strazis is the son of Eagal Ir Radin, the Worldlord of the Teluchi Islands."

"What!?"

She watched with some satisfaction as Ameron's jaw dropped agape, then turned away.

Soon, they were passing more refugees from Arendahj, citizens and slaves alike were running frantically along the banks of the river.

Then the tributary they were on joined with a massive river. Rounding a sharp bend, Arendahj came into view. It was still burning, and the towers without flames were blackened and still smoking. With a loud crash, one tower fell into another, taking them both down.

Sentar kept their craft near to the bank, his eyes scanning for the invaders. There was a sound of fighting upriver behind them, but no living thing could be seen in the direction of the ocean. He finally steered out to the center of the river, where fast running water quickly accelerated their speed.

Some of the transparent bridges remained intact, and Phaedra marveled at their construction as they passed overhead. The waters were surprisingly clear, with no floating bodies or debris.

The way seemed clear to the open seas.

"Arendahj is gone," said one of the Shezendoa.

"Destroyed by a pitiful little army of men mounted on one-man skiers," Sentar scoffed.

Phaedra kept quiet when she saw armies of skiers camped on one side of the river. Because there was no movement, and their eyes were pointed straight ahead, the Shezendoa never saw them. Phaedra also kept her eyes straight ahead but sat up tall in hopes of catching someone's attention as her skier headed down the delta outlet toward open water.

Chapter Forty
Disgraced

Amoment of peace came to Strazis as he steered his skier toward his impending duel with Eirlik. It was a feeling of calm that he had only felt before when swimming with the terhali, determined to do his utmost to shape his own fate, yet ready to accept without fear whatever outcome befell him. Both time and his heartbeat slowed as his focus sharpened.

An irritation on his chest caused Strazis to pull his medallion out and examine it for the first time since the being of light had grabbed at it. Eirlik's challenge had come so soon after the encounter that he had never had time to consider what happened. To his astonishment, as soon as he touched the medallion, it began chiming the same melody he had heard the night before. Opening it, he discovered that the center was no longer empty but had somehow been filled with a mass of tiny mechanisms that were all interconnected—and working in a cascade of tiny movements.

It was another addition to the long list of impossible things he had experienced.

The only explanation he could imagine came from an ancient and often ridiculed scholar, who hypothesized that all light and energy were just other forms of matter. It had been such an audacious statement, so far beyond any known science, that Strazis had always remembered it.

That explanation gained credence when, rubbing his fingers across the irritation on his chest, he realized that the skin beneath the medallion was slightly burned.

Had he really encountered a being who could transform light and energy into metals and precision gears? It seemed preposterous, and even if it could be done, even if that explained *how* it was done—there was still the question of *why*?

The sound of a blaring horn cleared his thoughts.

It was time to confront Eirlik.

Strazis accelerated past the crumbling buildings of Arendahj but soon slowed again to maneuver between the sand and mudbanks gathered at the mouths of tributaries where they joined the river beyond the city's walls.

Then, on the far side of the river, he saw a strange new type of skier emerging from a tributary. It was filled with several Shezendoa—and a blonde-haired woman with golden skin. Even though they were separated by a good distance and several long cycles of time, Strazis was certain that she must be Phaedra. No other woman looked like her or sat with a back so straight and chin held high.

Strazis forgot all about Eirlik and pulled his shakara as he turned his skier to pursue the Shezendoa craft.

He was closing the distance when the Shezendoa passed around the island of Neth and Nean. Strazis saw that his armies camped on the far side of the river had spotted his pursuit and were launching skiers.

Then Strazis saw another, massive group appear from hiding behind the island of Neth and Nean, and realized that the duel had been a trick to lure him away while Eirlik launched a sneak attack on his beached men.

Eirlik and his men were closer to the craft that carried Phaedra and gaining on it.

The Shezendoa on the craft grabbed up their spears and took defensive positions around Phaedra when Eirlik and his men surrounded them.

No one said a word as he and his sister exchanged a look of distaste that Strazis did not expect. Theirs was no happy reunion.

"I am Sentar," the lead Shezendoa announced when Strazis bumped several skiers of Promessus out of the way as he arrived. Phaedra silently mouthed his name.

"I'm Strazis of Issandra," Strazis answered in the Shezendoa language, "son of the Worldlord of the Teluchi Islands."

"What are you people saying," Eirlik demanded. Having understood some of Strazis' reply, he pointed at Phaedra and then to himself. "That's my sister. I'm the next Warlord of Promessus," then he gave a snide leer to Strazis, "and the next Worldlord of the Teluchi Islands."

"I don't care," Sentar replied in Shezendoa, while tightening his grip on the spear with one hand and slipping the other to the hilt of his sword. "What do you want?"

"Again," said Eirlik to no one in particular, "that's my sister."

"I see you understand the common tongue of the islands," Strazis observed. "So... use it. Phaedra, what's going on?" He could not tell if her silence was out of fear or intended to frustrate her brother.

"We rescued her from the Black Assassins," said Sentar in the common tongue,

"and we are taking her back to her father in Promessus. Let us pass."

"Now, that I understood," said Eirlik. "Who are you people?"

"We are Shezendoa," Sentar answered.

"Men speaking your language are the ones who took her," said Strazis, keeping his skier between them and the open sea. He noticed that Baron, Nara, and Farsun were approaching with reinforcements, but still some distance away.

"It's a big land. Many people speak our language. Our master rescued her, and now we are returning her." He looked directly at Eirlik. "And we'll do it ourselves, because we expect to be rewarded."

"I'm sure you do," said Eirlik. "Let them pass. I've got business right now to attend to with a traitorous murderer, and Phaedra doesn't seem to have any complaints."

"Wait," Strazis insisted. "Who is your master? What's his name?"

"Gaebel."

Strazis then saw the pleading look in Phaedra's eyes.

"You're the betrayer," he said to Eirlik, "if you leave your sister with these men. Because Gaebel is the man who attacked Kalikantari!"

Sentar threw his spear the instant his master's name repeated, but Strazis swung his skier to block the throw, kept the throttle open, and made a full 360-degree spin. He then leaped aboard the Shezendoa craft. His shakara gleamed as he defended against Sentar's sword.

The other Shezendoa shouted and charged at him with their spears, which he either parried or kicked away. Then he lunged with his shakara, cutting down two at once.

Eirlik cursed as the Shezendoa started to fall. While they were far superior fighters to the guards of Arendahj, their skills were no match for Strazis. The Shezendoa pushed Phaedra behind them, to the far end of the boat.

Surging his skier forward, Eirlik grappled Phaedra about the waist and snatched his sister off the boat before the embattled Shezendoa realized what he was doing. He threw her over his lap in an undignified fashion as he sped away.

"Spare Sentar," Phaedra called out to Strazis. "He was good to me!"

Sentar had other ideas and continued to press his attack with a fervor that left Strazis few options as he beat down the blade of his opponent. Sentar refused to accept defeat or capture and leaped forward to impale himself on the shakara.

As the only man left alive on the Shezendoa craft, Strazis looked up and saw the horror in Phaedra's eyes.

"Can you hear me, Strazis?" Eirlik called out. "I'm taking my sister back to Promessus! I'm done with this place. And there's no need for us to duel, now that you've attacked Phaedra's escort. Everyone has seen that you're clearly insane! You disgraced all of Issandra when you wouldn't even spare her friend!"

Sheathing his blade and throwing a loop around the hilt for extra security, Strazis dived into the water and swam for his skier. He was climbing aboard when his men arrived.

"What did he mean about you being disgraced?" asked Baron.

"You know Eirlik," said Farsun. "You can always tell when he's lying. His mouth is moving."

Strazis bowed his head.

"I came here to conquer Arendahj," he said. "Eirlik did that. I came to save the slaves, and Eirlik got them killed with his haste. I didn't even know the slave-masters had a weapon like that, but I should have. I was as hasty as Eirlik. Arendahj certainly didn't have many more weapons, as evidenced by how easily the city fell. This city was never a threat to the islands."

He pointed at the bodies in the craft that Nara's men were chasing down before it could drift away. "It turns out that they were the true enemy. And we still know nothing about them."

"Wasn't that Phaedra who Eirlik rescued?" Nara asked. "Surely she can tell us what we need to know."

"Eirlik... rescued?" Farsun said to Nara with his head cocked in disbelief.

Nara nodded in understanding, and Farsun shook his head.

"Even from a distance," said Baron, "I can tell she's grown into a beautiful woman. Maybe the most beautiful I've ever seen."

"Whoever she is, we can get her back," urged Farsun.

"Phaedra," Strazis confirmed. "That's her. And no, I've told you before that I won't pit islander against islander. It's amazing, she returns after all this time, only to find that Eirlik and I are still squabbling.

After all the failures of this quest, Eirlik may be right. I am a disgrace."

"Wait," Baron moved his skier closer to Strazis. "You may have lost Arendahj... and Phaedra, but the men who followed you to victory in combat know who you really are and respect you. As a matter of fact, they're a little in awe after that incident with the light on the island of Neth and Nean. You never did say what you did to make it go away, or where it came from."

"I really don't know," Strazis replied, "on either count. I did nothing. Release your prisoners, collect trophies of war and then return the armies to the Teluchi Islands. There's nothing more for us here. No one left to rescue. I'll ride back alone... I won't put my disgrace on the men, and I need time to think."

"You're no failure," Baron argued.

"Alone?" asked Nara. "You can't cross the western ocean alone."

Strazis shrugged. "I've done it before."

Chapter Forty-One
Gaebel's Awakening

The hollow flutes and stringed instruments of the musicians hidden in the shadows filled the auditorium-sized banquet hall with eerie music.

Seated with Tracus at a table laden with exotic foods and alcoholic drinks, Gaebel motioned to the Shezendoa standing guard at the entrance.

Ameron was dragged forward, shivering in fear and carried by guards holding each of his arms.

"Tasson, take off his chains," Gaebel or-dered. "That quivering ball of fat is no threat. And then clear the room—except for the musicians. Tell them to play something livelier."

The music quickly reached crescendo heights.

"On your feet, Ameron," Gaebel motioned for Tracus to remain. "Face me like a man."

"Greetings, greetings, merciful Gaebel," Ameron held his hands together like a man in prayer as he stammered and watched Tracus record his words with parchment and quill. "I have come to swear my allegiance to you. The men accompanying me gave your men the completely wrong impression when we met. After Arendahj fell, I was definitely coming straight to you."

"Don't lie," Gaebel rose and began pacing in circles around Ameron. "Your only thought was escape. The only thing I want to know is what you have to offer in exchange for your life."

"The fall of Arendahj?"

"How could that happen?"

"Well, it began with this peculiar slave." Ameron gestured at Gaebel's skin. "He looked a lot like you. The men who captured him said he'd been living on an island, running with the wavana... like a werebeast."

"Continue." Gaebel feigned disinterest.

"He wore a medallion, like yours."

"Similar to mine?" Gaebel pulled his medallion into view and held it forth. "Tell me more about your slave. What does he have to do with the fall of Arendahj?"

"We tested him severely. He was actually

able to rebuild an ancient islander skier—completely on his own, with no help."

Gaebel involuntarily raised his eyebrows.

"Then he later used it to escape. But, before that, he told our spy about how he intended to return and destroy Arendahj."

"How could a slave be a threat?"

"We didn't believe it, either. I still couldn't believe it when he actually did it."

"A slave brought Arendahj down? How?"

"The golden girl Tasson was escorting explained it to me. It turns out that Strazis was the son of Eagal Ir Radin, the Worldlord of the Teluchi Islands."

"A golden-skinned islander?" Gaebel returned to his seat and dropped down hard. "With a medallion?"

"Yes," Ameron replied.

"The boy whose name wasn't on the list." Gaebel looked at Tracus. Then his attention returned to Ameron. "How could a rabble of islanders take down Arendahj? What happened to your defenses?"

"You were always our main defense," Ameron bowed his head. "The legend of the Nameless Ones, the Black Assassins, always kept us safe."

Gaebel smiled.

"Now let me tell you some interesting things," Gaebel looked at his medallion. "This is more than a music box; it provides me with a form of empathy—puts me in touch with the workings of the Universe."

"Universe, my Lord?" Ameron obviously had no concept of the word.

"Call it a gift of the Moon Gods. It gives me their knowledge. I'm sure you've heard the legends, Ameron, about how the Moon Gods once walked this world and did war with their children who, like me, were born from matings between the Moon Gods and human women. The islander named Strazis must have been like me. How he came to Kalikantari at such a young age is a mystery."

Tracus scribbled furiously and started on a fresh sheet of parchment.

"I met him once," Gaebel rose and resumed circling Ameron. "Thought he was eaten by a terhali. But that boy is not what I want to know about."

"I'm at your service," Ameron bowed clumsily from lack of practice.

"When I awoke from a long sleep, you Shezendoa thought of me as your god. I promised to take all the old machines that you could not understand and make them work again. The islander's skiers are a perfect example. They use only a fraction of what those skiers can really do."

Ameron nodded as though his chin were spring-loaded, waiting for a question.

"Then I heard that Arendahj was competing with me to restart the old machines. In fact, I heard that you found the key I was looking for, and you kept it a secret."

"We did, yes." Ameron then hastily added, "But we never figured out how to use it. If you promise not to kill or torture me, I'll happily tell you where it is."

"You found it on the Isle of View!" Gaebel exchanged a look with Tracus.

"Philandreas found it." Ameron collapsed to his knees, his head ogling about as if his neck were broken while he tried to keep eye contact with Gaebel.

"How?"

"He said it came in a vision given to him by Neth and Nean."

"A vision?"

"Philandreas had many of them. One vision told him to unearth the rock on the delta island, where the giant carving of the doorway to Neth and Nean was discovered. The runes carved into the doorways tell how, at a predetermined time, it will open to grant Neth and Nean free access into our world. Only Philandreas could read them, and he never revealed when that time would come. He said that it would be soon, and it was his duty to make preparations for their coming."

"What else did you find on that island?"

"Ancient books of knowledge that told us how to build the transparent bridges so that Neth and Nean's worshippers could freely reach the island."

"So that's where you learned that. What else did his visions reveal?"

"Where to find and how to wake you."

Tracus abruptly stopped his writing and looked up in surprise.

"Me?" asked Gaebel. "I'm no worshipper of Neth and Nean."

"Neth and Nean work in mysterious ways." Ameron bowed his head. "Philandreas said you were a Moon Child who would become Neth and Nean's greatest servant. And, once again, Philandreas was right. Arendahj rose to great power while your Black Assassins kept our enemies disorganized and scattered—until now. You became so powerful yourself that Philandreas began to fear you and those

Shezendoa who served you."

"I never understood why," Gaebel's face became a mask of anger that reflected his tone of voice. "Everything I've done was for the benefit of the Shezendoa and Arendahj. I returned the Golden girl, Phaedra, to the islanders in an attempt to stop them from attacking you, but they moved much faster than I anticipated. Tell me what you found on the Isle of View?"

"Will you spare me? I don't understand why you're getting so angry?"

Gaebel drew his knife.

"I just told you how I sent Phaedra back to the islanders, for your benefit. I wanted to keep her for myself!"

Ameron covered his mouth as he tried to stifle spontaneous whimpers of fear.

"You saw her. You saw how beautiful she is!"

Gaebel's blade flashed at the same moment a drum sounded, and the music stopped.

The fingers covering Ameron's mouth could not contain the blood suddenly gushing from his mouth, and he slowly collapsed to the floor. He held up a pleading hand that slowly fell with each successive heartbeat.

"I'm free, now," Gaebel said to Tracus. "It's like a cloud has been lifted from my mind. All the time I spent concentrating on Arendahj's needs was a waste."

"What are your orders?" Tracus asked.

"I want an army. Not just more Black Assassins, but a damned army. We're going to the Isle of View to accomplish what I have been trying to do for far too long, but not for the Shezendoa. We're doing this for me!"

Tracus nodded, rose, and headed for the door, stepping over Ameron as his feet kicked for the last time and his body finally stopped quivering.

"But first," said Gaebel, "there's another matter."

Tracus paused. "That is?"

"The girl, Phaedra..." Gaebel paused when, through an open window, the scream and calamity of an animal caught in the jaws of a predator sounded briefly, followed by an eerie silence.

He saw the eyes of the musicians all go wide with fear.

"I want her back," said Gaebel. "Tell Tasson to trap a gatakmo and prepare him to travel. Take Phaedra's bedsheets to give it the scent, and then contact our man in the islands. Promise him whatever he wants."

"What about your promises to the Shezendoa?" Tracus asked, so softly that it was easy for Gaebel to ignore him.

Chapter Forty-Two
The Gyre

Strazis lingered in the ruins of Arendahj after his army departed. Charred embers and scattered bodies were everywhere, and huge flocks of scavenger birds filled the skies in rolling waves as they were drawn to the feast.

He stepped over a dung snake left in the streets by a warrior from either Promessus or Andera, right next to a woman who had been stripped naked, molested, then mur-dered and left to rot. It was beyond brutal. The islander culture that he had always revered now disgusted him as much as had Arendahj.

Returning to his skier, he headed down the river and, when faced with an open, em-erald sea, looked south and hesitated for some time. With a shake of the head, he threw off the rudderless feeling that had suddenly overwhelmed him and set his course eastward.

At the Isle of View, he saw a small cluster of skiers moored at the water's edge and moved closer to investigate. Seeing the banner of Keton, he realized that Nevil Daa Nara had claimed it as the most westerly of the Teluchi Islands.

Looking at the islander banner flapping in the wind, he made a decision without thought as his hands mechanically steered his skier away from the Isle and to the southwest.

Losing himself in the isolation of water and sky, Strazis was stunned by what he saw when the mainland once again rose be-fore him. Instead of polluted skies and the desolation of destruction he had expected, he discovered a world of clean air, teeming with life. Songbirds filled the skies, while herds of strange animals roamed the beach-es, and the waters beneath him were filled with fish. It was nothing like how the li-brary books had described the western reaches.

On the horizon, the sun dropped as the Shadowy Moons once again chased it from the sky, and waters were painted with bright colors that seemed to form a path that beckoned him to follow it to the shore.

Anyone else would have considered this to be a sign from the Gods that could not be ignored.

He sat, inwardly debating his options, until night had fully fallen and the pathway offered by the sun vanished.

He was not certain why he eventually turned his skier back to the east, but he did so with authority as he opened the throttle up.

During the days that followed, Strazis dallied several times on the waters, hoping to discover a current that might lead back to the Teluchi Islands, but all the currents led either west or south. He began to wonder if the Moon Gods might actually be real and if they were sending him a message.

Even more of a mystery was why he kept ignoring them.

After several days without sleep and fighting to stay awake, Strazis was dozing when a loud roaring noise roused him.

His eyes snapped open to complete disorientation as a parade of ancient spires jutting out of the water spun past in a repeating and ever-accelerating pattern. Looking over his shoulder, he realized that he had wandered into a legendary gyre. Once trapped, no skier had ever escaped from one of these whirlpools.

Feeling fortunate that his skier had been oriented with the nose pointed at the outer edge of the swirling waters, he opened his throttle full up, but all he accomplished was to slow his descent into the vortex.

Strazis refused to panic as his heart slowed and mind relaxed. Keeping the throttle fully opened, he closed his eyes and thought about the time in Arendahj when his skier had somehow risen off the water and sailed over the sea gate.

Taking in deep breaths and letting them out slowly, he ignored the deafening roar of the water ringing in his ears. Then there came a sudden jolt that threw him back into his seat.

Strazis opened his eyes and realized that he had not only pulled free of the gyre's grip, his skier was rising like a soaring bird in an upward arc that took him so high that he cleared an ancient spire that had been shattered. Had it not been, he would have crashed into the side. His skier then glided gracefully back down to the water, where it jolted wildly as he began careening at full power between the tilting towers.

Not until he had reached the far side of the cluster of spires was he able to fully slow. Once he did, he turned back and gazed at what was left of the ancient city slowly crumbling away into the gyre.

Rather than lament another mistake that nearly ended in tragedy, Strazis found solace in a pair of epiphanies. Most profound was that he now knew where he was. These ruins and the gyre were well known to islanders, being located southeast of Promessus, close to Tyle. Legends told that a great battle between armies of skiers had taken place here not long before Eagal Ir Radin became the Worldlord, resulting in so much cannon fire that the vortex had opened up and swallowed both armies. The gyre had continued to grow ever since.

The other revelation was the realization

of an opportunity for sleep. Strazis tethered himself to the jutting masonry of a collapsed spire and passed out immediately.

Waking with the first light of a new dawn, Strazis took the opportunity to explore the ruins. He made certain to stay well away from the gyre as he cruised beneath a pair of spires that had collapsed into each other to form a gateway. Unable to read the well-worn writing that had been carved into them, he wondered sadly what arts and history might lie beneath the water, destroyed by rolling waves.

Then Strazis heard the faint sound of metal clashing against stone. The noise was regular and guided him to a skier chained to the waist of a statue of a woman being held aloft above the water by a score of stone hands. The skier was pointed away from him, and the shifting winds and waves had caused its pontoons to bump repeatedly into the statue, slowly obliterating the face.

A terhali broke the water next to Strazis' skier, holding its head high as it gnashed its teeth along one of his pontoon skis, then abruptly slid away and out of sight. It was unusual to see one of them in crowded waters, but the reason for its presence was soon obvious when Strazis saw the dried blood trailing down the side of the skier.

Moving up beside the craft, Strazis finally got a look at the rider, sitting slouched with his hands clutching the clotted blood that covered his stomach.

It was Dextran of Promessus. His lips were curled back, revealing gritted teeth locked in a death grin. He had evidently suffered a stomach wound and had done everything he could in a useless attempt to staunch the bleeding.

Strazis realized that Dextran must have been in a delirium of pain to end up where he was, for Promessus was far to the north. Then he saw that the compass had been smeared with blood. The more Dextran had tried to clean it, the more he had obscured it.

What concerned Strazis was how such a thing could have happened. It was well known that the only possible match for Dextran in combat was Eagal Ir Radin, and it was long speculated that a fight between the two could have no winner.

Suddenly, Strazis forgot his own concerns and regrets, filled with anxiety for the Worldlord. Tethering the Warlord's craft to his, he scrambled aboard and across Dextran's body, attempting to free it from the mooring. But Dextran had wound and entwined the chain so haphazardly, it proved difficult to undo.

Pausing a moment to consider how best to unravel this puzzle, Strazis became distracted by the thin waist and perfect body of the statue, which reminded him of his last sight of Phaedra. It was easy to picture her face in place of the one missing from the statue.

Even though they had never really spoken, since that night she had come to his rescue, he had felt a bond with her that he could not explain. The romances he had laughed at as a child might have called it a chaste love.

He realized then that she was the real reason he had decided to return to the Teluchi Islands, and his feelings of being rudderless vanished.

Strazis determined that he would finish the conversation he had tried to start with Phaedra so long ago on Kalikantari, regardless of whether Eirlik and the whole of the Promessian army stood between them.

Chapter Forty-three
A New Worldlord

The sea gates of Issandra were closed, and burning kettles of oil had been placed all along the crest. From them fumed billowing clouds of differently-colored smoke, while nearby drums sounded a steady beat.

As he approached the side gate, Strazis could see that people were gathered around the lagoon for a ceremony. From the center of the lagoon, he saw the last wisps of smoke from a funeral pyre.

"What happened?" he demanded of the guard when he discovered that the side gate was also closed.

"Eirlik of Promessus is our new Worldlord," said the guard as he looked to his companion for instruction. The other guard only shook his head in confusion.

"That can't be. Eirlik was forbidden from ever again stepping foot on Issandra."

"The Worldlord issued a decree overturning that, right before he died," said the second guard. "Since then, Eirlik has killed all challengers."

"Or had them killed," the first guard added as he looked around to make certain no one else heard.

"What happened to Eagal Ir Radin? Open and let me pass!"

"My Lord Strazis," the second guard said as he quickly complied, "such things aren't for me to tell."

"Tell me anyway!"

"Murdered," said the first guard.

"Found dead on the docks," the second added.

Then both guards saw the body on the skier Strazis had in tow.

"Is that—?" They looked at each other, stunned.

"You can't go in there with him like this!" said the second. "You'll be killed!"

The warning came too late, as Strazis was already through the gate.

He crossed the lagoon on a direct line for the docks beneath the Worldlord's tower, where he saw skiers with familiar banners gathered.

Eirlik was there, too, sitting proudly on the Worldlord's skier, dressed in his finest armor and wearing a white-plumed helmet as he prepared to take a celebratory ride around the lagoon. All the inhabitants of Issandra had gathered to cheer their new Worldlord.

Strazis could see Eirlik's back stiffen when Eirlik saw his skier approaching. But Eirlik appeared to remain calm, making no reaction even when his dead father was discovered on the skier Strazis brought in tow.

"I found him by the vortex," Strazis explained before swords were drawn.

El Cee Baron's arm reached out to help Strazis up the moment he had docked. His eyes were tortured by something he could not express.

"I heard about Eirlik," said Strazis as Nevil Daa Nara joined them. "How did my father die?"

"By knife," said Baron as Nara produced a blade. "That one."

Strazis took the blade in his hands, turning it slowly, running his fingers across the designs on the blade. Then he reached to stop the men carrying Dextran's body away.

"Lay him down," he instructed.

Eirlik suddenly sat up, intrigued.

Running his fingers over Dextran's outer gear, Strazis found something he had noticed when climbing over the body in order to take it in tow. He pulled back a leather flap to reveal a pocket that hid an empty knife scabbard.

Nara leaned and compared the knife's length and breadth to the scabbard.

"It's a match," said Strazis.

"That doesn't change anything." Farsun shouldered his way down the dock that was rapidly becoming crowded. "It won't stop Eirlik from claiming the title of Worldlord. Eagal Ir Radin died while we were all at Arendahj. Since we returned, Eirlik has defeated all challengers in fair combat."

Eirlik grinned broadly and pulled his blade from its scabbard to show the blood he had not bothered to clean.

"He hasn't taken the coronation procession yet," Strazis asserted. "I claim my right to challenge!"

"You have no right," Eirlik scoffed. "You've returned in disgrace. You have no honor with which to claim the title of Worldlord."

"I don't care about that," Strazis replied. "Your father killed mine. If you won't take the challenge, then we have a blood feud between us that can only be settled with combat. You can't deny that!"

"I can, because I don't recognize your claim," said Eirlik. "Dextran didn't even die here. Where did you say you found him? By the gyre?" He looked around to his supporters. "We all know what happened here. Strazis murdered my father. I'll see him executed for that."

"That's a stomach wound." Baron pointed to Dextran's hands, locked in rigor around his midsection. "It would have taken him a long time to die from that."

"And the Worldlord's blade did have blood on it," added Nara, "but we never found a body. Judging by the rigor, your father has been dead for several days. The timing matches."

"Strazis couldn't have done it," Farsun asserted.

More warriors from Promessus who had seen the disruption to the planned festivities began pouring down to the dock, with men from Vanessa marching steadfastly at the side of their conquerors. Calarn and his men from Andera were closer and the first onto the dock.

"Regardless of how my father died," Eirlik argued, "Strazis is disgraced. I forthwith banish him forever from all the Teluchi Islands!"

Calarn cocked his head to one side.

"Does our new Worldlord have to put down an uprising on the very day of his coronation?"

"He's not the Worldlord yet," Baron replied with an almost casual tone as he gestured toward those at his side. "None of us have taken an oath to him."

"What about our treaties?" Eirlik demanded.

"Those were with Eagal Ir Radin and Dextran Taa Constous. Not you. After the grove of trees serving as the Avenue of the Dead was planted outside the city, the Warlord and the Worldlord were the last links to those treaties."

"And we haven't forgotten how you planned to ambush us at Arendahj," said Farsun.

"I have no idea what you're talking about," Eirlik retorted.

"To keep the alliance together," said Nara, "prove yourself with one final challenge."

"Eirlik, if you won't respond to my claim of a blood feud," said Strazis in a firm and clear voice, "then I once again challenge you to combat by skiers—for the title of Worldlord!"

Chapter Forty-four
And One Stood Alone

"Strazis must be given a chance to rest," Nevil Daa Nara demanded. "He just crossed the western ocean alone."

"And Eirlik just defeated three challengers," Calarn countered.

"We'll fight now," Strazis asserted.

"There's another option," Calarn drew his sword and prepared to thrust. "I could kill you now!"

In one swift motion Strazis pulled his shakara and cut Calarn down before he could make another move.

"Damn," said the swordsman from Andera as he fell to his knees, "you really are that fast." Gripping his bleeding arm, he tried to rise, but slipped in his own blood and fell off the dock.

Eirlik took one look, strapped the chin strap of his helmet, and without another word sped his skier right over Calarn. Warriors from Andera had to dive in to rescue their island's champion swordsman.

The sight of Eirlik heading out onto the lagoon astride Eagal Ir Radin's skier—the finest in all the islands—flushed anger through Strazis' veins. He remembered the look of horror he had seen on Tanith Woanan's face the day she watched Eirlik run him over in a similar fashion. Then he touched the jeweled pommel of the shakara the Worldlord had given him. This time Eirlik did not have every advantage.

"Tell them to beat the drums faster," Strazis said as he unmoored his skier.

Nara and Farsun nodded while Baron passed the order, motioning for the dock to be cleared. The trio then hastened up the stone steps to get a good vantage point while the drums pounded rapidly in unison.

As he often did, Strazis kept his seat straps unfastened. This would be a fight to the death, and he wanted every bit of mobility he could get.

To fight a sudden wave of weariness, he leaned and reached over the side of the skier to scoop up a handful of water from the plumes of his skis and splashed it on his face. Nara had been right about there being a toll from his long journey across the western ocean. He was glad for the moment of respite he had enjoyed the night before.

The beating of the drums continued to increase in tempo as Strazis positioned himself on the far side of the lagoon, opposite Eirlik. He unconsciously reached for his medallion, not realizing it until it began to chime, all the time wondering how he could possibly aim liquid fire at the Worldlord's skier. Then a fresh breeze brushed against the dampness of his face. It was a small thing but seemed to reinvigorate him. He pulled his helmet from the equipment compartment and strapped it on.

That movement signaled the beginning of the combat, as Eirlik began racing at him with reckless speed and firing his cannons prematurely, just for show.

Strazis moved forward to meet him, but with a conservative, controlled speed. Not wanting to use his cannons, Strazis dropped his hand to his shakara, then to his Sticks, and finally onto the hilt of his knife. He then threw his head back and let loose the howl of a hunting wavana.

As the two craft hurtled into striking range, Strazis changed his bearing and veered to one side an instant before Eirlik's cannon fire evaporated the water where he had just been. But Strazis knew that Eirlik was familiar with these tactics from their many encounters on the training waters of Kalikantari, and how it would only delay the inevitable. His only chance was to draw Eirlik closer.

All along the lagoon's edges, the crowds moaned their disappointment and began issuing jeers and calls about how all the previous challenges had already been concluded by this time. Strazis pretended to have made a wrong turn that allowed Eirlik to close on him.

"So, Lord Coward!" Eirlik called out. "Still the same old tricks? Still afraid of me?"

Then Eirlik did something Strazis did not expect; at the last minute Eirlik seemed to realize that he was being baited, drawn close in for hand-to-hand combat, and veered away.

"I saw what you did to Calarn," he shouted.

This completely confused the crowds, but Eirlik quickly regained the upper hand because of the speed and agility of his craft.

Strazis did not try to dodge the cannon fire this time, racing directly at Eirlik and spinning his skier at the last second, letting his engine take the hits. Smoke filled the air. He finished his spin and continued right back on course toward Eirlik.

The baffled crowds fell silent.

With his engine quickly consumed by the corrosive fire eating through its workings, Strazis experienced a unique thing as, for the first time, his skier began to lose its mysterious power.

To no surprise, Eirlik kept his distance as Strazis' skier began to drift and sink, the pontoons compromised. The engine went under first, and the forward section tilted up. Strazis climbed onto the nose of the craft, stripped off all his heavy armor and held his hands out to one side.

"I accept it!" he called out.

Cannon fire shrieked straight at him.

Strazis knew what to do, as if he had practiced it, then realized that he actually had.

Springing high into the air, he cleared the liquid fire as it raced past, then turned in the air to dive gracefully into the water. Once underwater, he drew his knife and placed it between his teeth, and swam even deeper. He could see shadows lurking in the water, knew that there were reasons no one ever swam in the lagoon, but ignored them.

He stayed down a long time, while above him, Eirlik's skis created a circle of light and steadily lost speed as the time elapsed became improbable for most islanders to survive. Eirlik had no idea about how predictable he had become, having never known an adversary who persisted as Strazis had done.

Strazis finally began to stroke powerfully for the surface, flexing every muscle in his arms, chest, and legs. As he barreled upwards, gaining ever more speed as he went, the scabbard of his sword bounced off his churning legs. He timed his rise to intersect perfectly with Eirlik's course and most of his body breached when he broke the surface and collided with the skier.

Strazis saw Eirlik's jaw go slack as he rolled up the nose of the skier and over the windshield into the rider's pit. He then made a single, quick motion with his hand, and Eirlik began gasping and clutching at his throat.

"Always go for the head or the throat," Strazis said as he calmly unfastened Eirlik's straps. He then pulled Eirlik from his seat, raised him into the air above his head, and turned to face the nearest crowds. He threw the would-be Worldlord from Promessus like garbage into the water.

Something from below snatched the body almost instantly.

Half-collapsing into the seat, Strazis watched as a cloud of crimson bubbled and expanded on the water's surface. The cheering from the crowds seemed hollow as he mentally processed everything that had just transpired.

When he finally moved the skier in the direction of the tower dock, the crowds strained their necks for a better look as they crowded in that direction.

Elsewhere on Issandra, high in the Worldlord's tower and far away from any window overlooking the spectacle, Eirlik's sister Phaedra turned her head when she heard the drums finally stop and trumpeting horns announced the new Worldlord.

To Be Concluded in Cirsova # 13!

Michael Tierney is known to wear a mask when traveling abroad. His hobby is underwater photography—especially sharks. Michael Tierney's credits include myriad Wild Stars titles, Tarzan and the Mysterious She, the weekly online strip Beyond the Farthest Star, and the Edgar Rice Burroughs 100 Year Art Chronology. His Robert E. Howard Art Chronology is coming soon. He has also collaborated with Cirsova publishing to restore the near-lost All-Story Weekly works of Julian Hawthorne.

Vran, the Chaos-Warped (Book 2)

By DAVE RITZLIN

Ripped by magic from the frozen world of the primitive cavemen, Vran finds himself in even stranger environs! Can he track down the foul wizard Foad Misjak within the halls of a giant castle that is teeming with cannibals and magically animated statues!?

Chapter I
Citadel of Dreams

Vran felt himself falling through a void of impenetrable blackness. But was he falling? Without a frame of reference, he could be soaring, or hovering, or not moving at all. At times it seemed as if any of those possibilities might be occurring, or perhaps all of them at once. He was trapped in a prison which deprived him of all his senses. Naught he saw and naught he heard. He resigned himself to a fate of wandering the void eternally, for nothing seemed to matter.

After Vran made his dismal prediction, the darkness gradually began to recede. He felt like one does in the moments after waking from an odd dream, when awareness has returned but before the powers of cogitation have been regained. Perhaps all he had experienced recently *was* nothing more than a dream. Demons, wizards, cave girls, goblins... They certainly did not seem real to Vran in his current state.

He opened his eyes. Where he was, he had no idea, but it was evident his current environs were nothing like a cave in a far-flung world of frost. He stood in a man-made chamber, furnished with finely crafted tables and chairs of wood. The temperature was refreshingly mild compared to where he had been last.

Vran checked himself for broken bones or other injuries and found none. His sword remained with him, as did the tezbou. It was still wrapped around his arm, asleep but breathing gently.

In the dim light, Vran could see that the chamber was untenanted. At least there was no sign of Misjak, Twar, or other enemies nearby. He exited the room via a wide archway and found himself in another chamber similar to the first. Vran continued on in the same direction, heading for what appeared to be a source of natural light in the distance. As he walked, he wondered if he was back on Nilztiria, in some noble's palace. If so, explaining his presence here would be difficult.

At the end of the series of rooms was an

immense hall, wider than the entirety of Misjak's manse in Otoro and doubly long. The ceiling was at least six times Vran's height, by his own estimate. Vast windows lined the far wall, letting in a dazzling amount of sunlight. Numerous tables surrounded by exquisitely-carved high-backed chairs were arranged throughout the hall. It would make an excellent site for a grandiose feast, easily capable of accommodating hundreds of revelers, but apart from Vran, the hall was empty.

Vran crossed the hall, hoping a glimpse through the windows would reveal some clue as to his location. Instead of enlightenment, what he saw offered amazement and stupefaction.

Far below the castle lay a vast forest. So far below, in fact, it was almost incomprehensible to Vran—the distance between himself and the ground was well over a mile! The castle must be the size of a mountain!

How could such an immense structure of stone be built by human hands? Sorcery must have been involved, no doubt, but even then… Vran grappled with this for some time before he noted that the hue of the sun was a healthy yellow. Therefore it was a certainty he had not returned to Nilztiria. Or perhaps he was still lost in a dream.

Vran stuck his head out the window again, intending to take in the whole of the landscape, but was struck by a sudden feeling of vertiginousness. He gripped the window's sill tightly until the sensation passed. After recovering, he made a second attempt. This time, craning his head to the left, he saw a tree of mythical height standing beside the castle, its crown hidden somewhere amongst the clouds. Intrigued, Vran was compelled to investigate further. He traversed the length of the hall to its end and opened the window. There before him was the immense tree, towering over the castle, its branches close enough for him to touch. Hanging from those branches were appetizing fruits which very closely resembled red apples. Vran felt the pangs of hunger, for it had been quite a while since he had last eaten—in fact, he could not say how long he had gone without supping, for the amount of time he spent in dimensional limbo was unknowable. He carefully extended his arm and snatched one of the fruits.

He paused before taking a bite. What if it were poisonous or otherwise detrimental to his constitution? He debated it in his mind, and hunger won out over caution. His worrying had been for naught, for he found it nourishing and satisfyingly sweet.

Vran picked a few more fruit from the tree and ate them while he continued his exploration of the castle. He had yet to encounter another living creature, hostile or otherwise, but it seemed implausible that such a gigantic construction could be entirely without occupants. Still, after travelling the corridors of the castle for hours, he had not met another human being. Vran wished for paper and a writing utensil to map the place, but he quickly realized only an expert in cartography could create a chart of any value.

The immensity and complexity of the architectural work was stunning. Vran pondered what sort of intelligence was capable of designing a building of such monstrous proportions. And where was its creator now? More questions occurred to Vran. What of the area surrounding the castle? What lay beyond the forest?

This line of thinking led Vran to wonder where his sworn enemy Foad Misjak might be. Had the winds of chaos transported him to this castle as well? If so, they must have deposited him somewhere far from Vran's vicinity. It might take months of exploration before they reencountered one another.

Vran noticed that while many of the myriad hallways were carpeted with dust, others were free of it. This would indicate that someone, or something, was nearby. He trod more lightly, more warily.

The swordsman came to a grandiose staircase, wide enough to accommodate an army, leading upward. He ascended it one flight, hoping that investigating a different level would yield more fruitful results.

At first glance, the new floor bore little difference from the one Vran had materialized on. He came to a great hall much like the one below, but more sparsely furnished. Also, tellingly, there were no accumulations of dust on the floor.

The walls to Vran's left and right each contained a multitude of high oaken doors. Vran tried to open one on his left, but it was stuck. He pressed his bulk against it and, after a strenuous time, eventually forced it open. Looking into the windowless room beyond he saw that the door had been barricaded by a square table. More importantly, hanging from a chain attached to the ceiling was a lantern—and it was lit!

So the castle was inhabited after all! But by whom—or what?

Vran reached up and removed the lantern from the chain. He believed it would prove useful in the near future.

Opposite Vran was another door like the first he had passed through. This one opened easily, however. Beyond was a group of four scraggly-haired ruffians seated at a table, their heads turned toward him. They were clad in what had once been fine garments of samite, but these were now torn and rumpled. They rose, reaching for their long knives and clubs. One pointed at Vran and shouted, "It's him! Green eyes!"

How do they know of me? Vran wondered. But little that mattered now, for he was about to fight for his life. His blade sprang from its scabbard.

One of the hostile men shouted to the others, "Get reinforcements!" Two ran off. Vran flung the lantern at one of them, knocking him prone and setting him ablaze, but the other escaped through a door on the far side of the room. The other two who remained advanced menacingly, licking their lips, seeming to care little for the plight of their burning compatriot.

Vran easily parried a knife-thrust from one of his opponents and cut him down with a lightning-quick riposte. The other's jaw dropped. He backed off, aware that he could not match the martial skills of the swordsman. He concentrated solely on defending himself from Vran's darting blade. While such strategy was sound, it availed him not, for, as was inevitable, one of Vran's blows found its mark and pierced his chest. As he fell to the floor, the man who had fled burst back into the room, accompanied by a dozen comrades.

In spite of his superior abilities in swordplay, Vran knew he could not stand against a force of such overwhelming numbers and made the tactical decision to retreat. He backed away through the door, brandishing his blade. The ruffians followed, but not too closely. None wanted to be the first struck down by that dexterously-wielded weapon.

A scuffling sound from behind Vran alerted him to another presence. Turning, he saw a man in the main hall dressed similarly to his attackers, but his countenance showed no trace of hostility.

"An enemy of the westerners is a friend of mine," said the stranger. "Come with me—quickly now, more are coming!"

Vran made a quick lunge, driving the point of his blade into the heart of his foremost opponent, then dashed into the main hall. He hoped that by causing these men—"westerners," evidently—to stumble over their fallen comrade, he could gain valuable time to escape. The futility of his action became readily apparent as many doors on this side of the hall were thrown open like floodgates, deluging the room with new enemies.

"That's Dorg with the green-eyed one!" one shouted. "Don't let either escape! We'll dine well tonight!"

The one called Dorg ran to the far side of the hall, and Vran followed closely behind. They passed through a door, and then Dorg led Vran through a bewildering labyrinth of rooms, halls, and chambers. Vran immediately perceived he had no hope of retracing their path if necessary. Fortunately, Dorg seemed to know the area well.

As they ran, Vran said to Dorg, "One mentioned dining well. Do they mean to eat us?"

"Cannibals run rampant in this part of the castle," replied Dorg.

This answer unsettled Vran. He greatly disliked the notion of being hunted for his meat like a deer.

They did not waste breath on further discussion, for there was no telling when the westerners might discover them. Sometimes they thought they heard their pursuers nearby, and Dorg would immediately alter his path. They came to a room with no apparent method of egress, but Dorg knew of a hidden passage obscured by curtains. After that, the sounds of pursuit faded, then disappeared.

After a dizzying run through a seemingly-endless maze, they finally came to a large steel door containing a peephole. Dorg rapped upon the portal and cried, "It is Dorg, let me in!" The door creaked open, and Dorg and Vran were allowed entry.

After they crossed the threshold, a guardsman slammed the door shut behind them and barred it. The room beyond was large and filled with people, all dressed in the same oddly ragged finery that the westerners wore. They looked upon Vran with astonishment.

"I found him fighting the westerners," Dorg announced.

A man with a thick, gray beard and thinning locks said, "Are you the one known as Vran the Chaos-Warped?"

"Some call me that," admitted Vran. "How did you know me?"

"All will be explained in due time," said the elder. "But here you may put your sword down."

"I'd prefer to hold on to it for a while longer," said Vran.

Of a sudden Vran felt a sharp point

against his ribs. Dorg, a knife in his hand and a sneer on his face, said, "You don't have a choice. Drop it."

Chapter II
Someone to Eat

With no alternative open to him, Vran released his grip on his sword. The elder came forward and bound Vran's wrists tightly with a length of hempen rope. The betrayed swordsman stared at the denizens of the castle with all the menace and hatred he could muster. Many turned away from those unnatural green eyes, but Dorg appeared unfazed.

"Take him to the kitchens," ordered the elder.

Dorg picked Vran's sword off the floor and pointed to a door on the right with it. "That way," he said.

Vran turned and spit in his face.

Exasperated, Dorg lifted the blade as if to strike off Vran's head, but the elder shouted, "Hold! Do not harm him, especially not his head!"

Dorg snorted. "Very well... I'll just tenderize the meat," he said, and forcibly drove his knee into Vran's groin. Vran staggered backwards, gasping for breath.

The elder's face darkened with disapproval. "No more foolishness, Dorg." He pointed to two other unkempt men. "You two, bring him to the kitchens and make him ready." Each man grabbed an arm and dragged Vran through the door.

The room beyond was in fact a kitchen, albeit one in such disarray it looked as if it had been ransacked by vandals. Various cooking utensils lay about the floor, as did piles of bones—human bones. The entire area reeked of noisome odors, in spite of the large open windows which looked on the surrounding forest. Steel hooks depended from the ceiling.

"Why are you doing this?" gnarred Vran. "Explain!"

Dorg cleared aside a stack of unwashed plates from a table and set Vran's sword down upon it. He pulled up a rickety chair and seated himself, facing Vran. "I owe you no explanation, nor anything else, but I see no reason not to tell you. One of your acquaintances, a certain Foad Misjak, has put a bounty on your head."

"Misjak is here? In the castle?" exclaimed Vran.

"Yes. He appeared not long ago, warning us of a dangerous madman with bizarrely-tinted green eyes. He offered his aid to whichever clan could bring him your head. Once we do so, he will lend us his sorcerous power and eradicate our rivals, the filthy westerners."

"Who are these westerners you despise so?"

Dorg leaned back in his chair. "Years ago, they were part of the same group as us. How we all came to this castle, I don't know. But a dispute arose between two of our leaders. Some sided with one, the rest with the other. The differences became irreconcilable, so the clan split in two. We hold the eastern halls of the castle as our territory, and our bitter enemies reside in the west."

"What was the nature of this dispute?" asked Vran.

"That doesn't matter."

"I would think the reason for endlessly fighting against your former compatriots would matter greatly."

"You won't be thinking anything for much longer. Soon we'll present your head to the wizard—after we dine on your flesh, that is."

Threats always inflamed Vran's ire. In spite of his bound hands, he lunged at Dorg, but the two men restraining his arms held him back. Still, Dorg recoiled, a look of exasperation commingled with fear on his face.

"We can't have any of that," said Dorg. "Hang him up."

Vran's captors produced another thick cord of rope and wound it around his ankles. Ungently they hoisted him and hung him upside-down from one of the hooks. Satisfied that it would bear Vran's weight, Dorg dismissed the other two.

"You won't be able to cause much trouble for us now," said Dorg. He turned away and started to make preparations for cooking his captive, beginning by lighting a fire beneath a large vat filled with a dubious-looking liquid.

With blood rushing to Vran's head, sensations of wooziness overcame him. Once again, he thought he was dreaming. Was this magnificent hold with its crazed inhabitants truly real? Did he, in actuality, lay unconscious in the goblins' cave, this castle merely an invention of his fevered brain?

The cave... He remembered now, for the first time since awaking in this massive citadel, that Misjak had killed the girl Olo in that cave, and he had been unable to prevent it. Pangs of despair wracked his mind. He wondered how it was possible to have even temporarily forgotten her.

Thinking of the cave girl and the moments they shared in what seemed like a previous lifetime caused Vran to recall another denizen of that frozen world: the tezbou. He slipped a finger under his shirt sleeve and found the small reptile still comfortably wrapped around his forearm. It stirred at his touch. With the prospect of escape now viable, Vran shook off misery's grasp and began to take action.

He coaxed the tezbou forth from his sleeve until its chin rested on the ropes restraining his wrists. He tapped its head, and a flaming tongue darted out, setting the ropes afire. Vran twisted his neck, looking for Dorg. From his vantage point, Vran saw the cannibal was still engrossed in his work. Hopefully, by being so close to the boiling cauldron, Dorg would not notice the smell of smoke emanating from Vran's person. Still, Vran knew he must act quickly.

With a great feat of abdominal strength, Vran raised his upper body until he was able to grasp the hook from which he dangled. He touched the burning ropes around his wrists to those binding his ankles, igniting them as well. The heat grew intense, but Vran gritted his teeth, refusing to succumb to the pain. Once the ropes frayed sufficiently, he tore them away and dropped feet-first to the floor.

The sound of Vran's landing caught Dorg's attention. The cannibal made a dash for the table where he had placed the sword, but Vran intercepted him with a flying tackle. Fists flew as the two men crashed against a wall.

No match for Vran's size or strength, Dorg resorted to underhanded tactics. He used his knee to hammer his enemy's groin as he had done once before. Vran staggered backwards.

Sensing an opportunity, Dorg made another run for the sword, but Vran grabbed hold of his shirt. Dorg turned around and swung a clenched fist at Vran, who retaliated in kind. The two traded more blows, with Dorg getting the worst of it. The cannibal, desperate for an advantage, thrust a finger in Vran's eye.

Vran covered his aggrieved eye with his right hand while he defended himself with his left. He swung wildly, and though he failed to find his mark, the tezbou sprang from his sleeve onto Dorg's face. It sank its fangs into the cannibal's nose.

Dorg screamed in pain, not because of his punctured flesh, but due to the searing tongue which licked him. He grabbed the tezbou and attempted to rip it away, but Vran dealt him a blow to the skull mighty enough to leave him bereft of his senses.

The tezbou hopped off Dorg's face and scrambled back up Vran's arm. Vran knew he had to dispose of the cannibal quickly, and attempted to lift him bodily with the intent of dashing his brains against the floor. Dorg resisted as best he could, and his struggling caused Vran to stagger backwards against the wall. A sudden insight came to Vran. With the cannibal still in his grasp, he turned towards the window and heaved Dorg through it. Dorg wailed as he plummeted, his limbs flailing impotently. Vran watched with much interest, for he had never seen a man fall such a great distance before.

Although Vran had regained freedom of movement, he still remained deep in the cannibal-dominated territory of this castle of madness. Fighting his way out with brute force seemed a dismal prospect; the task would require some degree of stealth. Still, it would be foolish to go unarmed. He recovered his sword and placed it in its scabbard. He also grabbed the largest and sharpest of the kitchen knives and stuck it in his belt as an extra precaution.

Vran explored the cookery, searching for other exits. The only other door in the room apart from the one he entered through was on the side opposite the windows. Charily he opened it, revealing a pantry stocked with ordinary items. It would not even be of use to Vran as a hiding place, for it was too small and cramped.

The sound of men approaching came from the hall. Vran was faced with a choice: stand and fight, or flee? The former would lead to certain death, although many would perish with him; he would ensure that. The latter seemed impossible... but things are not always what they seem.

Vran hastened to the window through which he had defenestrated Dorg. He remembered seeing a ledge alongside the exterior of the structure, but was unsure as to its width. Examining it now, he believed it would be able to support him as long as he exerted caution. He climbed out the window just as the door creaked open.

Vran inched along the ledge away from the windows. He heard the cannibals voicing their consternation at his and Dorg's disappearance. "How could he have escaped?" shouted one angrily. "Search the room—search everywhere! If the westerners find him first, we're doomed!"

How long would it be before one of them thought to look out the window? Vran knew it could happen at any moment, and it would be best to put as much distance as possible between him and the cannibals before then. But speed was out of the question. He crept down the ledge at a snaillike pace, for one misstep would cause him to splatter on the forest floor as Dorg had.

Disaster of another type struck: the ledge suddenly came to an end! A portion of it had crumbled, eroded by time and the elements. The ledge continued beyond, but the gap was far too wide to jump even if there had been enough room for Vran to land safely.

A commotion came from the windows. Vran had been discovered!

Vran's green eyes darted left and right, up and down, desperately seeking some method of reprieval. There were no handgrips with which he could scale the castle, and he could go neither forward nor back. However, one possibility presented itself, although it came with incredible risks.

Standing a moderate distance away from the castle was an enormous tree, like the one Vran had gathered fruit from earlier. Vran thought he had a fair chance of reaching it if he leapt. But a slight miscalculation would result in a horrible, horrible death.

With the cannibals drawing nearer, Vran was forced into action. He steeled himself, then sprung off the ledge with all the strength he could muster. The cannibals, astonished he would dare such a feat, halted and stared with mouths open.

For a moment, Vran felt his body soaring, eaglelike. Then the descent began.

Vran refused to look down at the crown canopy thousands of feet beneath him. He stretched out his arms, reaching for a thick branch jutting from the tree's bole. As he

fell he came tantalizingly nearer to it. Would he be able to grasp it in time?

Yes!

Vran hoisted himself up on the limb and straddled it. He laughed and made rude, mocking hand gestures at the awestruck cannibals on the ledge. They began to confer among one another. Vran suspected that, having seen him accomplish what they previously had thought impossible, some might attempt to duplicate it. He must show them the folly of such an idea.

Vran snatched one of the red fruits growing on the tree and hurled it at the cannibals. The missile struck one of the men in the jaw, knocking him off balance. He made one futile attempt to grab the ledge as he fell, but his fingers slipped, and he plunged to his death.

"Do not follow!" Vran warned. "I have plenty of ammunition!" He reached for another fruit. The cannibals knew they were beaten, and they edged back to the window. Vran watched them disappear inside and, smiling, took a bite of the fruit.

From his vantage, Vran was able to view the entirety of the castle. The roof was not far above the floor where the cannibals made their habitation—seven or eight stories, Vran estimated. The castle walls stretched nearly to the horizon in either direction, with thin, spindle-like towers placed at various points. Once again, Vran marveled at the forces necessary to construct such an edifice.

Now that Vran had evaded the cannibals, the question remained of what to do next. Climbing down the tree was a risky proposition, to say the least, for there were no branches below him for at least a hundred feet. There were, however, many above him, and one had grown quite close to a window in one of the uppermost floors. Up he went.

Vran threw a leg over the branch and scuttled along it toward the open window. It easily supported him at first, but began to sag the further along it he moved. It seemed fairly sturdy, but there was no way of knowing if it would snap. Vran hurried onward, refusing to look down. He arrived at the branch's terminus safely, but the window was now above him, just out of arm's reach. Gingerly he placed one foot against the wall for leverage, and bounded upwards. He grabbed hold of the window sill and scrambled inside.

Vran coughed, for this chamber contained nothing but a thick layer of dust. In spite of the discomfort the unclean environment caused his lungs, Vran sat down and relaxed, for he was glad to have something solid and unyielding under him. The absence of madmen thirsting for his blood was favorable as well. Maybe he would take a brief nap here...

No. With Misjak present somewhere in the castle, he must be on his guard at all times. Most likely the eastern cannibals had informed the wizard of their encounter with him by now. How could he think of rest at a time like this?

Suspicions arose in Vran's mind. Perhaps the nature of the castle warped its inhabitants' minds. Why else would the cannibals act so illogically? Maybe the castle was built by madmen... or mad gods. Perhaps it was nothing more than a mad god's dream...

Vran shook his head. Such speculations were frivolous and would lead nowhere. His time would be better spent exploring the castle. He stood up and entered the next chamber.

This room was wide, spacious, and, like the previous, filled only with dust. Each of the four walls contained an archway. Vran continued forward, investigating more and more rooms. He discovered nothing but emptiness.

Vran laughed aloud. "Whoever built this castle didn't seem to care to furnish it," he said.

Moving on, he spent hours passing through chambers and corridors, and still found no sign of life, or even a single tangible object. Finally he came to something of interest: a sculpture of an armored warrior, carved from pure white marble with remarkable detail. The statue stood alone in the center of a hall, leaning on its sword. A helm with small decorative wings covered its head. Vran came closer to admire the artisan's workmanship.

When Vran was but an arm's length away, the statue began to *move*. Vran was so surprised by the phenomenon that he failed to dodge the blow aimed at him. The flat of the statue's blade struck his head and knocked him to the floor, unconscious.

Chapter III
Hearts of Stone

A repetitive thundering sound brought Vran back to wakefulness. He opened his eyes and discovered himself in the grip of the statue that had attacked him. The animate statue was carrying him like a sack of barley, its arm about his waist, squeezing more tightly than was comfortable.

Vran's head still ached from the blow. Confused and groggy, he moaned, "Ugh… where am I?"

"You are intruding in the castle of Felst Dragoriat," answered the statue in a cold monotone. This reply shocked Vran out of his state of disorientation, for he had assumed the statue to be an automaton, incapable of speech.

"What? You talk? If you understand what I say, put me down!"

"No. I must bring you to King Lotorr, who will pass judgment on you."

"Judgment? I've done nothing wrong! Release me now!" Vran said. He struggled to break the living statue's hold but would have had greater success trying to push a weighty boulder uphill.

"If you are innocent, you have nothing to fear, for our king is just. You shall have a fair hearing."

Vran found the living statue's words less than reassuring. Would this King Lotorr be less mad than the other men and women of the castle? Vran had his doubts. In fact, he expected the worst. Fortunately, the statue had not bothered to confiscate his weapons, so if the situation necessitated violence, at least he would be capable of defending himself.

But until then, there was nothing he could do. From his position on the statue's shoulder, Vran had a view of various chambers receding as his imprisoner strode onward. Vran felt demeaned. If a human dared manhandle him thusly, an elbow driven into the back of his head would quickly remedy the situation, but against a man made of stone, such a tactic was useless.

The statue ascended a staircase of inordinate width. Each step it took echoed loudly throughout the halls. Vran twisted his head around, trying to see what lay ahead. All he could glimpse were more stairs.

"How much farther must you carry me?" he asked.

"Not far," said the statue. "We will arrive at the hall of the king momentarily."

"If it is such a short distance, put me down, and I'll walk the rest of the way."

"No."

"But—"

"No."

No sense wasting breath by protesting further, Vran thought. It was like arguing with a brick wall.

Vran looked back down. The steps stretched far below. Vran and his captor had already ascended a considerable distance from the floor, and there was no telling how much farther they had to go before reaching the head of the stairs.

As it turned out, Vran had not long to wait. Moments later, the floor became level. The statue placed Vran on his feet, turned him around, and prodded him forward. They were in an enormous hall, with numerous high windows to Vran's left, and many doors and archways to his right. At the hall's end, a giant wearing a crown sat enthroned. Unless Vran missed his guess, this was King Lotorr. Several figures stood near the throne, and as Vran closed the distance, he could see they were statues like his captor. Furthermore, the king on the throne was not of flesh and blood as Vran had presumed, but a statue as well!

"Ho there, Stong!" bellowed the king,

the marble lips in his white-bearded face moving as smoothly as if they were flesh. "What have you brought us?"

"Hail, Your Hardness. I discovered this intruder prowling about my sector," answered Vran's captor, who was evidently named Stong.

"An intruder, eh?" said King Lotorr. He leaned forward, examining Vran. "I do not recognize you, so I don't believe you are an inhabitant of the castle. What have you to say for yourself?"

Before replying, Vran straightened his back and met the king's eyes, which appeared to be orbs of ebony. "Before I tell my tale, I must warn you, Your, er, Hardness, that I am... under an enchantment. Any magical spells which are cast near me will have disastrous and unexpected results. I tell you this because you are clearly sorcerous beings."

"Very interesting," said the king. "While we, the stone-folk, were brought to life by the wizardry of Felst Dragoriat, we have no skills in the arts of spellcasting. So you have nothing to fear in that regard."

"Who is this Felst Dragoriat?" asked Vran.

"He is the wizard who built this castle ages ago. Such a grandiose citadel required extraordinary guardians, and we were animated for that purpose. Felst Dragoriat has..."

One of the living statues, carved in the likeness of a strapping, clean-shaven, youthful warrior, raised his voice. "Pardon, Your Hardness, but shouldn't we continue the interrogation of the stranger? We don't even know his name."

King Lotorr nodded. "Yes, you are cor-

rect. I have a tendency to forget myself and speak at length, as you are no doubt aware, ho ho!"

The stone-folk laughed. Stong whispered to Vran, "The king does not exaggerate."

"So then, stranger, your name?" asked Lotorr.

"It is Vran," said the swordsman, who was now feeling at ease. The affable nature of the stone-folk was a welcome surprise. "I come from a land called Nilztiria. Do you know of it?"

"As a matter of fact, I do," replied the king, to Vran's amazement. "But go on."

"In my travels, I encountered a despicable villain, a demonolater who victimized innocent children. I swore to slay him, but he is a wizard, and used his magic against me. Due to my, let us say, peculiar nature, the spell had the unintended effect of transporting us to different worlds."

Most of the living statues became slightly perturbed by this explanation, but King Lotorr showed no sign of unease. "An incredible tale, but I believe it," he said. "Now then, Vran, would you care to hear more of the history of the castle?"

"Of course."

"As I mentioned earlier, it was constructed by a wizard named Felst Dragoriat. He tasked us with the duty of guarding it from intruders."

"What of the cannibals?" asked Vran.

"The what? Cannibals, you say?"

Stong spoke. "He means the people who reside nine levels below us, Your Hardness."

"Oh, them," said Lotorr. "They are Dragoriat's servants and assistants—or their descendants, I suppose. They turned to cannibalism? Odd. But either way, we were instructed not to harm or interfere with them."

"And where is Dragoriat now?" asked Vran.

"That is unknown," replied King Lotorr. "Long ago, he disappeared. He frequently made sojourns to other dimensions, but from the last he never returned. Perhaps he found a world which was more to his liking than this one. A number of less pleasant possibilities spring to mind as well, but let's not dwell on those. In his absence, we continue to patrol the castle, searching for intruders, as he wished us to."

"How long has Dragoriat been away?"

"Oh, I don't know. Over a hundred years, I'd guess."

"I'm sorry to say it, but I doubt he still lives," said Vran.

"Why?"

"Humans rarely live to such an advanced age."

"Do they? Hmm. If what you say is true, Dragoriat must have extended his lifespan with magic, for he was far older than that. He imbued the stone-folk with life nearly five hundred years past."

Vran's eyes opened wide with astonishment. "So you believe Dragoriat yet lives?"

"Indeed," said King Lotorr, nodding. "He may return at any time, so we faithfully carry out his orders to guard the castle. Not an easy task, considering its size and our limited numbers. Speaking of which, here comes the last of us now."

All heads turned to the hall's entrance, where another living statue marched in. This one, unlike the others, was female. As she came closer to the gathering of King Lotorr's court, Vran could see she had been sculpted into a slender paragon of feminine beauty, yet with the musculature of an athlete. The sword she wore at her belt, like her scanty garments, was made of the same pure white marble that composed her body. As she strode forward, a waist-length mane of pale hair swayed behind her, as ordinarily as Vran's would, in spite of being mineral in nature. Vran marveled at the wondrousness of this enchanted being, even more so than he had at the other living statues. She seemed even more lifelike than the others, possibly because she wore little clothing or armor to conceal her form: nothing more than a very short skirt, a pair of boots, and a bejeweled bandeau around her bosom.

"Hail, Your Hardness!" cried the woman of stone as she approached. "My sector is free of trespassers, as always."

"Hail, Grenvette," answered the king. "I commend your vigilance. However, Stong has discovered a stranger, whom we have been questioning."

Grenvette laid her darkly painted eyes on Vran, and her face lit up with fascination. "Your eyes—they are beautiful!" she exclaimed. "They sparkle like emeralds!"

"Er, thank you," stammered Vran. "Most people find my eyes unsettling."

"I can't imagine why. They perfectly accentuate the rest of your handsome face," said Grenvette, gently brushing Vran's arm with her hand.

A flush of embarrassment came over Vran. A show of affection from a beautiful woman was always welcome, but how was he supposed to react when the woman was not of flesh, but stone?

"Are you this friendly to every stranger

who comes to this castle?" asked Vran awkwardly.

"Not at all, Vran," said King Lotorr, replying for her. "Grenvette had no liking for the man who arrived not long before you."

"There was another before me!" said Vran with alarm.

"Yes, he was scrawny and had an off-putting demeanor about him," said Grenvette. "Not like you at all."

"His name," said Vran. "Was it—"

"Foad Misjak!" answered a voice in the distance that was both familiar and repellant.

Chapter IV
Hall of the King

The iniquitous wizard Foad Misjak stepped forth from one of the many archways on the right-hand side of the hall, accompanied by his goblin lackey Twar. Vran immediately whipped his sword from its scabbard.

"Hold!" thundered King Lotorr. "There will be no warring in my hall without my say-so."

"But this devious miscreant is my sworn enemy!" protested Vran. "I beg you, O king, allow me to strike off his head and put an end to his appalling ways!"

"Nay," said the king of the stone-folk. "He will be allowed to speak and explain himself. Remember, you were granted the same opportunity."

Vran saw the truth in the king's words and sheathed his weapon, albeit with some reluctance.

"Now then," said King Lotorr. "Foad Misjak, come here and stand before me. I would hear what you have to say."

Two of the living statues stepped aside, allowing Misjak and Twar to pass between them. They approached the throne, casting glares of contempt at Vran.

King Lotorr addressed the wizard. "Foad, when we first met, you seemed courteous and genial, if a tad arrogant, so I allowed you access to Felst Dragoriat's chambers of wizardry. But now it seems you are a scoundrel. Vran has accused you of the crimes of demonolatry and child abuse. How do you respond to these charges?"

"They are all lies," said Misjak confidently.

"Lies!" shouted Vran. "You are the one who is false, you—" He moved forward in an aggressive manner, but Stong, anticipating the king's command, interposed himself between the two men.

"Once again, I say there will be no violence," decreed King Lotorr. "Do not forget it—that goes for both of you. Now, Foad, I would know how you came to be acquainted with Vran."

"I first encountered Vran when he invaded my home and murdered my brother," replied the wizard. "Before then, I had never seen him, not even once."

"Vran, is this true?" inquired King Lotorr.

"Aye, it is," replied Vran without a trace of remorse.

"How can you justify such actions?" asked the king. "It seems he had not in any way provoked you."

"As I said before, he and his brother had committed crimes most foul against helpless young ones, all to satisfy their disgusting sexual appetites. No honorable man could abide such heinous behavior."

"Disregard his lying words, O king," said Foad Misjak. "His tongue must be as sinisterly afflicted as are his eyes."

"I speak the truth!" insisted Vran. "Ever since the day of our first meeting, he has added more and more unspeakable deeds to his tally. I myself have seen him sacrifice innocent maidens to appease the repugnant demon he worships."

"I worship no demon!" squealed Misjak.

"Not any longer, since it cast you aside like the offal you are!"

Now, enraged by Vran's insulting speech, Misjak lost his composure. Before the wizard could confront his enemy, hands of stone grabbed him and held him back. Their intervention was fortunate for him, as he was no match for Vran either in physical stature or martial skill. But still he was determined not to let Vran go unpunished for his scandalous remarks.

"This is an outrage!" screamed Misjak. "King Lotorr, I demand you execute this murderous, delusive madman at once! He has harassed me continuously without provocation, killed my poor brother, and ceaselessly spreads dastardly lies about my esteemed person! Sentence him to death, I say, for the good of the world!"

"Hmm," said King Lotorr, placing a fist under his chin. "I have much to consider." He sat on his throne, unmoving, for a long while. The others stood silently, awaiting his decision. After ten minutes, Misjak's patience expired.

"Are you awake?" asked the wizard, irritated.

"Yes, of course. I am still pondering," replied the king.

As more time passed, Vran's concern grew. His life was in the hands of a rather eccentric being who had been created by magic. There was no telling if King Lotorr would pass judgment in his favor. The case was, essentially, his word against Misjak's. Who would the king believe?

Vran turned to Grenvette, who smiled at him. At least if the judgment went against him, he had someone to speak on his behalf.

After a great length of time spent in contemplation, King Lotorr raised his head and spoke. "It is clear that these two men, Vran and Foad Misjak, have both committed many injurious deeds against one another. At this point neither can claim to have been wronged more greatly than his adversary. Therefore, as their differences are impossible to reconcile, I declare that the matter must be settled with a duel. The nemeses shall be pitted against each other in a bout of fair combat, with myself as the officiator."

"Hah!" barked Misjak. "Fair enough. Let us begin now, for I ache to blast him with my most incapacitating spells."

The king shook his head. "No, the risk is too great due to the nature of the enchantment upon Vran. In this contest, no magic is permissible."

"What!" shrieked the wizard, now infuriated. "No magic? What sort of a contest would that be?"

Vran laughed loudly. "The sort everyone wants to see—one where I shear your loathsome head from your shoulders!" he said, drawing his sword.

"No, Vran," said King Lotorr. "No weaponry will be allowed either. This will be a test of pure physical might. You shall fight hand-to-hand, tooth and nail, without the aid of weapons, armor, or magic."

"Well, that is acceptable," said Vran.

"No! No, it is not!" yelled Misjak. "You promised a fair combat, King Lotorr. Vran has a clear advantage over me in terms of size and strength. If I cannot use my magic, how is that fair?"

"You make a good point," said the king, nodding. "But how else can the matter be settled?"

A crafty look came over the wizard's countenance. "Allow a champion to fight in my stead," Misjak said slyly. "One who is equal to Vran in physical power. Then we shall see a fair combat."

"Very well," said King Lotorr. "But where will you find such a champion?"

"I have my ways. I assure you I will have suitable competition for Vran within two hours."

"Then it shall be so," said the king. "In two hours' time, we will reconvene here, and the battle will begin. Stong, you are to accompany Foad Misjak while he searches for his champion to ensure he does not lose his way."

"Or try to escape," put in Vran.

"Well, yes. Remember, Foad, if Vran is victorious, your life is forfeit."

"Understood," said the wizard, glaring at Vran with extreme hatred.

"Vran, you will stay here in the hall," said Lotorr. "For the next two hours, you and Foad shall be kept apart. You will not be permitted near each other before the battle commences."

Vran nodded, but kept his eyes on Misjak as the wizard exited the hall through one of the many archways. The swordsman felt a strong temptation to disregard King Lotorr's decree and make a headlong charge at Misjak, but managed to resist.

With nothing else to do but wait, Vran made his way to the windows and gazed out upon the great forest. Seconds later, he found Grenvette by his side.

"Do you find the scenery beautiful?" she asked.

"I do. But the forest is so vast, I wonder how far it extends."

Grenvette shrugged. "Felst Dragoriat must have known, but he never told us. I have never been outside the walls of the castle."

"Still, you are probably more well-travelled than most."

"Really? How so?"

"In Nilztiria, most folk don't stray far from the village where they were born. And some of those villages are not much larger than this hall."

"Fascinating!" said Grenvette. "Tell me more of the people of your land."

"They come in many varieties. In the south, you will find swarthier folk, like the Jambootans and the Tul-Therans. To the north dwell the hardy Cytherans, who are of paler complexion."

"Like me?"

"Well, somewhat. Their eyes are ice blue, and their hair is as golden as the rays of your sun."

"Are their women lovely?"

"Very much so. In fact, I prefer them above all others."

Grenvette thought on that for a moment, then said, "I must leave you now, but I will return shortly." She crossed the hall hurriedly and passed through an archway on the opposite side. Vran wondered what business she had that necessitated such a sudden departure. There was no point in speculating, though, for the ways of the stone-folk were difficult to fathom.

He turned back to the window and thought on more important matters. It would not be long before he would have to fight for his life. Where would Misjak find an opponent for him? Among the cannibals? From what he had seen of them, Vran felt confident in his chances against one in single combat.

But Misjak was a guileful foe. He would look for any unfair advantage possible, no matter how underhanded. No matter what type of champion Vran would face, he must be on guard at all times for unscrupulous tactics. It would have been better, Vran thought, had King Lotorr assigned more than one guard to accompany Misjak, for the wizard doubtlessly had evil plans.

A while later, Grenvette returned, a painter's palette and brush in hand. She had colored her formerly white hair a bright yellow, and daubed blue paint over her eyes.

"Grenvette, what have you done?" asked Vran.

"I have beautified myself," she said proudly. "Now I look like one of the maidens of Cythera. What do you think?"

"Er, very nice," said Vran awkwardly.

"You like it? Oh, thank you!" Grenvette embraced him in her arms of cold stone. Vran gasped for air, for she gripped him more tightly than Stong had.

"Grenvette, release me before I suffocate!" Vran sputtered.

The stone woman did so and ardently apologized.

Eventually the appointed hour drew near, and Foad Misjak had yet to return. A grumbling arose among the living statues. In addition to their concern for Stong's well-being, they had been looking forward to the spectacle of combat and disliked the thought of being cheated of it. They looked to King Lotorr for guidance.

"This bodes ill," said the king. "Perhaps we should search for them."

"No need!" came the high voice of Foad Misjak carrying through the hall. He stood in one of the archways, Stong at his side.

"There you are, Foad," said King Lotorr. "We were beginning to grow concerned. Were you able to find a champion?"

"Yes, yes I was," said the wizard, grinning. "I have a champion who is fierce and ruthless. My champion fears no man. My champion lusts for violence, and that lust can only be satisfied by rending Vran's limbs from his body! He is none other than… Twar!"

"Twar!" Vran burst into laughter. "Twar, your goblin henchman?"

Misjak stepped aside, allowing a hulking brute to pass by him and enter the hall. The face of this bestial being was unmistakably that of Twar, but the resemblance ended there. This new incarnation of the goblin was equipped with an overabundance of muscle and sinew and stood as tall as Vran himself. He was clad in the same dirty furs as before, but with his new size, they only provided coverage for his loins.

"Yes, Twar!" he growled, beating his chest.

Chapter V
Fight Till Death

Stunned, mouth agape, Vran stared at this newly-formed monstrosity called Twar. Misjak cackled derisively at Vran's befuddlement.

"I can tell by the stupidity of your facial expression that you fail to understand," said the wizard. "While studying the grimoires of Felst Dragoriat—which King Lotorr graciously allowed me to peruse—I discovered a spell that rapidly accelerates growth. The previously puny Twar volunteered to be the recipient of the enchantment and is now the behemoth you see before you. And he will be the last thing you see, for you shall soon die by his hands!"

"And then I'll eat your dead body!" growled Twar, flexing the powerful thews of his arms.

At these threats, torrents of rage and hatred welled up inside Vran. "Foad Misjak," he snarled in a voice more ogrish than Twar's, "you son of a bitch! You despicable, reprehensible vermin! How many innocent women have you killed? How many innocent children have you raped?" Vran's face encrimsoned as he went on. "For far too long you've escaped the justice due to you—but no longer! There is blood on your hands, Foad Misjak, but tonight, I want to see your blood spilled—*and so it shall be!*"

King Lotorr applauded. "A very impassioned speech, Vran. But now you must divest yourself of your weapons so the fight can begin."

Vran unbuckled his sword belt and handed it to Grenvette, who fastened it around her slender waist above her own. The weight of two heavy swords at her hip did not encumber her in the least. Vran stripped off his leather coat, which he also gave to Grenvette. He began to unbutton his shirt, which caused the stone-woman's freshly-painted eyes to widen in admiration of his well-muscled chest. Vran doffed the garment and tossed it to her, heedless of her appreciation for his physique.

The tezbou, which had been comfortably resting inside Vran's sleeve, raised its head, curious as to where its covering had gone. Vran removed the reptile from his person and gently placed it on Grenvette's shoulder. It crawled down her bicep and wrapped itself around her forearm. She wondered what the small creature was, but Vran did not offer an explanation. His only concern was for bringing about the destruction of Twar and Foad Misjak.

Vran and the sorcerously-augmented goblin stood facing one another a few feet apart, awaiting the signal to begin. But first King Lotorr instructed the combatants in the rules of the contest. "As stated previously, this bout shall be conducted fairly. No weaponry or magic is allowed. Neither is attacking vulnerable parts of the body, such as the eyes. Outside interference will not be tolerated. The outcome of this duel will be determined strictly by skill and physical might.

"Stone-folk, form a circle around the two competitors, but give them enough space to move. This will be the boundary, and neither Vran nor Twar should be permitted to go beyond it." The living statues did as their king commanded. Grenvette stood at the king's right hand, with Misjak and Stong at his left.

"Now, when I give the command, you

may begin. May the best man win."

Vran and Twar drew closer together. Standing face to face, they stared into each other's eyes, neither one flinching. Although the goblin was now his equal in height, Vran was not intimidated.

King Lotorr clapped his large stone hands together once, resulting in a sound like an avalanche, and cried out, "Fight!"

Twar immediately hurled his enlarged body, shoulder first, at Vran like a spear. Vran sidestepped, avoiding the brunt of the impact, and struck Twar in the face with a clenched fist. The hulking goblin, more angered than injured, retaliated with a flurry of blows. Vran raised his hands to block the fistic assault then drove his knee into Twar's midsection. Vran grabbed the winded goblin by his legs and knocked him off balance, sending him crashing to the floor flat on his back.

Before Vran could press the attack, Twar kicked at him, then scuttled away. The goblin hurried toward his master Misjak, who whispered something in his pointy ear. A wicked grin spread across Twar's face.

Twar approached Vran, but this time with deliberation. The two combatants circled each other, each trying to guess his opponent's next move. When Twar's back was to King Lotorr, he moved in, arms outstretched. He lunged at Vran, intending to grab him and pin his arms to his sides, but the green-eyed warrior slipped free. In reprisal, Vran locked one arm around Twar's head. He curled his free hand into a fist and delivered a series of pummeling blows to Twar's skull, but the goblin trapped Vran's torso in his powerful arms and squeezed. Vran tried to struggle free from the goblin's

grip, but to no avail. Twar, careful to maneuver himself so that King Lotorr was directly behind him, quickly smashed his knee into Vran's groin. Vran grimaced with pain.

"Foul! Foul!" cried Grenvette.

"What do you mean?" asked King Lotorr.

"Twar hit Vran in the sensitive area between his legs!"

"Did he? I did not see that."

"It's true! The fight should be stopped!"

"Disregard her," said Misjak. "She is clearly mistaken. I explained to Twar in no uncertain terms that he was to follow the rules you set for the contest."

"Since I did not see the infraction, I will not intervene," declared King Lotorr.

This conversation went unheard by the two combatants, for they were too engrossed in their struggle for supremacy and could not afford to divert their attention. Vran, desperate to escape from Twar's bear-like hug, raised his arm and forcefully brought the point of his elbow down against the goblin's nose. He could feel Twar's grip weaken, so he repeated the maneuver. After a third time, the goblin was dazed enough to release Vran.

Twar staggered away while Vran caught his breath. Once more turning his back to King Lotorr, the goblin dipped a hand into his loincloth and withdrew a short length of chain. With great haste he wrapped the chain around his fist. Before Vran knew what his opponent had done, Twar punched him in the jaw.

The living statues, who, with the exception of Grenvette, had been watching the contest stoically and impartially, grumbled in disapproval at this display of unsportsmanlike conduct.

"A weapon!" shouted Grenvette. "Twar has a weapon!"

"He most certainly does not," sneered Foad Misjak while giving Twar a knowing look. The goblin swiftly placed the chain in his mouth and gulped.

The protests of the stone-folk grew louder, and King Lotorr ordered the match to halt. "Twar, come here so I can search you for weapons," he said.

"He hid the chain in his mouth," offered Grenvette.

Twar opened his mouth wide, and the king peered within. "I see no weapons," said Lotorr.

"Of course not!" said Misjak. "We fight fair, unlike Vran, who needs this painted hussy to intercede every time Twar gains an advantage! Now let's have no more interruptions!"

"Let the match continue," said King Lotorr.

Twar raced toward Vran, hoping to catch him before he could fully recover from the weighted blow. But Vran kicked at his shin, and the goblin, in his haste, tripped and fell forward. Vran pounced on him and grabbed hold of his left arm. He placed his weight on Twar and applied pressure, attempting to break Twar's elbow. Twar howled in both frustration and pain.

"Don't let him do that to you, you fool!" screamed Misjak.

With his free hand, Twar struck at Vran's head. Due to his awkward position, he could put little force behind the blows. Desperate to escape before permanently losing the use of his arm, Twar again resorted

to unscrupulous methods. He reached back and poked Vran in the eye, and the hold was released.

"Another illegal maneuver!" cried Grenvette.

"It must have been inadvertent," said Misjak.

Vran, clutching his eye, rose to one knee, while Twar scrambled to his feet. The goblin took advantage of Vran's vulnerable position by fiercely kicking him in the side of the head. Vran fell to the floor.

Twar straddled Vran and rained blows down upon him. Vran did his best to shield his face from the attacks. So furious was the assault, Vran could not afford to strike back, for if he dropped his defenses even for a moment, he would be knocked senseless. Instead, Vran suddenly shifted his weight and used the momentum to roll the goblin off him.

Twar continued to roll until he came near the feet of Grenvette. Both combatants rose, and Vran charged his opponent. Twar crouched, seemingly ready to meet his foe, but leapt aside before Vran could reach him. Vran was now headed straight for Grenvette and forced himself to halt before colliding with her.

"Behind you, Vran!" she said, but the warning came too late, and Twar hammered him with his mighty arms.

The goblin grabbed Vran by his lengthy hair and flung him to the floor. Twice he kicked Vran in the face. Vran was dazed, now, crawling on all fours. Blood dripped from his nose. Twar stalked him methodically, taking his time to deliver more well-placed kicks to his ribs.

Twar grabbed Vran's hair again and lifted him to his knees. Vran struck back weakly with a punch to his midsection, but Twar shrugged it off. The goblin forcefully hurled his clenched fist into Vran's head. After two more pummeling blows, Vran collapsed, his forehead bloody.

"Good, good!" laughed Misjak. "Beat him severely! Make him suffer before he dies!"

Grenvette covered her eyes momentarily, horrified by the beating Vran was taking. But she regained her composure and cheered her man on. "Get up, Vran! You can beat him!" But he did not appear to hear her encouraging words.

Vran lay flat on his back, seemingly insensate. Twar arrogantly placed a foot on his chest and laughed derisively. Misjak joined in, adding his voice to the hideous cachinnation. The stone-folk could no longer maintain their impartiality and decried this disrespectful act. Misjak and Twar reveled in their jeering and laughed all the louder.

But they did not laugh for long. Vran, with a sudden burst of energy, clutched the goblin's ankle and upended him! He twisted and wrenched, and Twar yelled in agony. The stone-folk applauded this turn of events, Grenvette louder than all.

"Ho, what a maneuver!" cried King Lotorr.

"No! No!" screamed Misjak.

Vran continued to apply pressure. He grinned at Misjak but said nothing. The implications were clear.

The goblin flailed recklessly at Vran with his free leg. By sheer luck, he managed to strike Vran in the nose. The impact caused Vran's grip to weaken, and Twar wriggled loose.

Now both man and goblin were on their feet, winded and unsteady. They began to trade blows, with Twar getting the worst of it. Vran rushed forward, but Twar, in an act of desperation, head-butted him. The two collided awkwardly. They both staggered backward, stunned, and collapsed simultaneously.

"What is this?" said Lotorr, moving forward to the edge of his seat. "Both competitors are down! Who will rise first?"

Neither Vran nor Twar had moved from where they had fallen. By all appearances they were unconscious.

"Get up, Twar, get up!" wailed Misjak, who had worked himself into a state of hysteria. "Damn you, get up and fight!"

Spurred by his master's frenzied screaming, Twar began to twitch. He rolled lethargically onto his side and attempted to regain his feet. But Vran was moving as well! The green-eyed warrior sat up and wiped the blood from his face, to the delight of the audience of living statues.

Now both Vran and Twar were standing, but unsteadily. The goblin lurched toward Vran, favoring his impaired ankle. Before Twar could take a swing, Vran kicked him in the gut, causing him to double over. Vran locked his arms around the huge goblin's waist and, with all the power in his limbs, lifted him off his feet. Twar squirmed helplessly as Vran turned him upside down. Vran dropped to his knees, forcefully smashing Twar's skull into the floor. The goblin's neck snapped on impact. There was no doubt he would never rise again.

Awed by this heroic feat of strength, the living statues applauded loudly. "I declare

Vran the victor!" said King Lotorr. Grenvette rushed to Vran's side and helped him to his feet.

"Misjak—where is Misjak?" stammered Vran, still woozy from the struggle.

King Lotorr spoke. "Yes, Foad, per the rules of the contest—" He looked around, but Foad Misjak was nowhere to be seen.

Chapter VI
Into the Vortex

"Misjak is gone?" said Vran. "But where? And how?"

"Did anyone see the wizard run off?" asked King Lotorr.

The living statues shook their heads.

Lotorr directed his gaze at Stong. "Foad was standing right beside you. How was it you did not see him depart?" he questioned sternly.

"I suppose I was too caught up in the action of the contest to notice," said Stong, with shame in his voice.

The coldness in King Lotorr's demeanor vanished as quickly as it had appeared. "I should not judge you too harshly, Stong, for I am as much to blame as you or anyone else. The excitement overcame all of us. But now we must waste no time in finding Foad."

"Where could he have gone?" asked Grenvette.

"He cannot be far, unless he used magic," said King Lotorr.

"If he had cast a spell, *I* certainly would have noticed," said Vran.

King Lotorr nodded. "Then let us search the halls and chambers of the castle for him. We shall each search separately, so we can cover more ground in less time. Vran,

after exerting yourself in combat, you will stay here and rest."

"The hell I will!" gnarred Vran. "How can I rest while that loathsome wretch roams freely? I'll hunt him down alongside the rest of you!"

"As you wish," said the king. "But I cannot allow you to go alone in your current condition. One of us will accompany you."

"I will!" volunteered Grenvette enthusiastically.

"Very well," said Lotorr. "Now, let us go!"

The stone-folk left the hall of King Lotorr, and each went their own way. Some exited via the grand staircase, thinking Misjak might be hiding on one of the lower floors, while others passed through the archways on the right-hand side of the hall.

"Which way should we go?" Grenvette asked Vran.

"Misjak said something earlier about Felst Dragoriat's chambers of wizardry. He's probably there, brewing up some foul deviltries."

"You must be right."

"Do you know the way?" asked Vran.

"I think so," said Grenvette. "It's not part of the sector I patrol, so I haven't been that way in a century or more."

"Well, lead on," said Vran. "And return to me my sword. I know I'll need it soon."

Grenvette unbuckled Vran's sword belt and handed it to him. "What about your shirt and coat?"

"No time for that now," he said as he strapped the belt around his waist and unsheathed his blade. "Let's move!"

The stone-woman smiled, delighted by

93

Vran's decision to remain bare-chested. She led him through a maze of rooms and corridors, striving to recall the best route to the wizard's chambers.

It was not long before Vran grew impatient. "How close are we?"

"I'm not sure," said Grenvette apologetically. "It's been so long I can't remember exactly."

"Think harder, woman!" said Vran. "The longer we dally, the more time Misjak has to plot our demise!"

Grenvette furrowed her brow in concentration. The contours of her face moved so naturally Vran was amazed they were sculpted from stone, and not truly flesh.

"I remember now!" Grenvette announced.

"Are you certain?"

"Yes. We must head east for a dozen rooms or so until we come to another grand hall, much like King Lotorr's. The chamber we seek should be in proximity to it."

"Good! Now let's hurry!"

Vran and Grenvette increased their pace. The rooms they traversed were very wide and sparsely furnished, like most of those in the castle Vran had seen. Felst Dragoriat, it seemed to him, cared little for decoration.

Vran tried to keep track of the number of rooms they passed through, but he lost count. He thought the total might be thirteen or fourteen, but he could not be sure. Just as he began to doubt the accuracy of Grenvette's recollection, the pair passed through a great archway. Beyond lay an immense hall, the far wall of which, like King Lotorr's, contained myriad egresses.

"Grenvette, we found it!" said Vran.

"Yes, but I can't remember which door leads to the chamber of wizardry."

"No need! Can't you hear it?"

Grenvette paused and listened. "No... What is it?"

Rather than answer, Vran crossed the hall. He put his ear against one of the wooden doors for a moment and signaled for Grenvette to come closer. "I can hear it quite clearly now. Misjak is chanting!"

As Grenvette approached she could hear the voice of the wizard emanate from behind the portal.

Vran tried opening the door, but it was locked. "Help me break this down," he said, throwing his shoulder against it.

"Stand aside!" said Grenvette. The stone-woman backed up, then charged into the door at full speed. It shattered to splinters from the impact.

"You're like a living battering ram!" said Vran, awestruck.

"Why, thank you," said Grenvette, batting her eyes coquettishly.

That Grenvette interpreted his statement as flattery was puzzling to Vran, but there was no time to ruminate on the intricacies of a stone-woman's mind. More important matters were at hand.

Beyond the demolished portal was a massive chamber, the purpose of which was made obvious by the plethora of wizardly paraphernalia strewn about. At its center stood Foad Misjak, reading aloud an incantation from an ancient grimoire he held in one hand. Beside him was an enormous bubbling cauldron, large enough to contain five human beings. His chanting did not cease upon the intrusion of Vran and Grenvette, but instead grew louder, faster, more panicked. As the recitation of the spell continued, the ceiling and walls of the chamber became obscured by clouds of star-speckled blackness.

Vran attempted to close in on his hated enemy, but a powerful gust of wind suddenly roared through the chamber, holding him back. The liquid in the cauldron, now alternating in color between radiant crimson and deep blue, rose and fell like tidal waves. Misjak clambered onto the cauldron's rim.

"He means to jump in!" said Grenvette.

"Where he goes, I follow!" shouted Vran, struggling against the windstorm.

Misjak plunged into the churning waters of the sorcerous cauldron. A whirlpool formed around him, sucking him down. As his head disappeared beneath the surface of the waters, the force of the winds lessened slightly. Now Vran was able to progress toward the cauldron unimpeded, and he made to leap in.

"Wait!" cried Grenvette. "You don't know what kind of danger it presents!"

"But I must!" said Vran. He dove and was pulled down into the swirling vortex of vibrantly colored waters.

Grenvette felt she had no choice but to follow, so she vaulted over the rim of the cauldron as well.

Beneath the surface, the alternating coloration of the waters was almost blinding. Grenvette reached out for Vran, hoping they would not become separated. She found Vran's arm and clutched it tightly. No sooner had she done so than the roiling of the waters increased, pulling them down far deeper than she thought possible, given the physical boundaries of the cauldron.

She, unlike Vran, had not previously experienced multidimensional travel and had no idea of what to expect.

The rushing waves carried them away, like a raging river of mystic force, to a destination unknown.

Vran's adventure concludes in the Winter issue of Cirsova!

D.M. Ritzlin is a Chicago-based author/publisher. He writes fantasy tales which mix action, horror, wonder, and gallows humor in varying degrees. His first collection of stories, Necromancy in Nilztiria, *was released in October 2020. Ritzlin also owns and operates DMR Books, the leading publisher specializing in sword-and-sorcery fiction.*

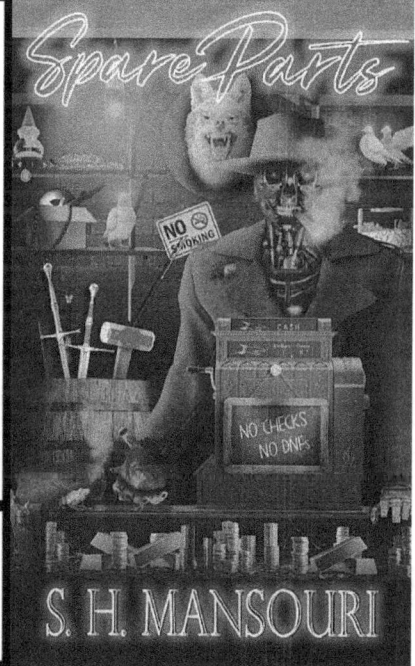

If dark, twisted tales of fantasy, science fiction, and horror are what you're craving, this debut collection from author S.H. Mansouri includes thirteen genre-bending short stories!

AVAILABLE NOW!
amazon

S. H. MANSOURI

S.H. Mansouri
@shamanwrites
Punches keys, hopes for clarity.
www.shmansouri.com

@atreyupress
atreyupress.com

Fight of the Sandfishers

By JIM BREYFOGLE

Celzez plans to denounce Teriz, a royal guard of Alness, as a traitor who shirked his duty as the city fell! Jalani hopes Mangos can stop him before it gets him killed!

Twenty-nine months after the fall of Alness.

I'm bored.

I wouldn't be writing this if I weren't. It's the first story I've ever written, and I don't even know how it's going to end.

Kat and I are riding in a merchant's wagon travelling to Hafiz. The merchant is Jalani, a young woman orphaned in the fall of Alness. The man who guards the wagon is Celzez, who also worked for her father. Celzez is from Hafiz.[1]

The wind is hot and dry, the desert stretching out ahead of us. Tall obelisks mark the highway, red sandstone taken from the quarries of Hafiz so travelers know the way even when sand covers the roads.

It's not the quarries that give the people of Hafiz their name, though. It's the lake. They catch *fallo* fish in the shallow, warm water lake that somehow exists in the desert. They dry the guts, grind them to powder, and sell them as a spice. So the people of Hafiz are called Sandfishers.

Celzez is a Sandfisher returning home to denounce another man. To denounce is to accuse somebody of being dishonorable. This will lead to a fight because honor is *very* important to the Sandfishers.

Jalani does not want him to do this. Although she's a prosperous merchant with many teamsters working for her, she's accompanying Celzez to try and change his mind. And sell some goods.

I've agreed to help her. Not that I really care—I try to avoid other people's fights—but Jalani is pleasant to look at, and I'm bored.

Hafiz crowds around the end of Xelin Lake. The red sandstone buildings form a crescent, the largest along the shore, then they get smaller and smaller as they get farther from the lake. By the edge of the city, they are nothing but shacks of salvaged stone with canvas stretched across to keep out the sun. It's not a large city, as cities go.

I rode up front with Celzez when the city first came into sight. Looking down from the dunes west of the city, our shadows lay in front of us.

Celzez held the horses tightly reined in,

---

[1] Jalani the merchant and her guard Celzez first appeared in *Sword of the Mongoose*, originally in Cirsova Vol. 1, #10 and collected in Tales of the Mongoose and Meerkat Vol 1: Pursuit Without Asking, out now from Cirsova Publishing! – *Ed.*

for the covered wagon slid in the sand on the steep dune face. While Hafiz lay close below, it would take until mid-afternoon to reach it.

"How long has it been since you've been here?" I asked him.

He held the horse's reins, staring down over the city, as if sorting my words and placing each one in his mind before answering.

"Seven years," he said.

Well, I thought, *it had been years since I left Arnelon, and I didn't have any plans to go back.* "Why now?"

He snapped the reins, telling the horses to go faster. They swished their tails together, almost as if they had practiced. The wagon wheels squeaked in the sand as they had the entire journey.

"The time is right," Celzez answered.

Obviously nobody felt the need to hurry.

Except me. "Why is the time right?"

Celzez glanced at me, not moving his head, just a quick darting of his eyes, and I sensed his disapproval. "There is a thing that must be done."

"So Jalani said. She doesn't agree. You want to challenge a man, but if the grievance is seven years old, why bother?"

"You are not a Sandfisher."

Just like that—I wouldn't understand.

I tried to think of what to say, but the silence drew out, leaving only the squeak of the wheels.

"It hasn't been seven years; two years, five months," Celzez said, surprising me with this gift of information.

I glanced over, expecting him to elaborate, but he did not, just kept guiding the wagon down the face of the dune toward Hafiz.

About two and a half years ago. What happened two and a half years ago? I had just left Arnelon, hadn't even met Kat—it seemed like an eternity ago. Stupid, I told myself. It wasn't what *I* was doing two and a half years ago, it was what Celzez was doing.

Two years and five months... it struck me, of course, Alness fell. Jalani and Celzez had been there when Rhygir's mercenary army took the city.

It shouldn't surprise me that something might happen in the plundering of a city that would make one mad. But over two years? And Celzez is just a hired guard. If anybody should want revenge, it should be Jalani.

I twisted around to look at her.

She rode in the wagon amongst the crates of goods, sheltering from the sun. Kat sat at the far back, her feet hanging over the edge, her hood up as protection against blowing sand.

I crawled into the wagon. "Did this offense happen in Alness?" I asked Jalani.

"Yes."

Kat turned her head, just slightly, but enough that I knew she listened.

"So why are you coming here?"

"This is where Sandfishers make denouncements," she said. "Once it is made, he wants to return to Alness to make his kill."

I shook my head. Celzez was coming here to *say* he intended to kill another man—a man not even in Hafiz. *Perhaps I can convince him this is a waste of time*, I thought. It certainly seemed so.

Jalani took a deep breath. "It is not just another Sandfisher." She looked down and brushed her leggings, hard, as though forcing the sand away from her. "It's a Kingsfisher."

The name sounded familiar, but I couldn't place it.

"The Kings Guard of Alness were called Kingsfishers," Jalani explained. "It was the honor of Hafiz that the King would draw a dozen men for his personal guard from the city. They were considered," her voice practically dripped irony, "*absolutely* reliable."

Obviously, they had not proven to be. I glanced at Kat. She still listened. "You know of the Kingsfishers?" I asked her.

"Every Alnessi knows the Kingsfishers," she said. "They were the King's best fighters, his most loyal servants."

I opened my mouth to ask another question but shut it. *Think,* I told myself. *You can figure some of this out yourself.*

I remembered Alness, the grey streets, the rubble, the smell of fire and death. I recalled the tales of fighting so savage it took weeks to secure the city. The King and his entire family had been killed, it was said, and if they died, their guards should have died as well.

Clearly that had not happened.

"A Kingsfisher survived," I said, "and Celzez wants to denounce him. Because he survived, or something else?"

"Something else," Celzez said. His voice was strong and angry, louder than I had ever heard. "Teriz, son of Razen, betrayed his King and his honor. He aided the invaders and even killed a Prince of the House."

I scratched my collar where sand stuck and rubbed with every move. I was still missing something. Celzez served a merchant. "Why do you care?"

Celzez did not answer. Clearly, if I had to ask, I wouldn't understand.

I looked at Jalani, but she just sniffed and brushed nonexistent sand from her leggings.

"Maybe he'll win," I said.

She shook her head.

Well, it will take a while to get to Hafiz and prepare to denounce. I have time, and I will need it, for Celzez clearly doesn't want to talk.

Hafiz looks deserted as the full heat of the day begins to simmer in the early afternoon. Occasionally somebody will venture out on some errand, but the streets are mostly empty. The sun reflecting off the lake will drive right through your eyes and make your head pound if you are unwise enough to look.

Celzez stopped the wagon in front of a small house with large windows, now shuttered against the heat. He led us to the door, which was open a crack.

Celzez pushed the door open and called out.

Inside, a woman carrying a deep bowl stopped in surprise. She asked a question I did not catch.

"Sharin," Celzez said, his tone chiding.

"Celzez!" The woman dropped the bowl,

and fruit rolled across the floor. She hugged Celzez, talking excitedly in Hafizi, laughing at the same time, even as tears ran down her cheeks.

A boy appeared in the other doorway, a lad about ten, with wild, dark hair and dark eyes. He frowned until the woman called to him, beckoned with her hands and spoke rapidly. A huge smile lit up his face, and he came forward, a little hesitantly, but Celzez swept him into the hug, and the three laughed together.

"My brother's wife, Sharin," Celzez introduced the woman. "And my nephew, Johin." Johin batted at his hand as he ruffled the boy's hair.

"Welcome," said Sharin. I could barely understand her because her accent was so thick.

Celzez spoke to Johin, a quick exchange in Hafizi, then said, "Johin only speaks Hafizi." He smiled at Sharin. "Sharin, too, mostly."

Sharin flushed but did not argue. She spoke to Celzez, and they launched into a prolonged conversation. It grew more and more animated until Sharin burst into an angry tirade. *Good,* I thought, *the more who oppose his foolishness, the easier it is to change his mind.*

It didn't take a genius to figure out she didn't like the idea of Celzez denouncing anybody.

Celzez cut her off with a sharp question, to which she responded indigently.

"You can stay here," Celzez told us. "It will be more comfortable. I will stay with the wagon."

It seemed strange that he still felt the need to guard in a city where, by all accounts, no one stole. But, I reflected, that was his job.

Celzez stroked his chin, spoke softly to Sharin, and nodded at her answer. A couple words sent Johin dashing from the house.

"He has gone to get a translator," Celzez said.

Johin returned with a slightly built man named Halmas. Halmas would stay with us until nightfall, then return in the morning. He would translate Hafizi for us, mostly for me, since Kat didn't seem interested.

Unlike me, Kat had made no promises. She did not argue with Celzez. Instead she seemed distracted, enmeshed in her own thoughts. If I was struggling to understand what would sway Celzez, she was struggling with something else entirely.

When Sharin took Johin to the market to buy extra food, Celzez drove the wagon to the caravan grounds, and I was alone with Jalani and Kat. I asked, "If this is about Alness, why now?"

"The north stirs," Jalani said. "There are rumors that one of the Princes survived. There is a feeling that something can be done."

Kat sat, leaned back in one of the corners. Sunlight slanted through cracks in the shutter to lie across her legs, but left her face in shadows. "Perhaps *that's* why Celzez chooses now to make his denouncement."

"I thought all the royalty died when Rhygir took the palace," I said.

"It was a large family," Kat said, "and there was much confusion that day."

99

Jalani nodded, her brows drawn together, uncertainty in her eyes. "Rhygir wants people to believe all the royals died."

"Do you believe it?" I asked. They were *her* monarchs, after all. I had no interest in whether they survived.

Jalani shuddered. "I have tried to block memories of that day. There was so much blood. For months, I believed everybody left in the city must have been killed." Her bottom lip started to quiver. "I *want* to believe one of the Princes escaped. But gods," her eyes misted over, and a tear stole down her cheek, "oh gods, I *watched* them kill the children."

I knew Celzez had saved her, taken her from the burning city, but I never knew she had still been there after the King had fallen and Rhygir was butchering the royals in the streets.

I glanced at Kat, unsure what to say, but she gave me no guidance. I cleared my throat. "Then the rumor is false. The royals are dead."

"There was so much confusion," Jalani whispered. "And there were twelve of them. Who can say they were all the right ones?"

"So," I said slowly, still piecing the thought together as I spoke. "Celzez could be doing this to help a surviving prince. If one survived," I added.

"He could." Jalani sniffed and wiped her cheek with the back of her hand.

"And Teriz was responsible?" I asked, remembering the name of the offending Kingsfisher.

"We saw him kill one of the Princes," Jalani said. She lifted her chin. "There was no mistaking it."

I nodded, starting to feel like I would soon have enough understanding to argue Celzez out of his denouncement.

"Which one?" Kat asked, her voice flat.

"Kalin."

"Kalin was thirteen," Kat said.

It suddenly occurred to me there was another Alnessi in the room. "Were you in the city when it fell?" I asked Kat. I couldn't see her face, for the shadows hid her expression.

"Yes," Kat sounded reluctant, whether to remember or answer I could not tell.

"You've never told me."

Kat stood up, prowled through the shadows around the edges of the room. "To what end?"

"To help me understand," I said. It struck me I did not understand. I did not yet understand Celzez, I did not understand Alness's dogged refusal to accept Rhygir's rule; and in spite of years of adventuring together, I feared I did not understand Kat. "To understand Celzez and all this anger simmering in the north." *To understand you,* I thought.

"Do you care?"

"Ye—" I bit the word back. It was easy to say, but did I care? Not just about Kat, who is like a sister to me, but about the Alnessi? Did I care like Celzez cared? Right is what you're strong enough to enforce, good is what benefits you; that is the way of the world. I know the fall of Alness troubles many, but I don't really understand why. Nations fall, people move on.

"Perhaps," Kat said in this silence, "that

is why I never told you."

I said nothing then, and I can think of nothing now. What might I learn if I were to ask, and why do I not? Why should I fear to be drawn and bound to the turmoil in Alness as Celzez inexplicably was?

In the morning, when the desert air is still cool and the air over the lake is warm, the *fallo* fish are close to shore. The men wade in the water, casting their nets and calling to each other. This is when the fish are caught, before the heat drives them to deeper water. This is the good time of day, when food is gotten and the work is light. The stench of processing the spice, or the sweat of mining red sandstone, comes later. The Hafizi savor early morning.

Celzez stood with one hand resting on a stone wall, looking over the water. He did not face me, but spoke as I approached. "Do you hear them, the fishers calling each other? When I am too old to fight, I shall return to wade in the shallows as I did as a boy. Time will stop, and all that moves will be the water and the wind and the fishers. The heat of the desert shall steal over me, and I shall go nap in the shade." He smiled at the thought. "I shall bake the mountain's cold from my bones."

He fell silent and after a minute slapped the wall with his open palm. "But there is much to do before then." He turned to look at me. "There is a man here you should meet. A man I admire greatly."

"Who?"

"An old man with enough honor for any three men."

He clapped me on the shoulder and went inside, once again leaving me with questions instead of answers. Only after we broke our fast and Halmas appeared did Celzez announce his intention to visit Inark.

"Inark?" Kat said. "He's alive?"

"You know him?" Celzez looked interested.

Kat shook her head. "No more than I know other Kingsfishers." She chuckled. "I do remember when he retired and a new Kingsfisher was selected to replace him. Though," she added, "I was very young. I'm just surprised to hear he is still alive. I assumed he was old then and would have died by now."

A Kingsfisher. A former Kingsfisher, really, but I couldn't help feeling a sense of anticipation, having heard so much about them recently. This would be his fight, not Celzez's. I added it to my list of arguments to use.

"Inark lost a leg serving Alness," Halmas explained, trailing a step behind as we crossed the wide street and approached a small house near the lake. "Like all the Kingsfishers, he is very well respected."

The door was open, and Celzez knocked on the doorframe. A voice called out. Halmas didn't translate the word or the words Celzez used to greet the old man sitting in the cool dimness inside.

The old man answered—Halmas began to translate, but the old man stopped him. "We need not use Hafizi," he said, "if there are others here."

He must be blind, I thought. We filed inside, blocking the light from the door and making the house even darker. The only light threaded through us to fall on the old man.

Inark turned his head so that it caught the light a bit, and I could see white clouds of age in his eyes.

Celzez bowed respectfully. "There are, Kingsfisher. Jalani, a merchant."

Why does he bow if the man is blind? I wondered.

Inark nodded greeting.

"Mangos, an adventurer." Inark nodded again.

"And Kat, an adventuress."

Inark started to nod, but paused. "Where are you from, Kat?"

She stirred, dropped her hood. It seemed her answer came from deep within her, and it took a long time for it to come out. "Alness. It is a common enough name, as I'm sure you know."

"Among the children, I've been told," Inark said.

"Even so," said Kat.

Inark bowed deeply to her. "And Halmas, who I heard at my door translating."

"Honor to you, Kingsfisher," said Halmas.

Inark snorted. "Are the rumors true, Celzez? Are you here to denounce?"

"I've only spoken of it to family and friends."

Inark chuckled, a dry and angry sound. "There have been stories about Teriz—but nobody knew for certain. Nobody *saw*, nobody could denounce. You were in Alness then, and you return here now. Of course rumors start."

"Tell him," I said. "Tell him it is foolishness." Inark turned his head toward me but did not answer. The silence drew on, grew long. *This place is filled with silences*, I thought.

"I reached the fifth marking stone," Inark said finally.

"What?"

"The day we heard Alness fell I reached the fifth marking stone before they found me and brought me back."

"You did not try again?" Kat seemed to already know the answer, and I felt she asked for my benefit.

She had spoken mildly, but Inark recoiled as though slapped. He dropped his head. "The second day, I became confused by the heat and lost my feel for the sun. They found me in the desert."

Again silence surrounded us.

"You do Alness great honor," Kat said.

"I failed them. I failed them by getting old." The bitterness in Inark's voice filled the room, enduring beyond his words and mixing with the next silence.

I tried to clear my thoughts. "What? Why?" This man did not owe Alness anything.

"Because I am a Sandfisher, and because I was a Kingsfisher. Age has robbed me of my honor, leaving me waiting to die."

He held up a fist, wrinkled skin covered with brown blotches, tendons standing out from his withered muscles. "Were I able, I would find out the truth..." He dropped his hand. "It would do me no good."

"I know the truth," said Celzez.

"Then you must act," said Inark. "You

must act before you no longer can."

I expected Celzez would rush off and make his denouncement, but when we left Inark, he merely turned toward his sister's house.

"Why *does* he wait?" I asked Halmas as we followed Celzez toward the main square. Not that I minded, I needed the time.

"Denouncements occur at sundown," he replied, "for that is a time of endings."

"Huh," I said. "Why should that matter?"

Halmas gave me a frown at odds with his usual stoic helpfulness. "It is a matter of honor. To kill a man without warning of your intention is murder. You must allow a man to defend himself. Or," he added, "another to defend him. There is a ritual."

It shouldn't have surprised me there would be a ritual, but why make it difficult? If you're going to kill somebody, just have at it. "What is this ritual?"

"You must stand on the denouncement stone at sundown and wait ten minutes."

"Ten minutes?" I exclaimed. "Why?"

"To prevent people from jumping on the stone and muttering their charge before anybody knows of it. And the charge must be spoken clearly in a loud voice."

"You may as well announce it to the world."

"How can honor be a private thing?" Halmas said.

I wasn't sure if he expected an answer, but I didn't have one in any case.

After a short silence he continued. "Somebody may challenge the denouncement. It needs be one with knowledge of the person's honor." He shrugged. "Then there is a fight."

"What if no one challenges the denouncement?"

"The man who made it will hunt and kill the man he denounced."

"If he can," I said, thinking at that point all the rules would be over.

"If he can," Halmas agreed.

So, I thought, *since Teriz was not here, he could not challenge Celzez.* "What happens if the first man doesn't hunt down the man he accused?"

"There is much shame and loss of honor in that."

The Sandfishers seemed to have covered everything. Still, Celzez would be free to hunt Teriz down without rules. That wasn't so bad.

Sundown. I glanced up. Almost half a day remained to fulfill my promise to Jalani. I felt a prickling down my spine as I realized I might not be able to change Celzez's mind.

Kat went I knew not where. Jalani returned to the wagon to sell her wares, urging me to keep trying. I had until evening when Celzez would utter words that could not be taken back.

Sharin and Johin went with Celzez to a small cemetery on the edge of the desert. Halmas and I followed along but stood back when we approached a lone grave in the shade of the red sandstone wall.

"My brother," Celzez said as he crouched next to it. Without apparently thinking, he tugged on a string about his neck, drawing something from under his shirt.

It looked like a shield, twice the size of his thumbnail, light-colored with an iridescence that I wasn't the only one to notice.

"Are you still wearing that?" Sharin asked. Halmas murmured a translation only I could hear.

Celzez nodded. Sharin snorted, curling her lip.

"What is it?" I asked.

"Nothing," Celzez said. He turned toward the grave in the shade of the wall. "Something my brother gave me. When we were boys." Halmas quietly translated into Hafizi, speaking to Johin, who watched with wide eyes.

"What is it?" I asked again.

"A *fallo* scale." Celzez rubbed it—a gesture so practiced and smooth I knew it must be a habit. He held it out to me, and I saw it bore the head of a kingfisher, nearly worn away. "He told me it was a shield. That it should remind me of my goal and someday I would trade it for a real one."

"There are no Kingfishers anymore," Sharin snapped.

Celzez shrugged. "It reminds me of the type of man I want to be."

"A man who would leave his sister-in-law and nephew alone in the world," she said.

"I shall leave you money."

"Damn your money! For years you have sent us money."

Celzez hung his head, staring at the grave. "You do not know," he said quietly. "You have not seen Alness. You have not seen the people suffer. They leave bloody marks when they walk. You have not heard Jalani cry in the night."

"Must I cry too?"

Celzez lifted his head and looked her in the eye. "No. Pray I do not fail."

We left the cemetery, Sharin and Johin returning home while the rest of us headed down to the caravan grounds adjacent to the main square and the lake.

Celzez stopped by the wagon and watched Jalani dicker with a customer. She pointedly ignored him and only glared at me. There was no reason to be there, so Celzez wandered over to the lake and kicked off his boots.

I took a deep breath. Now. Now was my best chance to try and change his plans. "There is no proof a prince survived," I said. "And if one did, you need not serve him." I licked my lips. "This will not make you a Kingsfisher."

Celzez smiled over his shoulder as he took a step into the lake. "I know."

"I promised Jalani I would talk you out of this. Think of her."

Celzez moved his feet, watching the waves he made disappear amongst the larger waves of the lake. "In Alness they call it Trust. It is the obligations the people have to each other, and some have special Trusts. Duties: the soldier's Trust to defend the country, the judge's Trust to be fair. The King's Trust to rule well."

A strange place of honorable fools, I thought. "You are not from Alness," I pointed out.

"No. I am a Sandfisher."

"Another Trust." I sneered.

"If you wish. A Trust to all those who take pride in what it is to be a Sandfisher.

And for those who were Kingsfishers whose honor was betrayed. There is a reason the Kings of Alness drew the Kingsfishers from Hafiz, and a reason we were willing to serve."

"You want to do this," I accused him.

He sighed and closed his eyes for a moment. "No. I *need* to do this." After a long silence, he opened his eyes and asked, "Whom do you stand with?"

His question caught me by surprise, and I had no answer. Celzez continued to wade in the lake, wandering away from me as I groped for words.

This story isn't turning out as I expected.

The Denouncement Stone sits in the square at the heart of Hafiz, next to the lake. It's about eighteen inches tall, just enough for a man to be seen by a crowd. Like the rest of the city, it is red sandstone. There are no carvings on it. Like honor itself, it is an unassuming part of Sandfisher life.

I had expected more.

Men already gathered in the square. Some browsed the wares of the shops and merchant wagons. Others talked in small clusters, but all knew Celzez planned a denouncement.

Celzez walked to the Stone, looking neither right nor left. He paused next to it, looked out over the lake, took a deep breath, and stepped up.

A few men dashed off. Their shouts drifted back, summoning friends to the spectacle. The others came forward, forming a circle around the stone. And they waited.

Celzez looked like a statue on a plinth, standing quietly, hands loosely at his side. More people gathered in the square. I looked for Jalani, but having failed to change Celzez's mind, she didn't want to watch the denouncement.

Inark came. He used a crutch, and the men made way for him so he could stand near the stone. He did not look at Celzez—it wouldn't have mattered—but he kept his head tilted as if listening to every sound.

Finally Celzez spoke. "I denounce Teriz, son of Razen, as an oath breaker. He—"

"No!" exclaimed a deep voice. A huge man stepped forward.

"That's Ranas, Teriz's brother," Halmas murmured.

Ranas stood nearly as tall as Celzez, but Celzez stood on the Denouncement Stone. Ranas shrugged off his robe, stood in billowing pants and a sleeveless vest. He wore metal bracers on his arms. "I will not hear of dishonor. Not in the same sentence as Teriz's name." He moved to the center of the square.

I moved so I could see both Ranas and Celzez's faces. Neither seemed surprised.

"I will not retract," Celzez said. It sounded like he read from a script.

"Then we shall test your words." Ranas stretched his arms and drew a scimitar of enormous size.

Celzez stepped off the stone, suddenly looking very small.

"Is Teriz as big as Ranas?" I asked Halmas.

"They are twins," Halmas said. "But Teriz is far more dangerous."

I didn't know if that was good or not. Better chances now, worse later. Ranas clearly knew his work. He had the strength to use his gigantic scimitar, and he moved it quickly as he loosened his muscles.

Celzez drew his own sword. The two saluted each other, and the fight began.

Celzez moved well, like a veteran fighter. He kept his feet under him, his weight balanced. He moved away when Ranas tried to close. He engaged Ranas's scimitar, tapping it without attacking.

Ranas swiped at Celzez's sword, but Celzez disengaged and lunged. Ranas stepped back and delivered a great, sweeping backhand, but Celzez recovered from his lunge and moved aside.

All very formal, I thought.

Celzez leapt forward, his sword twisting and cutting, again and again; but each time Ranas tapped it aside. Celzez came close, too close to cut. Ranas punched, sending him reeling back as the crowd murmured.

Blood ran from a cut on Celzez's face, staining his shirt. He parried the next blow, and the next, but the third tore his sword from his hands.

With his free hand, Ranas grabbed him by the throat. He lifted Celzez until only his toes touched the ground. He drew back his scimitar. Celzez's face was turning red.

Celzez kicked right for Ranas's groin. Surprised, the larger man dropped him and twisted to protect himself. Celzez stumbled toward his sword.

Ranas swung, catching Celzez behind the knee. As Celzez sprawled on the ground, Ranas thrust down with enough force to part his ribs and plunge the heavy scimitar into his heart.

Ranas jerked his scimitar free and used his foot to turn Celzez over. "The fight is over." He turned around, looking at each of the watchers. "My brother's honor has been defended."

Johin pushed through the crowd and raced across the sand to crouch by his uncle. *Don't do anything*, I urged him in my mind. He brushed the sand from Celzez's face. Slowly he reached down, pulled on the string about Celzez's neck, and drew out the *fallo* scale shield. He wiped it clean of blood.

No, no, no. I feared what he might do.

He snapped the cord and held the scale in his fist. Lifting his head, he stared at Ranas and reached for Celzez's sword.

Twitter: @MattPungitore

IG: matthewpungitoreauthor

His books are available on BookBaby and Amazon!

MATTHEW PUNGITORE has written essay-articles for the DMR Books blog. His essay "Gothic-Decadent Marks on Howard's 'Spear and Fang'" was nominated for The Hyrkanian of the 2022 REH Foundation awards. He is the author of "Wychyrst Tower," which appeared in Cirsova (Winter 2021). Matthew is the author of *The Report of Mr. Charles Aalmers and other stories.*

"The fight is *not* over."

The crowd murmured. I blinked, for Halmas spoke, translating words Kat had spoken. *She speaks Hafizi!* I realized.

Kat glided into the square and positioned herself between Ranas and Johin. She looked tiny.

Ranas started to laugh, but he saw something in her that made him stop. He hefted his scimitar and cut the air.

The men around me murmured. Halmas didn't translate, but I could tell they thought this an unfortunate waste of life.

"You cannot help," Halmas murmured, and I realized I had not just taken a step forward, but half-drawn my sword as well. "This is within the process. Should she die, you may act."

I knew Kat, had seen her fight a hundred times; but she looked so small, and Ranas had killed Celzez so easily.

Kat circled, Ranas turning with her, letting her do the work. She feinted, but he did not respond. She crept closer. He watched.

Suddenly, he swept his arm up, and Kat darted closer, raising her sword as if she would protect herself. Ranas swung down, but Kat was too close, he brought his arm down onto her sword, cutting deeply. Kat's left hand twitched, and a dagger appeared from some hidden sheath. She drove it into Ranas's side.

Ranas twisted away, the dagger caught in his ribs, swinging to keep Kat away.

She began circling the opposite direction. She flowed, she glided, she moved like a force of nature. Ranas followed her, blood dripping.

"Kill him," I growled.

She dove in, twisting and feinting. Ranas tried to follow her, but bad footwork put him off balance, and Kat grabbed her dagger and yanked it free. She swept past him, driving the dagger into his back. He arched up, and she dropped her sword to take the back of his collar. She yanked, over-tipping him. He tried to turn, but as he fell, Kat used her dagger to cut his throat.

Silence, another type of silence, the silence of surprise, filled the square.

"Do you accuse Teriz?" called a voice from the crowd, and the men murmured, agreeing on their right to know.

Can she do that? I wondered. I never asked if she witnessed Teriz's treachery.

Kat prowled over the paving stones like a cat looking over a gallery of songbirds, selecting its next meal. "I assert that Celzez is not a liar."

Another man stepped forward. Though not as tall as Ranas, there was a resemblance, a brother perhaps, or cousin. The man behind him grabbed his arm. "There's a difference. In what she said, there's a difference."

There was, I realized. Kat did not accuse Teriz, but left the accusation open. Celzez could not pursue it, so nothing would come of it. But would anybody push the question of Celzez's honor?

The first man paused as he looked at Kat, who grinned. Her grin sent a shiver down my spine, and from the crowd's reaction, I was not the only one.

By the gods of Eastwarn, I thought, *is he fool enough to take up this fight?*

He was not. He left, half-turned to show he was not afraid. I snorted at that lie.

I could not shake the feeling something had happened here. Something about honor and deciding whom you will stand with. Something that *mattered* to me. Given time, I might figure out what.

The crowd began to break up, and the men drifted away. The men furthest away leaving first, then more and more until only a few people remained: Halmas, who stood quietly next to me; Inark, who faced Kat with a question on his face but not his lips; Kat, her eyes hooded, thinking I knew not what; Sharin, who stood crying beside the Denouncement Stone.

And Johin, holding a *fallo* scale shield tightly in one fist, who slowly took his uncle's sword as his own.

Jim Breyfogle's Tales of the Mongoose and Meerkat Volume 2: The Heat of the Chase is out now from Cirsova Publishing! Find it on Amazon.com or ask for it wherever books are sold!
https://jimbreyfogle.wordpress.com/

Richard L. Rubin's
Short Story Sci- Fi Thriller

NOW AVAILABLE ON AMAZON!

★★★★★

*"Great read!!
Would highly recommend!!"*

★★★★★

*"Kept me intrigued
from start to finish."*

ROBBERY ON ANTARES VI

RICHARD L. RUBIN

The Wisdom of Man

By ADAM S. FURMAN

John Knox finds a victim of the experiments of a billionaire working to distill tachyons that can freeze time itself! Can he stop the mad project before it's too late!?

The heat sizzled over the brick sidewalks of Naperville, Illinois, obscuring the view of anyone strolling through the quaint and ordinary village. But the dank scent of metal in the air set a man on edge.

Jaunting off the main street came John Knox, a man with ghastly eyes and a crooked nose, who had gone on his morning constitutional to clear his head. Suddenly he stopped at the sound of a strained whimper echoing down the street.

Knox rested a weathered hand on the ivory handle of his revolver, and he peered down the alley next to him. The whimper repeated—a feminine cry from the shadows. He drew his gun and entered the alley, mindful of the dangers from nearby Chicago.

"By God's Grace," he whispered as an unnatural scene came into focus. He rushed over to a woman lying on the brick alleyway. "Miss, what happened here?" The air around her torso became blurry so that the caramel color of her skin seemed to meld into the street's red and black.

She blinked at Knox. "Who...are...you?"

"Don't worry about me, miss. I won't hurt you. Who did this?" He reached for her torso. "What is—"

"Don't touch me." The woman snatched his wrist—weakly—but Knox stared at her. "It was Suleiman."

"The billionaire?"

The woman nodded. "He's experimenting with the particles from the collider at Dodge Labs. Exotic particles." She inhaled sharply, eyebrows arched upwards in a pained expression. "Reality is just an illusion. Time is meaningless when it can be controlled."

Knox squinted. "You can't mean he's a time traveler, can you?"

The woman shook her head. "He tortured me, shot me, but slowed the time around my waist..."

Knox glanced from the woman's eyes to her stomach and back. "...So that any movement and you bleed out," he said.

"Or when the particles expire, I'll bleed out." She sniffled and her midnight hair shook. "I'm scared." She clutched Knox's arm. Her eyes held an unspoken request.

"I've got you," he answered. Knox lifted her shoulders, pulled her body from the time cloud, and held her tight as he offered up a prayer. Her body quickly went limp, and Knox set her down and brushed a hand over her face to close her eyes. "I prophesy a reckoning."

"**B**lasted idiots, the lot of you," a man said, cutting into the slab of steak before him. His neat pencil mustache danced along his lips as he chewed the savory meat. The restaurant had closed an hour before they arrived, but by arrangement with the owner—who was not his friend—his party had the place to themselves.

"It's fine, Suleiman," a deep voice answered.

Suleiman paused, and a drop of steak sauce landed on his cream-colored suit. "Look what you made me do," he said through an exasperated sigh. Suleiman set his utensils down and dabbed at the droplet. "You say these upsetting things, Sa'id—incompetent things—and it causes me to lose my composure."

"Suleiman, we're doing fine," answered Sa'id. He wore a foolish grin inside a thick beard. "Nobody knows about you, or what you're doing."

Suleiman exhaled sharply. "We don't know that, Sa'id, and that's the problem. Who is John Knox? A zealot—a fanatic, to be sure."

Sa'id scratched at his shaved head. "He's a crazy man—some say he has a magic knife. Nobody would believe Knox even if he said anything."

"He's killed four of our men." Suleiman slammed his fists on the table, rattling the dishes. "Crazy doesn't mean he's safe. It's quite the opposite. Make yourself useful and go stare at the sun."

"I'm sorry, boss. I just wanted—"

Suleiman raised his hand, and Sa'id fell silent. "He picks us off one by one. We have a rat among us. Must I be the only one who cares about what we're doing here?" Suleiman reached a hand into the inside pocket of his jacket and clutched a freezing glass vial. Suleiman shuddered, unrelated to the temperature.

"There's a snitch?" Sa'id asked, shifting away from him.

"There's no other explanation," Suleiman said. "Knox has systematically hunted the whole research team. Björn fell out a five-story window, Sal was shot in the hotel, and we found Charles in his rental car with the written threat."

"There's still me and Vasily," Sa'id said.

Suleiman's eyes narrowed. "We need to leave the country—fast. Where is Vasily, anyway?"

"He's out on the town."

Suleiman returned to eating until the front door opened. A tall man in a low-cut shirt entered wearing a grin of ecstasy. His eyes glossed over as he stumbled in and shut the door.

"Vasily, where have you been?"

The tall man staggered over to Suleiman's table and leaned his elbows on it for balance. He ran his hand through the blossom of dark curls on his head. "We were just at the club."

Suleiman noticed a shameful stain at the bottom of Vasily's shirt. "Who is 'we'?"

"Just me and Candy," Vasily answered and rubbed his nose.

"Have you been frequenting whores?"

Vasily's lips stretched into a frown. "That's such a backwards way of thinking about sex workers."

"Euphemisms attempt to mask the truth and, as a result, help nobody, Vasily," Suleiman said. "I trust you're using drugs?"

Vasily chuckled. "Are you my dad?"

"Your father failed in raising you, because he raised a scoundrel," Suleiman said. "What conversations do you have with Candy?"

Vasily jerked backwards. "That's my private business."

"I'll give you two some privacy," Sa'id said, sliding away from him.

"You'll not move another inch, Sa'id. Vasily, answer the question. Do you talk to her about us, maybe?"

"No, I never mention you. We talk about life," Vasily said, his eyes drooping into a cinematic moment that only existed in his mind. "Our wants and goals in life."

"You've known a whore for a few weeks and you're going to marry her?" Suleiman guffawed.

"She's the only one who asks me about *my life*," Vasily said. "You're right. I didn't have a father. I've talked to her about that, and how a research team is my family now, and how we're only in town for a little bit, that we broke Dodge Labs and were searching for a solution to—"

"Vasily, are you that thick?" Sa'id shouted with a clenched fist.

Vasily waved a meaty hand. "She dropped out of college...wanted to go into physics, but it was too hard. I invited her to the hotel and showed her around."

"We found the rat," Sa'id said.

"I'm not a rat," Vasily said.

"Did you mention that we're holed up in this restaurant because Knox found our hotel?" Sa'id asked.

"Knox? The restaurant—I mentioned—of course I mentioned this restaurant. We stay here ever since—"

"Go watch the door, Vasily," Suleiman said. The anger coursed through his veins, but he knew that impulsive actions exacerbated problems instead of solving them. He quelled his urge, burying it deep within his gut.

Vasily straightened, brushed glitter from his shirt, and set course for the restaurant door, where he promptly sat down to stare at the wooden blinds masking the black night beyond.

"He's a liability, Sa'id," Suleiman said while glaring at Vasily. "Take care of him, and then we can go. I've got some old friends in Minsk. We'll rebuild there."

Sa'id nodded and shimmied out of the booth. He drew a pistol from his waistband and sauntered towards Vasily.

Two blasts rang out from the door before Sa'id had raised his gun. Vasily shook from each blast, and crimson splotches soaked through his shirt.

The front door swung open, and a figure whisked inside. A black bandanna covered most of his face, but hard eyes pierced through to the carnage. He held a shotgun in his left hand and a revolver in his right.

One more shotgun blast sent Vasily skidding two yards backwards. Sa'id raised his pistol, but the figure aimed and fired three rounds to his head—all finding their mark.

The figure floated over to Suleiman's table and pointed the shotgun to his chest. "Aren't you gonna beg? They always beg."

"John Knox, I presume?" Suleiman asked, rigid in his seat. "A fanatic, to be sure. Thank you for taking care of Vasily and Sa'id for me. They had become too burdensome."

"Does loyalty mean nothing to you?"
Suleiman shrugged. "It is what it is."

"Hell's waiting for you," Knox said as he racked the shotgun. "Repent while you have the chance."

Suleiman waved his hand and leaned back into his booth. "If I may, why are you doing this? We didn't do anything to you— we never even heard of you before you began killing my team."

"You're so depraved that you can't remember your sins from a few weeks ago? An assistant from Dodge Labs died in my arms."

"Oh, her." Suleiman's lips curled to a smile. "What was she to you? Girlfriend? Whore? How much do I owe you?"

"Justice ain't for sale, scumbag. You murdered the girl using the occult, and I'm here to return the favor with bullets."

"The occult? Mr. Knox, are you trying to insult me with that word?" Within a flash, he drew a glowing beaker from his jacket pocket and set it beside his plate. "Do you know what this is?"

"No more sudden moves," Knox said.

Suleiman clasped the glass and lifted it to his eyes. "Tachyons, timeless particles, drawn from beyond this universe through modern miracles of physics."

"That's...firmament." Knox lowered his weapon to gaze at the cerulean fluid suspended within the cup.

"Who knew the ancients possessed such wisdom?"

"Do you know what you've done?"

"Perfectly, which is why I intend to continue," Suleiman said. "I assume you know about the destruction at Dodge Labs. No worry. It will only take a few years for sufficient particle colliders to be built. And I've got all the time in the world after that."

"You've committed an abomination," Knox said. "The firmament was isolated by the Almighty, never intended to enter Creation."

Suleiman nodded. "The science suggests otherwise. And with that, you'll have to excuse me."

"I don't think so."

"What, are you going to shoot me, unarmed and holding a vial of tachyons?" Suleiman touched the lid with a fingertip. "I'd caution against that. You see, a substance outside of time and space acts... predictably unpredictable."

Suleiman unclasped the beaker's cover and flung the substance towards Knox. The fanatic brought his shotgun up. As he pulled the trigger, the tachyons engulfed him. The blast rang out, slowed to a low rumble, and finally died to a perceptible nothingness. The tachyons fractured the air around him in tiny icicles until Knox became stiff while steel shot stopped mere inches outside his barrel with gas and flash fixed in the air nearby.

Suleiman slid out of his booth, careful to avoid the cloud that held Knox frozen in space-time, and adjusted his tie. "Farewell, my friend. I've got a laboratory to build. I suspect by the time I'm done, you'll be dead or—even better—will never have existed."

Knox pulled the trigger, but his delay became disastrous when combined with Suleiman's sleight of hand. The air fractured around Knox to the point where the businessman's sneer blurred. The shotgun rang out, but the cloud of substance surrounded Knox in a flash and seemingly dissipated at once. The slugs hit exactly where Suleiman had sat, but he was now nowhere.

Darkness encased Knox, and as he peered around, he noticed the entire restaurant appeared decayed. Dust lined the tables, windows were broken, and two skeletons each covered their own brown stain.

"The firmament." His words echoed in the air. A shudder traveled down Knox's spine. How much time had passed as he stood frozen, he didn't know. The mission remained. Suleiman still lurked out in the world, dangerously driven by prideful desires with at least one victim still calling out for justice.

The insatiable anger towards Suleiman remained, as if God Almighty whispered to him, revitalizing his determination to track down this beast of a man.

Knox's investigation yielded quick results. Over the last five years, an or-ganization in rural Belarus had constructed the world's largest particle colliders—the BAL Complex. As he traveled towards the Slavic countryside, daydreams related to the swift passage of time haunted him.

Still, his conscience pressed him forward to face Suleiman prior to the initial experiments scheduled at the BAL Complex. Despite his mind's protests, Knox knew Suleiman posed a danger to everyone. Vengeance began his hunt, and now duty sought its completion.

Knox knew nothing about science—or, at least, how Suleiman proffered science—so the religious statue of a four-headed man outside the BAL Complex headquarters was unexpected. While Knox became momentarily distracted with the foreign statue, a darkened blur moved on his periphery and slammed his head before he could draw his revolver.

A drone of hisses and beeps pounded at Knox's head. The factory of sounds labored beneath his mind until he produced a groan through a tightened jaw. Hushed murmurs echoed throughout the room, but Knox witnessed nobody speaking.

Before him hung spindly wires and cords, snaking up the walls and overhead, connecting drab silver to bland gold. The myriad tubes and wires led to a thick metal box in the front of the room. A clear vat appeared through the box's glass windows. An army of men stood staring at their stations, terminals that rose waist-high and shone with plain white screens.

Knox tried to move, but thick cords—not

unlike those that hung in the room—bound him to a chair. They pulled his arms back, straining his shoulders and rendering his hands useless. Knox needn't have checked, but knew that his shotgun, revolver, and Bowie knife had all been removed from their accustomed places on his body.

"Welcome, Mr. Knox," a familiar voice called. "It's been years since our last meeting. I didn't know you were a fan of the hard sciences."

Knox gazed around until his vision settled on a man with a beige suit. "Suleiman." The word scraped against his throat, resulting in a brief coughing fit.

"I'm surprised to see you, Mr. Knox, even if you did try to kill me. I'd thought time had gotten the best of you."

"You don't know what you're doing, Suleiman," Knox said. "I've come to put a stop to your experiment."

Suleiman scoffed. "It shows what little you know, fanatic. But then again, what can you do?"

"Persuade you to stop," Knox said. "Then, I'll avenge the poor woman you murdered."

"I'm not stopping this. Funding the BAL Complex is my life's work." Suleiman pointed a long finger at Knox. "As soon as I generate enough tachyons, I'll have anything—or everything. Time shall belong to me."

"You're playing with things you don't understand," Knox said. "The firmament belongs in eternity, not toyed with by a snake."

Suleiman snapped his fingers at a young man nearby. "Go, gag our fanatic. I'm tired of hearing his superstitious rubbish."

"Right away, sir," the man said and approached Knox.

"Just imagine, Mr. Knox, being able to have more riches than Louis XIV, to revel in Cleopatra's beauty—make her your wife, even—or become a Sultan." Suleiman inhaled deeply and closed his eyes. "The time's at hand." Suleiman turned his attention to a large monitor in front of him.

A man rounded Knox's seat and pulled a piece of fabric tightly around his head, overlapping his mouth so as to gag him. After another moment, Knox felt a cool weight in his right hand, a familiar blade of sharp steel—his Bowie knife!

"*Soli deo gloria.*" The whispered words caused Knox to notice the man, one with a lanky stature and thick auburn beard. He nodded at Knox, slowly, which Knox interpreted to mean he was a friend.

At once, Knox went about sawing at the ropes around his arms. Suleiman spoke with another man in a labcoat and turned to Knox's secret friend. "Are we ready, Dr. Warfield?"

Dr. Warfield nodded. "The experiment has been prepared for."

"We're far past the experiment stage, Doctor." Suleiman rubbed his hands together. "This is another extraction."

"To be clear, sir, we don't know what will happen—this procedure has never been attempted with colliders of this size."

"Stop with the posturing, Doctor, and get on with it."

Dr. Warfield nodded and walked over to his station, where he input instructions on a blinding terminal. The room soon thrummed loudly as if it were inside a rocket. When Knox thought the noise couldn't get any louder, the building trembled.

Knox felt a cord drop down his arm, and his wrists suddenly had a wider range of motion. He strained as Dr. Warfield and Suleiman approached the metal receptacle and peered at the glass vat inside. The complex noticeably shook, now, and the vat collected trace amounts of sky-blue liquid—tachyons.

Suleiman jumped. He grabbed hold of the metal box and embraced it, squeezing it as he would have hugged his child. Suleiman turned to face Knox, revealing a wild-eyed expression, and called out something unintelligible.

A siren barely registered over the commotion. The lights flickered and dimmed until an amber glow oscillated over the men's faces. The air crashed, echoes bounced from the corners of the rooms and settled atop the metal box, and the light bent around that fixed point so that the wall behind appeared to fold until a sphere mirrored the room.

"What's going on?" Suleiman yelled at the scientists.

Knox worked quickly to saw the ropes from his wrists. He freed one arm and, with the panic unfolding within the room, he could work faster without worrying that he'd be caught.

The supercolliders powered down, and the only sound in the room came from the mirrored sphere. A breeze tickled Knox's face. Warm and wet, it circled around the room, whisking papers off a desk. The breeze intensified so that it blew Knox's hair, growing into a gale so that chairs fell over and scientists struggled to remain standing.

The sphere widened and revealed a deep scarlet light inside. It beckoned Knox to rise and bade him good fortune—power, sex, riches. There would be no more pain that needed healing, no more crime that screamed for justice, and no more loneliness that begged for companionship. Knox could have it all. The answer—the opportunity—unfolded before him.

He finally freed himself from the binding, clutched his Bowie knife within his right fist, and stepped towards the orb that offered him his heart's desire. With a glance around the room, he witnessed everyone else standing with mouths agape at the enticing entity—everyone except Dr. Warfield, who averted his gaze.

Dr. Warfield's discipline stirred something within Knox, a resolution and fortitude for the people's true well-being. Knox struggled against the gale winds and grabbed Dr. Warfield.

"We need to shut this off," Knox said, sheathing his knife.

"It's too late," the doctor said. "An entity approaches."

Knox glanced at the widening orb. Movement flickered on the other side. "My guns! Where are my guns?"

The air crackled with a deep voice. Words sang on a twisted chord, dispelling any peace that yet remained in the room. And an ungodly chorus of ancient tongues spewed forth harsh clicks and throaty growls: *Arise, come Baphomet! Arise, come Baphomet! The Six Princes of Sheol bid you well. Arise, come Baphomet!*

The building quaked, and a large human hand pulled the orb's edge from within. Soon another joined it until it widened the orb enough for a head to fit through. The head, a goat's likeness, forced its way through, stretching the portal so that the figure could stand, revealing a bronze human body with brilliant feathered wings.

The chorus sent Knox's hair on end. The entity's appearance took the breath out of him, and a sudden flutter in his chest strained his focus.

"Warfield, my guns."

The scientists were released from their baleful hold. Suleiman's jaw dropped, and his face twisted inward as his mind tried to comprehend the sight before his eyes.

Baphomet, a god among men, the fiend who reveals forbidden knowledge to mankind, extended a hand towards them. They stumbled backwards, just out of the demon's grasp. Knox and Dr. Warfield ducked behind a nearby terminal, while Suleiman scrambled out the door and towards safety, if one could indeed be safe from a demonic angel.

The demon responded in a raging snort, clasped its fist, and smashed the tachyon receptacle. The force thrust the scientists into the air, their insides ripped out, but the tachyons held them in a timeless suspension. Natural sounds in the room ceased— killed by witchcraft. The hellish choir grew, and Knox felt the worry bear down at him,

trickling out from his chest to his arms and legs.

Cool metal fell into his lap, and Knox realized it was the gun barrel of his shotgun. Dr. Warfield handed Knox his revolver, and the smooth ivory handle calmed his nerves.

"Shut the power off," Knox said. "I'll cover you."

Dr. Warfield pulled two M1911 pistols from beneath his coat. "I can handle myself. You're not the only one on a mission."

Dr. Warfield sprinted towards the power terminal, avoiding the horrors hanging in the air. He unleashed a hail of bullets that peppered Baphomet's wings. The demon turned its attention towards the gunning scientist.

Knox stood and fired six rounds into the demon's chest. Each bullet hit its mark, but the monster was unfazed. He shoved the revolver into his holster and grabbed the shotgun.

Knox racked the lever and pulled the trigger, sending a slug into Baphomet's face. It groaned and gazed at the fanatic through narrowed eyes. Knox fumbled with the lever action and stalled when the fiend struck him. He skidded across the room and bashed his head against a wall.

He staggered, holding an arm against a wall for balance. The room spun around him as the demon refocused on Dr. Warfield. Knox searched the floor for his shotgun, but came up empty. Dr. Warfield stepped away from the terminal just as Baphomet reached for him. The man emptied his gun on the copper hand, and the demon recoiled.

"It's done," Dr. Warfield said.

Terminals faded to black and, though dark arts already kept sounds stifled, the air grew peaceful. Baphomet's portal, too, was affected by the power loss. The sphere collapsed, tightening its circumference and volume to the point where it pressed upon Baphomet. Baphomet grabbed hold of the portal's edge to stabilize it.

Knox filed six more bullets into his revolver's cylinder. He cocked the gun and shot directly at the demon's head. Baphomet recoiled into the portal, the sphere shrinking along with the retreat. It roared and tore the portal wide enough to stand once more. Crimson lightning crackled from its hands as its muscles rippled against supernatural forces.

"He's coming through." Dr. Warfield ran to Knox's side. "There's no stopping him. We need to leave—to warn the others."

"How do you warn people of a monster they don't believe in?" Knox drew the Bowie knife and skillfully tossed it so he held it by the blade. "*Sola fide.*"

Knox drew his arm back and threw his Bowie knife at Baphomet. The knife arced through the air, end over end, flying past a fresh mess of bodies. It struck the demon in its left eye and glowed bright.

Baphomet threw its horned head back and ejaculated a throaty groan. It let go of the portal and grasped at its face. The sphere buckled, digging into its flesh, and it realized it had mere seconds until it would be cast back into Sheol.

Baphomet lunged towards Knox and Dr. Warfield. The portal shrank, and its oversized wings now kept it from reaching the duo. With only an arm outside the portal, it roared and pounded at the floor. The arm flailed, searching for them—or anything—to cause mayhem, catching machines on either side of the portal.

The portal became small so that Baphomet could only be seen as a scarlet shadow within the sphere. The orb snapped shut, and nothing remained in the air. With the sphere's disappearance, the surrounding sound returned, consisting of a siren's wail and hissing hoses.

Knox scrambled towards the destroyed metal box, searching. "Where's my knife?"

"This place is coming down." Dr. Warfield tugged at Knox's jacket. "We need to leave."

Knox cursed Baphomet and turned to follow Dr. Warfield out of the complex. On his way out, he noticed a dull tube of metal with flecks of maple wood—his shotgun. He shrugged. Knox picked up his shotgun and exited the supercollider complex, wishing that he had his knife instead.

"This is where we depart, friend." Knox slapped Dr. Warfield on the shoulder. "God be with you."

"And also with you," Dr. Warfield said.

The duo eyed a bloodied man in a beige suit frantically hauling himself across the sidewalk fist over fist.

"I've got business to finish," Knox said.

"Farewell. Watch out for the pockets of firmament," Dr. Warfield said. "There's some that made it outside."

Knox followed the bloody trail to the man fumbling on the ground, who had just reached the four-headed statue. Knox grabbed the man by the collar, picked him up, and threw him against the statue's base.

"Suleiman... Where are you off to?"

"I'm just going to—there's a thing over—" Suleiman trailed off into crazed laughter. Shreds of his jacket fluttered while he cackled. "That was unbelievable, Mr. Knox, truly fascinating."

"You dismissed everything I warned you about."

"Well, hey, I'm a believer now." Suleiman shrugged, nodding at the collapsed BAL Complex behind him. "I know there's things out there, wicked things—powerful entities. Even now, I wonder if fairytales and myths aren't the truth, and modern man isn't—"

"You've done enough." Knox struck Suleiman across the jaw.

"Only God can judge me."

Knox stared hard into Suleiman's eyes. "That should terrify you, but there's no fear in your eyes." Sunlight glared at him from a few feet away, a pocket of firmament sizzling in the air. "Stand up."

"I can't."

"Get." Knox smacked him again before shoving him away from the statue's base. Suleiman staggered forward, complaining of an injured leg.

Knox whirled Suleiman around and fired four bullets into his stomach at point-blank. Suleiman stumbled into the cloud of firmament, and Knox steadied him.

"I've planted four lethal shots into your belly, scumbag. Luckily, this firmament will preserve your life. But if you move, or if the firmament expires, you're gone."

Suleiman's jaw quivered. "Why?"

"I asked you the same damn question about the lab assistant," Knox said.

"I hope you burn in Hell," Suleiman said through his pain. "You hypocrite... You're the same as me, just as bad."

"You're wrong, Suleiman. One of us regrets that our paths have crossed, and the other lives for it."

Knox turned and headed towards the Minsk skyline. Suleiman's protests grew louder with each of Knox's steps, until suddenly Suleiman's voice ceased. Knox didn't even give the crumpled body a final glance. He had already formulated a plan to get his Bowie knife back, and he was sure he'd see Suleiman shortly.

Adam writes action-packed stories, still playing catch-up from discovering the pulps at an older age. When he's not at his day job, he fosters the glimmer of wonder in his children's eyes. Follow him on Twitter @AdamSFurman.

New Troops for Old: Jerry Pournelle's Janissaries

By J. COMER

The field of military science fiction owes a great deal to the late Jerry Pournelle (1933-2017). Pournelle, a Korean War veteran, worked for Boeing and wrote columns on computer use, eventually being the first author to write a novel on a word processor. His numerous collaborations included *The Mote In God's Eye* (1974) and *Lucifer's Hammer* (1977), both with Larry Niven. Pournelle was also the author of fourteen solo novels, inspired not only by Heinlein, but by Poul Anderson and H. Beam Piper.

In the *Janissaries* books, Pournelle explored a question handed to him by Jim Baen: if UFOs were real, what would they be doing?

Pournelle concluded that aliens would be doing something unlawful in their own society. But what? To Pournelle, author of the non-SF thriller *Red Heroin* (1969), it had to be *drugs*. American soldiers abducted by UFOs were taken to an Earthlike world, Tran, to grow a narcotic called *surinomaz*. The aliens do this every six hundred years, so Tran has Venetians, Celts, Romans, and Scythians, each new group being brought in to grow drugs in a "Time" of apocalyptic climate change. This allowed Pournelle to base much of the series on European military history, as he did when writing the CoDominium novels. Unfortunately, the military-history and technological aspect of the novels grew until the original idea was almost forgotten.

A human pilot, born a slave to the aliens (one of the titular 'Janissaries')[1], takes the soldiers to the new planet. (Bermejo did beautiful illustrations for the first novel.) Once the American soldiers reach Tran, they find the human pilot's girlfriend (an American), pregnant and abandoned, and she quickly befriends Rick Galloway, the series' main character. Together they forge an alliance and defeat Romans, rival natives, and a mutinous officer of Rick's troops. They start a university. Rick marries a native noblewoman and...we're done. No drugs, no more aliens.

The puzzled reader is free to turn to the sequels, co-written with the late Roland Green, the author of *Wandor's Journey*. In

---

[1] The Janissaries (*yeni ceri*, "new troops") were Christian boys taken as tribute to the Ottoman Empire, forced to convert to Islam, who had 'no father but the Sultan, and no family but each other'. Goodwin's *Lords of the Horizons* provides a very readable portrayal of these developments.

the second book, the young native king marries a charming Roman noblewoman, and the technological efforts of Rick's University progress. Rick's wife starts a team of under-aged assassins (huh?). The human slave pilot Les returns...and more battles. While the military part of the novels is well written and grounded in European history, the reader will be distracted when two human slaves of the Galactic rulers talk in an 'interlude.' The Janissaries of the Turkish empire rebelled, after all, and ended up ruling. Is this going to happen in space? And while Rick and company plant some drugs, and even trade them for a shipload of goodies, the whole 'apocalypse' plot is still on hold when...the book ends.

Pournelle and Green penned a third book, subtitled *Storms of Victory* (1987). The wars continue, now with Scythians ("Westmen") invading as the planet's climate changes. Technology progresses as the Americans introduce new ideas. (Pournelle's colleague S. M. Stirling has virtually made a career out of this trope). But the 'Time' has not yet come, and neither have the aliens eager to buy dope. Instead, a mad prophet appears and leads a horde to attack the heroes. Rick and his wife have marital problems and Rick has hemorrhoids a lot. They fight another big, big battle. And...the book ends.

And there matters stood for twenty years. This reviewer once asked Roland Green about it, over beers at Murphy's with the late Scott Palter, and Green was non-committal, saying that the sequel would have to involve the return of the aliens and the "Time" of doom, which sounded like *fun*. Some years later, Pournelle's blog announced a fourth Janissaries book written without a collaborator. It was being written, and written...and then, in 2017, Pournelle died.

Philip Pournelle, Jerry's son, and David Weber, author of the Honor Harrington books, finished and edited what Jerry Pournelle had left as the fourth Janissaries novel, *Mamelukes* (2020), thirty-three years after book three came out. The plot is thoughtful and reminiscent of Burroughs at his best: Rick is banished while, on Earth, human agents gather people to aid him and pack three McGuffin-loads of books and tools to fuel an industrial revolution on Tran. The mysterious Agzaral, slave Janissary of the Galactics, masterminds this mission, which needed to be a separate novel, frankly. Some Gurkhas come to Tran (?) and are fetishized in a sort-of-offensive way. The 'Time' begins as the oceans rise, and we get a long, long subplot about a Venice-like city, whose people speak modern Italian (This is less likely than Pournelle's space drives!) and are plagued by pirates. There is a well-done battle scene against the pirates. Rick is acclaimed as Warlord of Tran, a la John Carter. And the book ends.

So what happened to the aliens and the drugs? What happened to the apocalyptic climate change and the revolt in space? Sadly, Larry Niven tells us: after treatment for brain cancer, Dr. Pournelle could no longer write fiction. The heartbreaking story is in the preface to *Starborn and Godsons* (2019), the final book of the "Heorot series." Niven and Pournelle sold *Burning Mountain*, the last book in yet another series, back to the publisher. *Mamelukes* suffered in this process, and any potential for ending the main dramatic arc of the series was lost. Presumably, Weber and Philip Pournelle did not feel as though they could write the (at least one) additional novel's worth of narrative needed to close the main plot from the first book. In addition, the series is badly dated. Rick's mercenaries need to be told that the Cold War is over, and that such and such has happened on Earth. The newcomers to Tran point up the degree to which the original *Janissaries* is a work of the 1970s and a reaction to Vietnam.

This reviewer regrets bitterly that he cannot give these four books his endorsement, as dearly as he's loved other work by Pournelle and Pournelle's collaborators. The series as a whole is, like its author, a product of its time. The UFO craze of the 1970s has shifted to pure conspiracy mania as cell phones cause the number of UFO sightings to drop.[2] The Cold War is over, and the CIA-soldiers-in-Angola plot will need to be explained to any readers under fifty. The Fermi paradox makes a galactic empire of aliens very unlikely. The War On Drugs is visibly an unjust and racist struggle, and Earthlike worlds are *rare*. And remarks such as "nobody ever got raped in an upper bunk" weren't adequate even in the Vietnam era. The word "no" may be uttered in an upper bunk as readily as elsewhere.

The *Janissaries* books are masterful military SF, but the mission crept out of sight across the decades. Recommended to fans of war stories and of Pournelle's Piper-esque tales.

J. Comer is a writer and a teacher. He lives in Texas.

---

[2] https://www.sfgate.com/science/article/UFO-sightings-down-extraterrestrial-intelligence-6481669.php;
https://www.inverse.com/article/33878-ufos-flying-saucers-roswell-incident-aliens-are-real-debunk

A Long Way to Fall

By DAVID EYK

A murder has occurred on a colony cylinder under hostile occupation: a young officer has been found mangled, every bone broken—how did he fall from the axis?!

When I emerged from the courthouse that beautiful fall afternoon, the crisp air smelled of falling leaves, the sort of smell that puts a jaunty spring in your step. A stiff breeze billowed my coat and tousled my hair and reminded me to don my hat. Long wispy clouds obscured the By and Cy purlins above, so if I squinted and shaded my eyes (and didn't let *too* much of a spring into my step, accounting for the Coriolis effect), I could almost imagine I was back on Earth and not crawling around inside a big tin can. I'd done my civic duty and I felt like a million grams. I was ready to go home, put my feet up, and take a nap. The sleep of the just, I hear they call it, and I figured this was my chance to try it out.

It was the perfect sort of day, I mean, taking one thing with another, and I was feeling fine. You wouldn't have known there was going to be any trouble except for the ominous growl coming from the mob gathered at the foot of the courthouse steps.

"Good afternoon, gentlemen," I said, tipping my hat at the lead elements as I descended the steps.

The first of said elements, a squat, powerful, middle-aged man with a square jaw and the look of a dockworker about him, got in my way. "You ever consider taking a vacation, outworlder? Go see the old place?"

I looked him over and didn't much like the view. He had a silver crescent pinned prominently on his breast. "Yeah, I consider it. But you know how it is. The bills keep coming. The kid needs braces. There's a war on." I leaned in and lowered my voice. "Occupying force, nervous about spies. You know."

"You don't have any family."

I straightened up and said louder, "That's a dirty lie. Doc Bren Sax is my family."

"You don't have any kid, neither, and he don't need any braces."

He had me there. I smiled wide. "I didn't know I was talking to a fan. I missed your name."

He sneered. "Nobody you want to know, outworlder. You stay out of our business, we'll stay out of yours."

I nodded solemnly. "That's my plan, exactly. Go home, take a nap, stay out of your business. First thing on my agenda."

"You *should've* put that first, before narcing on the Councilman."

I glanced back at the courthouse. "Oh,

that?" I looked back at the crowd. Come to think of it, lots of them had that silver crescent pinned somewhere. I hadn't placed the Councilman as the Silver Guard sort. I filed it away for future reference. "I'll have you know I'm an orderly, law-abiding fellow. When the court tells me to appear, I ask 'what time?' and I put *that* on my agenda, right at the top, in big letters."

"You're a dirty snoop, and you've worn out your welcome."

Also true, but I couldn't let him win them all. Everything about the case was public record now anyway. "Look, it's just his tough luck his wife hired me to check in on him. Not my fault he had a big mouth 'round his mistress about all those grams he was taking under the table."

He scowled. "You make us look like fools in front of the Akkas."

"My pop always told me two good ways to not look like a fool: one, don't do foolish things, and two, don't hang around with other fools. Good day, then."

I pushed past him. My pop also said there was a third way: to keep my big trap shut. I always counted myself as doing pretty well with two out of the three.

The mob was looking uglier and uglier throughout this exchange of pleasantries, and I figured if I wanted a chance at that nap, I needed to get my back to a wall right quick.

Then, to my infinite relief, the Akkas showed up, a little squad of bloody-red Accord uniforms that commanded the attention and rifles that made a man stand up a little straighter. Now, as a rule, I realize you're not supposed to feel a sense of relief and gratitude when the occupying force shows up with guns, but I was mostly considering the clear path they'd opened up in the mob with their little wedge.

The major at the center of his espatiers had a loud, booming voice: "This is illegal gathering. One minute you have to disperse and to your businesses return."

I smiled, tipped my hat again at the fellows with the silver pins, and aimed myself in the general direction of out of there.

"You Ransley Banden?" It was the major with his too-loud voice.

There's such a thing as being *too* popular. I stopped short. The mob was dispersing, but some still watched me. "Folks around here call me 'Ras.' You're *not* from around here, so you can call me 'sir.' I also answer to 'hey you' if you prefer."

The major smirked. "You they told me about."

I smiled and tipped my hat. "Good day, then."

"Hold," he said. "I meant to hire."

I was walking.

"A murder has been," he called.

I couldn't help but toss off behind me, "Sheriff's office is across the square."

"They care not. My man he was."

I hesitated mid-step, but kept going.

"I want to know how tell his wife and son."

I stopped, and sighed. Hell, what did "they" tell him, anyway?

I admired the architecture while the major and his squad caught up.

"Major Sanderling, of Titan."

"Call me Ras."

We started walking.

"Lieutenant Robin was good man. He they found outside Cesun, near forest. Beaten, very bad, unrecognizable."

"That narrows it down to about half of Vulk."

"See, already we make progress!"

"The other half would have simply made him disappear."

Sanderling sighed. "I know we are not popular."

"You figure that out on your own?"

He shook his head and plowed on. "The last man Robin seen alive with was local woman, name is Lide."

You had to watch out for those local women. "Pretty blonde, hangs out in dives down by the port?"

"Yes, I am told."

I stopped and looked at him. He really was an ugly fellow. I couldn't help but like him. "Let's talk fees. Five thousand gees retainer for the week, plus expenses."

"Yes, of course." He held out his hand to shake.

I looked at his hand and wished I'd started at ten thousand. "I'll talk to Lide and visit the coroner. I can't promise anything."

He dropped his hand awkwardly. "Of course, of course, I know."

"How do I contact you?"

"Here is card."

I pocketed it and walked away.

I studiously avoided looking at the two fellows who had peeled off of the dispersing mob to follow me at a distance. Asyn had plenty of angled shop windows for observing a tail.

I walked quickly and smoothly down narrow streets, adopting that native cat-like gait that reduces bobbing of the head. No spring in my step after all: my head was spinning quite enough already, thank you.

Sunport wasn't that far away from the courthouse. As much time as I spent around it in my line of work, I avoided looking at it. It loomed, a mighty bastion that stretched up into the clouds and left and right as far as the eye could see. Which wasn't far. It gave me vertigo to look at it close up. My eyes, trained on terrestrial buildings, couldn't make sense of it, even after all these years.

Lide was a loose woman of low family, the sort of family that was barely tolerated by the Asyn community only because they dedicated themselves to fleecing outworlders. I knew her twice over, once being warned about her by Doc, and twice it being my business to know her type.

I lost my tail when I stopped in at a bar to ask directions. I keep a running account of favors with most of the barkeeps in the Sunport district. Kyes knew straight away who I was talking about and where she lived.

On my way, I meditated on the sorts of women that are known immediately by name in a town of eighty thousand souls. I decided I preferred a humbler sort.

I was relieved when my tail showed up again, both of them in front of me, just short of Lide's building. Now I knew what *they* were up to, at least. The minds of criminals and terrorists run in deep and rather predictable tracks. They also tend to get upset if you point this out.

"Good to see you again, boys. I had a feeling you were going to turn up over here. Is Lide in?"

The first one scowled. It was my friend from the steps, the dockworker. "Get lost, outworlder. You don't belong here." His buddy had a nice and shiny silver crescent on his breast too.

"Sorry, I haven't gotten lost around here in a long time. I've adapted too well, I guess."

He looked confused, then his scowl deepened. "Just get out of here," he clarified.

I shrugged. "Nah, the pay's too good. Besides, I'd be shirking my civic duty." I held up my hand and ticked through three fingers. "Bringing in outworld money, pulling one over on the Akkas, *and* getting justice for a widow and an orphan besides." I spread my hands and shook my head. "Sorry, no can do."

Sometimes talk of that sort will buffalo a tough guy. It's always worth a shot, mainly as a perk of the job. More often than not, though, it just makes him mad, which can also be helpful.

"Let's get 'im, Cor!" he replied.

I mentioned I'd been happy to see both of them in front of me. Every once in a while you meet fellows like this who actually know what they're doing, and they like to set up little flanking traps. Not so these guys. The first one rushed me while Cor looked on, curious to see if he'd be needed or not.

Fighting in a spinning habitat is fun if you know what you're doing. In my first few months on Vulk, I'd found a local dojo to learn all about it, and I still go back regularly to stay fresh. Throw a guy spinward (*fingerward,* the locals call it), he hits the ground fast and hard. Throw him anti-spinward (*knuckleward,* they say) he flies a little farther and is guaranteed to land a bit awkwardly.

Even the locals tend not to be very good at it unless they practice.

I sent the first guy flying to knuckles, just to give me some time to work through the rest of the queue. Cor, looking a bit disappointed, manfully put his fists up. I swept his feet out from under him with a fingerward kick, the sort where you hit the ground a wee bit later than you expect to. It always hurts.

Then I dusted myself off and kept walking. They didn't follow.

Lide let me in with a sardonic smile. "I didn't kill him," she said.

"Now, that's interesting," I said. "Kill who?"

"Lieutenant Robin, the Akka fellow you're here to ask about."

Lide was the sort of woman who made a man glad to be alive when he saw her. She wore a simple green skirt and light blouse so as not to distract from the rest. Her soft, pale skin and the platinum-blonde hair she wore in a long braid were unusual on Vulk, which tended to darker complexions. Outworlder blood, to be sure. Living this close to Sunport, she'd probably crinkle up and die young from radiation, but for now she was too good to be true.

The hardness in her eyes confirmed it.

"I didn't kill him," she recited. "He killed himself."

"What, he beat himself up with a big stick?"

"No," she sniffed, "he jumped."

"Jumped," I echoed. "From what, a tree?"

She rolled her eyes at my stupidity. "From the axis."

I didn't have time to digest that because a big fellow in a powder blue constable's uniform barged in right then. My eye darted to the silver crescent pin that flashed on his breast, right below the Asyn crest.

"All right, buddy," he said. "Scram."

"Now hold on," I said. "I'm not done talking to the lady. I'm just asking her a few questions."

"Lide, is this guy bothering you?"

She nodded. "Get rid of him, Bick."

I shrugged. "The lady says scram, I'll scram." I looked at her.

She pouted. "What are *you* looking at? Get out."

I got out.

I stopped at a public box to call Major Sanderling's office and get a few details. Then I caught the Sunport roundabout over to the Cy purlin and transferred to the subway. I stared out the window of the train car. Vulk's neighbor, Heff, lumbered into view, surrounded by stars, turning endlessly, then fell away again as we spun farther on. I had to look away after a minute—the wheeling stars always made me dizzy. But once you've lived on one of these big cans long enough, if you don't look you can almost forget. Almost.

Acceleration is acceleration, whether it's a planet-sized mass making gravity or a spinning cylinder imparting tangential velocity to the poor schlubs crawling around on the inside. Something was bothering me about what Lide had said, about Robin falling from the axis. I wanted to see the place where they found him.

I reached the station I wanted on the outskirts of Cesun and took a hike. It's always peaceful and quiet out there. The rich folks all live underground, and I saw not a few picnickers enjoying the commons, which are kept like some kind of endless country garden. Myself, I always felt funny walking around on top of some industrial titan's bedroom. But I see the justice of the arrangement.

I found the axis road that Sanderling's office gave me and walked starward, toward the forest. Just sun of the trees, the road petered out into a brief sort of meadow. They'd found Robin a few yards past the first trees, sort of wrapped around a trunk. Rough ending for somebody's picnic, not to mention the lieutenant's life.

I stood at the edge of the forest and looked back to Sunport. From here, nearly ten miles away, it didn't look so bad, just a funny round wall, obscured by clouds. I could just make out the axis point, a dark round circle. For a moment, I thought about how it was all spinning round that point, cities and trees and gleaming lakes and industrial titans and me, and the vertigo made me look down at the meadow grass again. Lide's assertion taunted me. How the hell did he fall from *there?* Ridiculous.

I hiked back to the station, then took the connections back to Asyn. I figured on stopping by Doc's next. He had his clinic a few blocks starward and knuckleward, not too far from the Aybee window lake.

I get my exercise on these cases.

"Doc Sax in?" I asked the lady at the front desk. The waiting room was usually empty this time of day.

She smiled and sent me back.

Doc looked up from his desk when I entered and smiled his wide smile. He was short and compact, like most Vulkas, with a bald liver-spotted pate and tufts of white hair above his ears. He'd been close to retirement age for at least a decade.

"Ras! Good to see you. I didn't expect you to drop in."

"Good to see you, too, Doc."

"Have a seat, won't you?"

I sat, hat in my lap, and braced myself for the next question.

"Found a girl yet?"

My lip twitched. As my Patriarch, he had a vested interest in seeing me married. If nothing else, in order to get me out of his house. Well, technically: I usually slept on a cot in my office and visited the homestead on Sundays to attend church and eat dinner with the family.

When I saw him one on one, though, this was the game we played. "No, Doc, that's just not on my radar right now."

He pursed his lips and shook his head. "That's a shame. I just met an eligible woman yesterday who'd be perfect for you…"

"Doc, I need your help on a case, actually."

He quirked a fluffy white eyebrow up. "Oh?"

"Murder."

He twitched. "That's not your usual kind of case."

"No," I pressed on. "An Akka lieutenant. Sheriff's not interested, hard feelings and all."

Doc nodded. "I see. Not many here *would* be interested."

I waved my hand. "Yeah, I know, there's a war on. I noticed. But the CO wants to know what to tell the wife and kid."

Doc's eyes widened with understanding. "Ah."

"Would you come see the body with me?"

"I won't be able to do an autopsy. I'm not licensed for it with the city."

I shook my head. "I don't need you to, I just need a professional eye to look and tell me what you see. As a favor."

Doc nodded. "I can do that."

Doc's been doing me favors for a long time. Heaven help me the day he calls them in.

At the coroner's office, the guy at the desk had a silver pin too. I indicated it. "Did I miss the meeting when they were handing those out?"

The guy gave me a funny look, then

handed Doc back his medical license. "Coroner's made his decision. Cause of death's blunt force cranial trauma. No autopsy."

"We just want a look," I said. I said it with a stack of grams. The guy gave me another funny look but took the grams and led us into the back.

Doc was giving me a funny look too, but I just smiled and shrugged. "Expenses," I muttered out the side of my mouth.

Our guide opened a cabinet and pulled the stiff out in his drawer. I really hate murder cases. Back in Angel City I had a buddy on the force, homicide. He drank too much.

"Just looking," reminded our guide.

Doc smiled a professional smile and looked.

"What I want to know, Doc, was it a guy with a baseball bat?"

He glanced up at me. "A what?"

"Was it a guy with a club?"

He shook his head, and kept looking. "No," he said, in a distant, detached voice, "not unless he was patient and thorough."

He looked some more. I had to look away a few times. Did I mention I hate murder cases?

Finally, Doc looked at me. Even he looked a bit green. "This looks more like he was hit by a cargo dolly, knocked into a wall, then rolled down a flight of stairs. Neck first. There's not much that *isn't* broken."

Doc's not one for jokes, except when he's being dry and professional.

"That's what I was wondering. Thanks, Doc." I looked at the guy with the pin. "We're done here."

We'd just rounded the corner into the front office when I saw a constable coming in the front door. The guy saw me and immediately turned tail right back the way he came.

I found this interesting. "Thanks for your help, Doc. Need to catch up with that fellow. I'll swing by later."

I didn't stop to hear what Doc said. I was already across the room and crashing through the exit myself.

If a guy sees you and turns around or hides his face, that's what we call in the business a "tell". If he runs, we call it a good way to get some exercise. Opinions on the best response vary; it's highly contextual, but usually I like to chase them, just on general principle. That is, I like to find out where they're going.

My man was running, so I obliged him.

Running on Vulk is always a challenge to my outworlder thews. When I was a kid on Earth, running fast was simple: you just run until you reach your goal or get tired. Here, it's that plus a game of rock-paper-scissors: go fingers, it makes you heavier; running knuckles makes you lighter. Run to sun or star, it makes you drift and trip easier. Running round a corner, you'd better remember which way's which, or you'll end up kissing pavement.

Locals know all this in their bones. I'd had to practice.

My new friend the constable probably figured on me being a flat-footed outworlder. He was also out of shape.

I caught up to him after the third block. "Yoo-hoo, Constable! You dropped some money back there!"

Involuntarily he glanced back at me, and I nearly tripped in surprise.

It was Bick.

I jogged up alongside him, friendly-like. "Nice day for a run. Don't you love this weather?"

Bick was in no condition to answer, so he stopped to catch his breath. I gave him a neighborly minute or so. Besides, I needed some time to suck oxygen myself.

When he looked a little more composed, I figured it was time to commence the grilling. "What were you doing back there, anyway?"

"None of your business," he growled.

I shrugged. "I was just curious why you ran."

"Y'weren't supposed to see me," he muttered at the ground. He looked me in the eye, then. "Why're you sticking your nose in this, anyway? Aren't you Yoonie?"

I nodded. "I was, at least. I'm *persona non grata* around Earth these days."

"Huh?"

"They don't want me there."

"I don't blame them."

"Neither do I, and *I* don't want to be *there* either. So it's worked out pretty well."

He scowled, the expression settling in comfortably on his face. "Still, why're you helping these Akkas? They don't belong here, less'n you do."

"I don't care a whit for the Akkas. I wish they'd go home where they belong, but I get that they can't right now, and I appre-ciate that they're occupying us rather than shooting missiles. Better courtesy than the Yoonies gave to Phlox, so I hear. They'll leave eventually."

"Yeah, they'd better. But why are you *helping* them? The sheriff told us to leave it alone."

I cocked my head. "Now *that's* interesting. You realize a kid died, right? Might've been murder?"

"So? It's a war. Lots of kids die."

I just looked at him, with a bit of curl to my lip, then looked pointedly at the crest on his uniform, and the pin just under it.

He glanced down and reddened. "Look," he said in a quick mutter, "I didn't have nothing to do with that. I believe Lide, but she's at it again. Silver Guard's trying to find a way to push the Akkas out. That much I believe in. But some of 'em get too impatient. I don't like it."

"What do you mean?"

But he'd shut his mouth and gave a quick little shake to his head. I nodded. "Thanks anyway."

I figured I could fill in the blanks with some work.

I found Lide working an Akka-favored bar near the port. She was cozying up to a young Lieutenant. Looked like he'd bought her a drink, but he was downing a lot more than she was. I thought of Robin's face all black and blue and dead. I shuddered.

I sidled up next to him at the bar and leaned forward to look at her. She was always worth looking at. "Hey, Lide."

"Hey." Her voice was less than enthusiastic as she side-eyed me.

The lieutenant looked annoyed.

I pressed on. "I see you're busy, but you wanna catch a vid later?"

"Nothing new in the theater," she said as she gave me what I assumed was intended to be a discouraging look.

"Not since these Akkas barged in, no," I said.

"Hey," the lieutenant broke in. "You be backing off, forge-born."

I looked at him for the first time. I figured that was supposed to be a slur. "You talking to me, Jove-brat?" That was *definitely* a slur, and fighting words too. You didn't insult these guys' mothers.

He stood tall and faced me, cutting off my view of Lide. It'd been a nice view while it lasted.

"Say again?" he asked, not so politely.

I slugged him. Lide had known enough to back off a bit, so he ended up in a pile of chairs. It's hard to keep your feet in a fight in this place.

I glanced at Lide. "Shall we move on?"

She gave me a look, one part venom, two parts appraisal. "Yes," she said. "Back to my place?"

I offered her my arm and escorted her out.

Back at her place, while she poured drinks, I glanced around to make sure Bick wasn't hiding in a closet. Call me paranoid, but the guy kept turning up like a bad token.

She invited me to sit on the divan and handed me a highball, which I accepted with thanks and set down untouched on the floor, there being no table. She sat down on a stool, just a little too close, and crossed her legs so the slit in her skirt showed just a little too much leg.

"I saw Bick down at the coroner's," I said.

"Oh?" She looked uninterested. "How was he?"

"Winded. Looked like he'd been running. The constables are letting their fitness standards slip."

She frowned and sipped her drink, giving me another of her sidelong glances.

"I saw Robin, too. He was in worse shape."

"Can't we talk about something else?"

I shrugged. "It's just eating me, you know. You say he jumped, but from what?"

She put on a sad face. "He was sad, missed his family. I thought I could cheer him up, so I took him up Sunport to the axis, to show him the view. Once he saw it, he wanted to fly out over it. I told him it was stupid, but he insisted, found the hatch and everything."

"He was drunk?"

She nodded.

I thought about it. Being drunk in zero-gee *can* make you giddy. If it was true, the poor fellow got his wish. A good ten-mile flight before he spiraled down into the forest. I winced at the thought.

She alighted from her perch on the stool and joined me on the divan, draping her arm lightly over my shoulder. "Surely there's something more cheerful we can talk about," she said.

I looked at her. "Something Major Sanderling's office mentioned made me think."

She pouted. "What?"

"He's Fleet Operations and Logistics. Robin was in his command."

"So?"

"So, the fellow you were chatting up at the bar there, he had the same patch on his shoulder."

Her lip twitched. Her arm stiffened a moment, then she tried to cover it by beginning to idly caress my neck. "A silly coincidence."

I licked my lips. "Yeah?"

"Yeah." She leaned in a bit closer, gazing into my eyes. "You have such handsome, kind eyes."

My handsome, kind eyes rolled hard in their sockets. "Sister, you need some new lines." I grabbed my highball and stood up.

I took a swig of the drink. Scotch and soda, or something like it. Liquor here always had a funny taste to me. She was watching me like a cat watches a mouse. I noticed the top buttons of her blouse had come undone somehow, and I averted my eyes to notice something else.

There on a misplaced end table by the door, I noticed a little silver crescent-shaped pin. "Hey, you've got one of those too."

"One of what?"

I sidled over to the table and picked up the pin. "These guys. Popular fashion of late. I'm seeing them everywhere."

"It's Bick's. He must have left it there."

"Sure." I pocketed it. "I'll give it to him next time I see him."

Her eyes, dark and sultry one moment, were just dark the next.

I sipped the drink. "You seem confused, Lide, so I'll just out and tell you. I don't go to bed with murder suspects." I didn't tell her I didn't go to bed with anyone these days. I'm a one-woman kind of guy, but I've got to keep my reputation up.

Her face twisted in anger. "I didn't kill him. He killed himself."

"Yes, you mentioned that earlier. You didn't stop him, either. Who knows: maybe you opened the hatch for him? Maybe you gave him a helpful push?"

She managed to compose herself with a perfect little pout. "You don't have any witnesses."

I shrugged. "Maybe I do."

Her face was not only pretty, it was very helpful, animated as it was. Now I was pretty sure there were others with her at the time.

While she worked on that, I polished off the drink and set it on the kitchenette counter. This was starting to smell like some kind of Yoon Intelligence honeypot scheme, and maybe I would be smarter to back off. I was feeling pretty tired, what with all the exercise I'd had that day. The sleep of the just was still calling me. I figured I'd head home, skip the nap and go for a full night's worth.

I turned to say my good-byes. She was still watching me closely, and I found my mouth didn't work right. She was smiling, a smug sort of smile I didn't like one bit. I took a step but stumbled. I figured I must have been more tired than I thought—the spin didn't usually do that to me. I tried again, and that's the last thing I remembered for a while.

I awoke in a dark room, lying on the softest bed imaginable. I tried to sit up and realized I was bound and gagged. I wasn't lying in a featherbed, but brushing gently against a bulkhead in microgravity. Moving made my head pound. Whatever Lide had slipped in my drink left a nasty hangover.

I heard voices, and then the main event arced into the room: Lide, changed now out of her skirt and blouse (though she'd kept the smug smile) into a brown jumpsuit that was more catsuit; Bick, looking miserable; and two others, whom I felt pretty sure were Cor and his friend the dockworker who'd followed me around town that afternoon.

"Whall," I slurred, "I'm honnnored. Ya didn't hafta bring th'whole gang…"

"Geez, Lide, how much did you give him?" scolded the dockworker. He looked to be the leader.

"The usual," she said. She shrugged. "It wears off pretty quick. He's faking."

Annoyed, I dropped the act. "All right, what's the deal? We're on the same side here, you know."

"Did you hear that, Bick?" asked the leader. "He said 'we.'"

Bick had stationed himself by another bulkhead, away from the others. "I heard him."

The leader got up in my face. "You work for the Akkas, you're not one of us."

"I'm not working for the Akkas, they're just paying me; I'm working for Mrs. Robin and her kid. They deserve to know what happened."

"They're Akkas, too. Should've kept Dad home if they didn't want him killed."

"All right, so we're not all on the same side, but I'm not an Akka. My side's got a sword and a blindfold. What's your side? You're not Yoonies. All these silver crescent pins, I'd swear before a judge they're new this week."

He grinned. "You like them? A friend over at the Forge fabbed 'em up. We're the local chapter of The Loyal Order of the Silver Guard."

I smiled. Just as I'd figured. Guerrilla fighters, part of the organized resistance against the Accord now that the Yoon was on the ropes in the war. I'd heard they'd been started by the last remnant escaped out of the destruction at Tycho City.

The leader had taken his pin off and was turning it over in his fingers. "It's a shame you're so tied up right now," he said. "We're recruiting."

"Under different circumstances, I'd join in a heartbeat."

Then his face twisted. He took the pin and jabbed it into my chest. The force of it bounced me off the bulkhead and sent him sailing across the room.

"Ow!" I said. I had taken on a slight spin as I traced a lazy ballistic arc back to my original bulkhead. "That's a lousy trick."

He caught himself on the opposite bulkhead and smirked. "That's for this afternoon."

Bick and Lide looked on in wide-eyed

consternation. Cor looked bored.

Lide spoke up. "Let's get this over with, Alf."

"All right," said Alf. "Bick, Cor, grab him."

Bick looked away. "I'm stayin' out of this one."

Alf shook his head in annoyance and waved dismissively. "C'mon then, Cor."

I didn't like where this was going. Whoever had done my trusses up had done them right, but I struggled gamely anyway. They grabbed me and towed me into the next compartment: the Sunport axis airlock, as I'd feared.

Long ago, when Vulk was being built, before they'd spun up, they'd transported material through a large gap in the axis. Before they'd pumped in the initial atmosphere they'd capped the hole with an enormous cargo airlock, big enough to hold a fair lot of cargo. While the rest of Sunport had accreted around and beyond it, it was still an airlock. The axis pressure in the main habitat was low enough that, while it was breathable, the lock was still needed to equalize pressures.

"Seal it up," said Alf.

Bick had stayed in the other compartment, so Lide sealed us in. Alf gave her a nod, and she palmed the switch. Compressors sounded somewhere, echoing strangely through the big lock. My ears popped. It felt hard to breathe.

They towed me up to the center of the big hatch, where a smaller man-sized hatch was mounted alongside some nice ports for catching the view. The view *was* pretty

spectacular, with all twenty miles of insular Vulk stretched out all around you.

I swallowed. "I'm glad you plan to untie me. I find it hard to fly without my wings."

Alf chuckled. "Don't worry, we're going to untie you. That way, it's just another tragic accident."

"You don't think the sheriff's going to get a bit suspicious?"

He grinned. "Of course not. You're an outworlder. Plenty more of you are going to die like this before it's over. As long as we don't get *too* obvious about it, good citizens won't ask questions."

They lined me up with the man hatch and held me while Lide began to untie my bonds. The moment my arms were free, I started bucking and punching. While they were busy trying to hold on to me, my hand shot into my pocket and pulled out the pin I'd found in Lide's apartment. Alf grabbed my arm, but I got free again just long enough and quickly jammed the pin into *Alf's* chest. There, see how *he* likes it.

He didn't like it, not one bit, and I almost struggled free when he let go. But Cor was quicker in freefall than he had been in pseudogravity, or maybe I was slower with the lack of oxygen, and in a flash he had me in a solid lock.

Lide slapped the hatch open. Little gusts of warm wind blew my hair around, and I wondered what had happened to my hat.

There was a cage, something like a colander, projecting out from the man hatch. Beyond that, empty space for twenty miles. Two thick guy lines attached to the cage on either side and receded into the distance.

The lack of oxygen must have been getting to me because all I could think about was those guy lines. Twenty miles of line, stretched taut! What the hell were they made of? The mind boggled. Or at least mine did.

I thought about those guy lines. And the other safety lines I'd learned about in my original safety orientation they used to make outworlders go through.

Cor was arguing with Lide about something. Alf was cursing like a, well, like a dockworker, and dabbing at his chest with a handkerchief. I don't know what he was so upset about. I'd forgotten all about my own memento of the Silver Guard.

Cor still had me in that lock, with my arms useless at my sides. He pivoted so I couldn't see out anymore. I think he was trying to get us both through the man hatch by hooking a foot on the edge of the hatchway.

"Alf! Dry up and give me a hand here."

Alf was still muttering imprecations, but he turned his attention to me. I greeted him with both feet, a solid push straight off his chest.

Microgravity's a great place to get a good feel for Newton's laws. For every action there's an equal and opposite *reaction*. Alf went flying across the vast airlock while Cor and I, at twice the mass, went at about half the velocity. We caromed off the hatchway, Cor first. That knocked the wind out of him and let me get my arms loose. When we spun out into the cage, I grabbed wildly and caught a handhold. Cor slammed into the cage next to me, lost his grip completely, and tumbled out into the void.

My bowels felt pretty loose as I watched him go spinning after he glanced off the safety line. The first winds caught him and sent him spiraling off around and around. I silently wished him good luck.

I turned back to the hatch, and there was Lide, wedged in the hatchway with a little pistol leveled at me. Her lip curled, and she fired.

The little pea-shooter didn't have much of a kick, but the sudden sharp burning in my shoulder took me by surprise. I lost my grip, started to tumble, and grabbed madly for a guy line. Caught it, though the shoulder hurt like hell, and wrapped myself around it. Looked up.

Lide was lining up another shot.

New plan. I swung my legs out, folded like you see those gymnasts do, and looped around the line before letting go. No really, I had a plan—almost anything would be slightly better than playing target practice with Lide. I knew roughly where the safety line should be. I sailed through empty air, praying fervently that I'd been right.

The line came fast and caught me square in the gut. I did my best to ignore the sensation of having nearly been sliced in two and wrapped myself around that line like it was life itself.

As quickly as I could, I pulled off my shoes, stuck one under my left armpit, held the other in my right hand, looked back at the cage about ten yards away, and readied myself.

Sure enough, Lide leaned out, gun in front. She looked decidedly less sure of herself as she scanned for me.

I whipped a shoe at her. Way off. It sailed past her head. I readied the next one, mentally adjusted my aim for the Coriolis effect. She fired, I flinched. No hit. With a grunt, I threw my other shoe at her. I've never been prouder of any throw: it hit her square in her pretty face. Even better, the gun went flying, but she didn't. She disappeared.

That was when I made the mistake of looking down. Or out. I don't know what direction it was, but it was two miles to the ground. To the wall. To the place where all the buildings and people were.

It took a minute to master myself. My shoulder hurt like the very dickens. I focused on the cage and the twin guy lines. I just needed to jump back. How hard could it be? I'd done it once without even thinking about it.

The problem now was I had too much time to think. I fought vertigo as I painstakingly arranged myself on the safety line, feet hooked beneath me. The gentle push of the Coriolis effect had me shaking in frustration: I wouldn't get a second chance if I missed this time.

I jumped. I caught the guy line—another few inches and I would have missed entirely. I pulled myself back into the relative safety of the cage...

Just in time to welcome Alf back into the match. He'd found a sturdy-looking pipe somewhere, which he brandished in one hand while he stayed himself on the hatchway with the other. He had a red blossom on his chest and an angry scowl on his face.

"I told you to stay out of this, didn't I, outworlder?"

"You did," I admitted. "I guess I'm contrary that way." I shrugged with my good shoulder.

He grunted and came flying out of the hatch, swinging that pipe at me.

The funny thing is, these guys were always underestimating us outworlders. As a dockworker, Alf had lots of practice flying around in microgravity and moving heavy things. But that dojo I mentioned earlier? We spent every other month up at the axis, practicing in the weird freefall there.

There's this neat trick I learned—my instructor called it an "Oberth maneuver" which always made the pilots mad—where you push off, grab a guy who's coming at you like that, do a little do-si-do and let him fly off in the direction he was originally going, with most of your extra momentum added besides. If you do it right, of course.

Did I do it right? Well, I'd like to say I did, but I'd be a liar. I ended up slamming myself against the hatchway and getting a nasty knock on my bad shoulder, but I managed to grab onto a railing and look for trouble again.

Trouble was sailing out into the void with a confounded look on his face.

I took the opportunity to slip back inside the airlock and seal the hatch. Lide was still on the loose, and I'd had enough microgravity for a bit. Besides, I wanted to see Doc Sax about my shoulder. Maybe look into that vacation trip.

So what killed Lieutenant Robin? The ground, or a tree; it's hard to tell which at this point. That's the proximate cause, though. What ultimately caused his death? Well, he ended up on the wrong side of the hatch at the axis, but that's proximate too.

Somebody killed Robin. It could have been Lide and her cronies, if they pushed him out the hatch the way they were going to push me; they had the means, motive, and opportunity, after all. It could have been Robin himself, as Lide's story goes, drunkenly thinking he could fly. It was certainly Robin himself when he betrayed his wife for a few minutes with a pretty face.

But aren't those proximate causes too? Lide wouldn't have been seducing young Accord officers, and Accord officers wouldn't have been lining up to be seduced if they'd stayed home with their wives and kids, or at least if they'd left Vulk alone.

And the Accord wouldn't have formed, and they wouldn't have sent their young men to die in this stupid fashion if some fool Yoon captain hadn't wiped out a million souls at Phlox with a handful of missiles.

Did the war kill Robin? Yes. Did Lide and the others kill Robin? Probably. But no jury would've convicted them, and no prosecutor would've risked the lynching.

Did Robin kill Robin? Isn't every man complicit somehow in his own death, pre-senting himself at the proper time and place of slaughter?

What do you tell a wife and kid when Daddy's not coming back after all, or at least not like he said he would? What do you tell a wife, who's got to deal with the grief and anger and disappointment while she's still raising her kid? What do you tell a kid who's going to grow up without a father, who's going to grow up hating whoever or whatever killed his dad?

What's more, what do you say when it's not the wife and kid you're saying it to, but an occupying enemy who still needs to be countered and resisted?

"Well?" said Sanderling, after he'd paid me. The five thousand was nothing compared to his signature on my travel documents to Mars.

"A couple of thugs jumped Robin up at the axis. I tracked them down, and they're certain not to do it again."

He frowned. He'd seen the news same as I had. "Is all? There was woman."

I shook my head. "I don't think it's worth mentioning her."

David Eyk (rhymes with "like") writes more thrilling science fiction at www.salvageofempire.com.

Fall of a Storm King

By MISHA BURNETT

The dangerous job of piloting in Saturn's rings requires altering one's perception of time! Luther is one of the best until a minor injury costs him his certification!

A pebble in retrograde holed Luther's skimmer, and he flamed out, all control lost, fuel spraying in a torrent, pinwheeling through the ecliptic in a series of collisions. After the first dozen impacts, he lost consciousness, and his last thought before darkness was, *this is it, this is how a storm king dies.*

But it wasn't.

By blind luck, his mad course through the B ring didn't strike any rocks big enough to crush his skimmer, and the small impacts drove him up into a polar orbit, spinning above the storm zone and into the traffic lane where a cruiser from Titan was able to scoop him up, battered and torn, but still alive.

He woke up in a hospital in New Harriman, held down by layers of regenerative collagen and Titan's eighth of a gravity.

Confusion, but no panic at his strange surroundings. No sense of motion, no alarms, no skin-tingling sensation of pressure loss. An angular room, white painted stone walls, containing Luther, a bed, some kind of equipment console, glowing with displays, a net of cables and tubes connecting the three items.

Thinking: *I got to a hospital on a rock somehow.*

Thinking: *They'll know I'm awake.*

Thinking: *Someone will come in and check on me.*

And then, while he waited, Luther reconstructed what he could of the last moments in his skimmer.

The impact had come without a collision alert, which meant that the object must have been small, and fast, and come up behind him. Small, because anything bigger than twenty centimeters across would have shown up on the skimmer's instruments. And if something that small had hit the electrostatic field, it would have been deflected away from his path, so it must have come up behind him, through the 30-degree cone directly behind the engines that the generated field didn't cover.

And fast, because Luther had been doing nearly 30 klicks a second when he got hit.

Well, it happened.

The skimmers were designed as well as the state of the art allowed, but in the end, working the storm zone wasn't anybody's idea of safe. They said that less than a third of storm kings survived five years working the zone—five system years, that is. Twenty years subjective.

138

Footstep.

In the hallway outside.

Then another.

Luther tried to take a deep breath to relax, but whatever was regulating his breathing wasn't set up for deep breaths.

Another footstep.

A poke, obviously, but then it would be, wouldn't it?

Luther waited while the footsteps came to the door and the door opened. Slowly.

Outside of the storm, everything happened slowly.

The doctor came in, saw that Luther was awake, and started talking right away. She was a small dark woman in a white suit and scarf. To Luther's eyes, she walked like she was underwater.

"Hello. I. Am. Doctor. Vumonupali. You. Are. In. New. Harriman. Major. Medical."

Luther nodded, exaggerating the gesture and moving with deliberate slowness.

"You've received. Some extensive. Injuries."

Luther concentrated, trying to recapture the mindset he used when he had to talk to pokes. It had been a while. *They aren't stupid just because they're slow,* he reminded himself. *Try not to get impatient.*

"At the moment we've got you on a metabolic override," the doctor went on. With an effort, Luther was able to hear the statement as a sentence and not a string of unconnected words. "Once we're sure you're stable, we'll return control of your body to your autonomic nervous system."

Luther nodded again. He swallowed, tried to speak. "How bad?"

She understood his words. "You broke a lot of bones, tore a lot of muscles. I'll leave you the details on your chart." She pointed to a flat display nested in the clutter of medical hardware. "Your injuries are responding well to standard regenerative treatment."

That sounded positive.

Then the doctor went on. "Unfortunately, you've also sustained some brain damage from hypoxia. At the moment we don't know how extensive it is, but I have to prepare you—there is a high probability that it will impair your ability to pilot."

Luther felt cold. *Impair?* he thought, *what exactly do you mean by "impair"?*

The doctor caught his mood. With a grave expression of professional concern she said, "You'll have to make some adjustments."

Luther was in bed for nine days—nine twenty-four hour days. Over a month for Luther.

The hospital made allowances for the six-hour day that Luther's accelerated metabolism required, but it was clear that they were making adjustments to something they saw as abnormal. They didn't get many storm kings, even here on Titan. Accidents in the storm zone tended not to leave injured survivors.

As far as the staff was concerned, Luther took four two-hour naps and had twelve snacks during what they saw as one day. From Luther's point of view, they moved with agonizing slowness. The staff walked like they were wading through mud, and every conversation was a trial of endurance.

System time. Poke time.

Dr. Vumonupali, at least, seemed to grasp Luther's perspective. She was a neuroendocrinologist and understood—academically at least, even if she couldn't experience it—what had been done to Luther's time sense and metabolism. She downloaded a variable speed playback widget for video feed so that Luther could watch Titan soap operas at four times their broadcast speed.

They weren't any less banal that way.

Bone and muscle tissue take time to regrow, even with modern regeneration techniques. Luther's altered hypothalamus didn't make his tissue knit together any faster—he healed at the same rate as a poke.

It just seemed longer to him. Terribly, horribly long.

"It's a shame we can't reverse your acceleration," Dr. Vumonupali said during one of her visits. "It's been much too long, of course; your brain would never adjust."

Adjust. There was that word again. As time dragged on it became clear that Luther's left hand was not regaining sensation or full range of motion. Central nervous system tissue—even now—could not be regrown. The nerves in his hand and arm came back to life, but the delicate connections in his brain were unplugged and would remain so.

The two smallest fingers on Luther's left hand were numb, and they stayed curled up unless he pulled on them to straighten them out. Such a small thing, an inconsequential thing, hardly noticeable.

It was enough.

The storm zone—what pokes called Saturn's rings—was arguably the most dangerous environment the human race had yet attempted to enter. A case could be made that the extreme temperatures on Mercury or Pluto would kill a man faster, but that was largely the province of automatic machinery. Either the equipment worked, or you were dead in a split second.

The storm zone was different. It required constant vigilance. The storm kings' skimmers wove their way through a maelstrom of rocks from the size of grains of sand to goliaths that would be considered moons anywhere else. Mining the zone, scooping out a dozen valuable elements and getting them back to the processing stations, took absolute control over one's ship—and that meant absolute control over one's own body.

Luther had lost control over two fingers of his off hand and it was enough to cast him out of the heavens.

NOTICE OF CHANGE TO YOUR SPACECRAFT PILOTING LICENSE: From the Trans-Jovian Transit Authority. This is to serve as official notice that due to reported medical issues, your license to operate extra-atmospheric equipment is limited in the following ways...

The next two thousand words or so boiled down to: *You're not a storm king anymore.*

He could still legally fly—just not in any zone of space that was considered to have a "high to extreme risk of collision." That included most of the asteroid belt and the vicinity of the outer planets and their trojan points. In one dense legal document, his universe shrank down to a ball that stopped at the orbit of Mars.

He could still live in the storm zone and work in one of the support services for miners, ore processing or food production—as a passenger. Stuck on some rock unless a real pilot took pity on him and gave him a lift.

This was all explained to him by a cheerful young man from the relocation service.

No thanks. Better the accident had killed him than to live like that.

"What will happen to me?" Luther asked dejectedly. He had already gained the habit of pausing between each word so the pokes could understand.

"Your trip home is guaranteed by your insurance," the young man said around a cheery smile, as if he were telling Luther he'd won some prize. "First class transport to Olympus City!"

"*Send-me-back-to-Mars?*" the words came out in a garbled rush, all his speech discipline forgotten, "*They-can't-do-that!*"

As it happened, they could.

Short of killing the crew and taking over the luxury liner—something that Luther *did* consider more than once during the long voyage—he had no way of avoiding returning to the world of his birth.

"OUR FIRST STEP ON HUMANITY'S JOURNEY TO THE STARS" was in meter-high letters on the arch above the main concourse.

As Luther gazed up at the words, the automatic luggage cart burdened with the two trunks that held all of his belongings stopped obediently behind him.

"The problem with Mars," Luther said under his breath, responding with a quote of his own, "is that there really isn't any reason to be here."

The line was a remark by Tiaisha Washington, ex-president of Tharsis, which had been covertly recorded during an unguarded moment and had formed the basis of her opponent's election campaign, costing Washington her third term.

A politician should never speak the unvarnished truth, and it was true—there really wasn't any reason to have a colony on Mars, except that no one wanted to admit that the cyclopean expense of giving the red planet a breathable atmosphere had been wasted.

Humanity didn't need the room. By the time that people could walk unsuited on Martian soil, extra-solar habitats had reached triple digits and Ganymede had already celebrated O2 day—starting later and with much less, but a smaller world and better technology.

You could grow food on Mars—but not as easily as on Earth. You could mine Mars—but the asteroids were better for that. Mars was the solar system's second place choice for just about everything. It made a convenient place to change ships when traveling from the inner to the outer system, but most of that traffic went through Deimos and Phobos without ever touching down on the Martian surface.

Even the prestigious Hesperia Flight Academy was a tacit admission that the burning ambition of the cream of young Martians was to find some way to get off the planet and never return.

Luther's first stop—before he even left the spaceport—was to register at the Pilot's Guild Hall with his newly issued license listing his restrictions.

The clerk was unimpressed.

"Your metabolism is going to be a problem," she said flatly. "Inner system travel runs on eight-hour watches, one on, two off. That's thirty-two hours subjective for you. I don't think we'll find a captain willing to either work you that long or rearrange the watch schedule to accommodate a pilot with brain damage."

"It's two fingers!" Luther struggled to keep his voice slow.

She handed back his license. "You're in our files," she said. "We'll be in contact." The last phrase was delivered in a tone that made it a lie.

Luther didn't have a family. He'd been raised in a communal creche, another failed experiment that—like the terraforming—had seemed like a good idea at the time. What friends he had made in the creche were scattered throughout the system. The creche itself had closed, he saw, and the building was now used to manufacture low-cost plastic toys for export to the asteroids.

He did have some savings, enough to last a year or so—a Martian year—if he lived frugally. He found an apartment near the spaceport, where everything was open twenty-five hours a day.

It was the counterman at All Nite Eats that ended up giving him his first decent lead.

"There's a guy you could talk to..." the counterman said, a little hesitantly.

"I'm not desperate enough for smuggling," Luther said. "Yet."

"Nothing like that," came a quick reply. "Perfectly aboveboard. But it's sub-orbital, short range."

"Shuttle?" Luther considered. It wasn't really flying, but he could do it, and it would pay the bills.

"Sort of. I know a guy who runs sightseeing tours, taking tourists around Big Ollie, down the Val Mar, things like that. See the wonder of the Martian landscape, you know?"

Luther chewed it over and then nodded. "If he pays, I'm interested."

Tarduk Mac was an outer system guy. He'd made a fortune on Triton in extreme low-temperature ceramics, went to Mars on vacation and had fallen in love with the scenery of Tharsis. He was impressed by Luther's background in the storm zone and hired him on the spot. Mac's Sightseeing Tours had four airbuses, and his pilots tended to be local boys who were just out of flight school and killing time until they could pull a shift on something interplanetary.

It turned out to be a good job. Cruises ran from an hour to four, depending on what the tourists were willing to pay. Mostly outer system guests, the *nouveau riche* of the Jovian satellites where new industries were being born daily to meet the needs of an expanding humanity.

Luther's craft was called the *Annie O.*

She was an ancient dropship, originally

built to ferry contract workers from Deimos to the surface during the terraforming project. She'd been extensively retrofitted with both a luxury interior and the newest safety features, but the outside retained the crude blocky functionalism of the early colonial era, and while the injectors had been retooled for modern chemical fuel, the controls were original equipment, designed to harness the massive reaction engine. What wings she had—little stubs that could be retracted into the hull like switchblades—were more for keeping the nose oriented than to generate lift.

She was a ridiculous relic of another time, an old draft horse brought out of retirement to pull a gaudy coach for tourists to gawk at the scenery. The chemical thrusters had been designed for surface to orbit, not short point to point hauls, and the yoke was awkward, with the aerial control surfaces slaved to the jets in a way that had probably made sense when the atmosphere was half its current density, but now seemed designed for turbulent instability. Flying *Annie* could be like trying to ride an elephant on ice skates.

Still, Luther loved the old beast, overpowered and undercontrolled as she was. When he opened her jets full out, she would *move*, slicing through the atmosphere like a bullet.

He learned to judge the mood and tolerance of his passengers. For the ones that just wanted to see the scenery—and Luther had to admit that sunrise over the vast chasm of *Valles Marineris* was breathtaking, as was the long shadow of Mount Olympus stretching across the plains—he took it nice and easy, narrating the landscape like a proper tour guide.

If the passengers seemed adventurous, though, he'd ask them if they wanted a more interesting ride. Never anything dangerous, of course, or even particularly difficult to his altered reactions, but he enjoyed giving the tourists a thrill, running through a few outside loops and spins while the passengers alternately laughed and screeched.

He got good tips that way, too.

There was a group from Ganymede that looked like it was going to be a typical sightseeing group, but Luther caught the way that Mac was deferring to the woman in charge, which wasn't like him. She turned out to be the Minority Speaker for the Ganymede Assembly, making her one of the most powerful people in the Jovian system. With her were two secretaries, a half-dozen bodyguards, and her teenage son.

Only the son and one of the bodyguards were going; the rest had business to conduct at the spaceport. Luther got the idea that the kid was going to drop dead of boredom if he had to wait through one more meeting, and so mom took pity on him and arranged the tour.

Luther was on his best behavior. Storm kings didn't have much in the way of protocol, but he'd watched enough video to be able to mimic a military bearing.

"Can we see the canyon?" the kid asked on the way to the dropship. He was gazing around the field with genuine interest, and Luther grinned in sympathy. All boys loved spaceships, even rich kids.

"We can see whatever you want," Luther said, "as long as it's in fuel range."

"What is your fuel range?" the bodyguard asked. He was eyeing the *Annie O* skeptically.

"We've got monster reserve tanks on this thing," Luther told him. "I can get you to either pole and back."

"We haven't got that kind of time." The bodyguard seemed to have no sense of humor at all. Probably part of the job.

The kid sat up front with Luther, and the bodyguard took the seat directly behind the kid.

"I'm Luther. What's your name?"

"Ajax," the kid said, then jerked his head to indicate the bodyguard. "That's Dean."

"All right, Ajax," Luther said, "Let me show you the Val Mar. Biggest hole in the solar system."

Once he'd made sure the flight harnesses were secure, Luther took off.

He did a slow banking turn around the spaceport first, giving the kid a good view of the triple peaks of the Tharsis mountains, with the bulk of Olympus looming behind them. Then he headed east until the canyon was directly below. It was still early enough that the floor of the canyon was in shadow.

The kid leaned to try to look beneath the ship into the dark emptiness, eyes wide.

"Want a closer look?" Luther asked.

"Yes, please," Ajax answered eagerly.

Luther cut thrust and let the *Annie* fall like a rock. It was one of his favorite tricks, and it never failed to impress the tourists. They plummeted from bright morning into midnight in seconds.

Ajax laughed delightedly. Behind them Dean grunted, and Luther took that as a sign of displeasure. He eased the jets back up to cruising speed gently, letting the ship's fall smooth out into a controlled glide down the deep canyon, a safe click above the rock-strewn floor.

"Can we go any lower?" Ajax asked.

"Sure," Luther said. He eased the *Annie* lower and feathered the drive flame. As the combustion temperature dropped, the exhaust glowed in the visible spectrum, bathing the ground below them in an eerie light.

Ajax stared, open-mouthed in wonder.

"Hang on," Luther said and rolled *Annie* until he was flying at about 30 degrees from vertical, with Ajax's window pointed down.

A quick glance back showed that the bodyguard Dean was frowning, so Luther eased back to upright. It was a ticklish situation. He wanted to please the kid, but it was mama who was paying for the trip, and the bodyguard was sure to report anything that he thought was dangerous. The last thing Luther wanted to do was get Mac in hot water with an outer system politician.

Ajax was easy to please, though, even taking it safe. He'd probably spent most of his life deep in Rostien City and was used to seeing landscape on a screen.

Luther took a side canyon and let *Annie* gain altitude until the sun broke over the canyon walls and was rewarded with a gasp of pleasure from Ajax at the dazzling view. Even surly Dean seemed impressed.

Luther climbed over the canyon wall and cruised over the highlands long enough to let his passenger's eyes adjust to the bright sunlight and then cut back to the main channel and dropped into the canyon again. This time he hugged the wall and let Ajax get a good look at the sheer stone as it hurtled by his window.

Luther halfheartedly started his usual spiel, going into the history of the terraforming efforts and pointing out where erosion had begun softening the sharp edges of the canyon, but it was quickly obvious that Ajax wasn't hearing a word he said and Dean couldn't care less, so he shut up and flew in silence.

Luther had been cruising the canyon for an hour and was about to ask Ajax if he was ready to turn back when the gunships dropped into the canyon and flanked him.

They were black disks, atmospheric craft with their lifting fans protected by armored skirts. Military craft, each one sporting a pair of recoilless automatic cannons but absent of any insignia.

Luther heard Dean releasing his flight harness and standing.

"What is this?" Luther asked.

"Just put her down nice and easy, rocket man," Dean said. He had a weapon out, a heavy pistol. "This doesn't have to concern you."

The three gunships were flying around the *Annie* in formation, one to each side and one dropping back behind her.

"You're taking the kid?" Luther asked.

"That's right," Dean said. "He'll be fine, just so long as Momma pays up."

Luther glanced at Ajax. The boy was wide-eyed and gave an almost imperceptible shake of his head. His lips formed the word "please."

"Sir," Luther said in his best no-nonsense pilot voice, "would you please sit down and reattach your flight harness?"

In answer the bodyguard tapped Luther's head with his pistol. "Down!"

"Suit yourself," Luther muttered.

Then he jerked the yoke, and *Annie* went into a vicious barrel roll.

Dean went flying and hit the wall, then the ceiling, then the other wall, then fetched up against the seats. The gun went bouncing off somewhere else. Luther didn't bother looking for it; he opened *Annie*'s throttle to full and punched up for the sky.

The gunships were expecting it, and they took off after him quickly—quickly by poke standards, anyway.

Luther broke the level of the surface into full sunlight still accelerating and realized his mistake immediately. There was a ship waiting up there, also military, an out-system destroyer.

How did they get that thing past the orbital watch? Luther thought, but he didn't waste time pondering the question. Instead, he pulled harder on the yoke and turned his climb into an inside Immelmann, dropping down below the walls of the canyon. Dean bounced around the inside of the cabin a little more. He was no longer trying to shield his head from the impacts, either unconscious or dead; Luther didn't much care which.

They won't bring that thing down here, Luther thought. *I just have to outrun the egg-*

beaters.

"Hang on, this might get a little rough!" Luther called to Ajax as he dove for the canyon floor.

The damned gunships were clinging to him like leeches. *Annie* could leave them in the dust, given time, but at subsonic speeds the fans had better acceleration. Then Luther caught flashes as the lead ship opened fire.

I thought they wanted to ransom the kid, Luther thought and pushed the thought away. Analysis could wait. He yawed hard left, then hard right, and the shells went wide, bringing down an avalanche from the canyon wall.

The lead ship crept closer. It was clinging to him too closely; it had to be computer-guided. No poke could fly like that.

Okay, if that's how you want to play it, Luther thought grimly. He cut the throttle down to full closed, and the thunder of the engines shut off. Momentum and a thimbleful of lift kept him from the canyon floor as he opened the throttle wide open again.

A cloud of atomized fuel and pure oxygen flooded the combustion chamber and out through the exhaust ports, unburnt. Still dropping, Luther kept the throttle open and the ignition off, pouring a stream of high quality explosive vapor straight into the lead ship's fan intakes.

Then, a dozen meters above the rock of the canyon floor, he kicked in the ignition.

The airship's fans probably survived the resultant fireball, but the control harness wasn't designed for that kind of heat, and the gunship executed a neat flip straight in-to the floor.

One down, two to go.

Then he was pulling up, weaving around a boulder the size of a small house and booming skyward.

There was more gunfire from the surviving ships, but Luther expected that and was jinking from side to side, up and down, being all over the sky, everywhere except where the pokes were pointing their guns.

Then he caught a glimpse of the huge silhouette of the destroyer above the canyon wall and dropped back down fast. That thing would have sky-to-sky missiles and *Annie* had no countermeasures.

If that destroyer gets a lock, I'm dead. No way to dodge a hunter-killer.

The gunships had learned from the fate of their comrade and were flanking him, one on each side. Still on computer control, but the pilots were running the override in real time, telling the computer what to do rather than letting it pick the strategy.

Their guns couldn't fire straight to the side, but if they figured out that one of them could drop back and nail him things could get dicey.

Luther didn't give them the chance. He cut the jets again and yawed the yoke hard. *Annie* went into a tumble, and a moment later Luther felt the impact as he struck one of the gunships broadside.

Now both of them were tumbling. Luther cut his jets back on full and rode it out and back into level flight without hitting the canyon wall.

The gunship didn't. It bounced off the wall and dropped hard. Before it hit the floor it managed to straighten out and cruised, following the contour of the rock but not attacking. Probably the pilot was knocked cold and the computer was left running the show without orders.

The last one had taken advantage of *Annie's* tumble to drop back and line up for firing, too far back for Luther to foul its fans with fuel like he had with the first one. Instead, he ran straight down, seeing the bright trails of cannon shells streaking over his head.

Down he dropped until he was close enough to the canyon floor to kick up a plume of dirt and rock. The gunship was still firing, but it was blind and Luther kept *Annie* bouncing back and forth.

Luther waited, counting under his breath. The gunship had one move open to it, to use its acceleration to get ahead of the cloud and shoot from the front.

At what he judged the proper moment, Luther hauled back on the yoke and popped up out of the cloud.

Directly into the belly of the gunship. He hit *hard* and kept going up, shoving the lighter craft upwards, and then pitched up as fast as *Annie* would go until the beast was standing on its tail. He tilted the gunship up, up, onto its side and further still, flipping the flying pancake until its fans were pointed at the sky rather than the ground.

Luther watched with interest as the pilot struggled. He knew that it was theoretically possible for an airship pilot to right an overturned craft in flight, but he'd never seen it done.

Thirty seconds later, he still hadn't.

The surviving airship was still cruising down the canyon like a truck on autopilot, so Luther opened up *Annie's* engines and ran for the end of the canyon and Olympus City at full throttle.

He glanced over at Ajax. The kid was white as paper, but managed a brave grin. Sometime during the trip he'd thrown up on himself, but he probably hadn't noticed it yet.

"Thank you for flying Mac's Sightseeing Tours," Luther said. "We hope you've enjoyed our tour of the majestic *Valles Marineris* and want to remind you to keep your flight harness in place until we are on the ground and the cabin has been opened."

The short fiction of Misha Burnett has been with Cirsova from the beginning. In addition to penning tales for the magazine he has collected stories into two volumes, Bad Dreams & Broken Hearts *and* Endless Summer. *His third Cirsova collection,* An Atlas Of Bad Roads, *will be available for pre-order through Kickstarter in July.*

Tripping to Aldous

By J. MANFRED WEICHSEL

An interstellar police investigator is in pursuit of murderer Richard Morales! But the trail leads to Aldous, an illicit party planet with a hallucinogenic atmosphere!

Dressed in a blue airtight uniform and standard-issue fishbowl helmet, I exited my interstellar police vehicle (IPV) and looked at the poor kids in the field below, wasting their brilliant young minds.

I was on Aldous to ask around about the murderer Richard Morales, who had been sighted here earlier in the summer. Personally, I wouldn't put much stake in anything anybody said they saw on Aldous, but the department has to follow up every lead.

Aldous is the most dangerous planet in the galaxy. Its atmosphere contains slightly more oxygen than Earth, but it is a certain other chemical in the air that attracts the crowds; one with psychedelic properties.

Travel to Aldous is strictly forbidden by the government of Earth, as well as the governments of most planets in the Federation. And yet every summer vacation, thousands of teenagers and young adults book illegal vessels to the forbidden planet. Participants call this annual ritual tripping to Aldous.

I looked at the crowd with pity. They were so young and had beautiful futures ahead of them, but here they were throwing it all away for nothing. None wore a helmet, gas mask, or breathing apparatus of any kind. And the worst part was they looked like they were having the time of their lives as they danced to the electronic music that blared from the speakers. It was so sad.

I figured this was as good a place as any to start my investigation, so I made my way down the hill, thinking I would ask some questions. But the moment the kids saw me, the music stopped and everybody ran from the field in a blind panic.

I was thinking my job would be easier if I could wear plainclothes, when I felt something hit my fishbowl. And then, again. I looked about and saw three blond teenage boys with serious looks on their faces. They could have been star athletes, but instead of throwing pitches, here they were, high out of their minds, throwing rocks at an officer of the law.

I reached for my stun gun, but another rock hit my helmet, and I heard a hiss. Maybe if the people of Earth didn't hate paying taxes so much, the force could issue better equipment.

I experienced the preliminary effects of the atmosphere immediately. As the boys ran off, they left motion trails in their wakes. I turned to return to the safety of my IPV, but with the simple motion of my head, the entire field became blurry with trails. I turned around and around looking for my vehicle but had lost my sense of direction. I removed my helmet, thinking it was obstructing my view, but more atmosphere hit me, and I became unable to make out any object at all because of the trails in front of me. I stuck my hands out and walked in a direction I thought would take me to my IPV. But I must have gone the wrong way because I didn't find it, and then forgetting what I was looking for, I continued like this for some time.

Suddenly, I wondered where I was. I had been walking mindlessly for some time, unable to see a thing. What if I was near a cliff? My heart pounded in my chest with the thought that a single step could plunge me to my death. In a panic, I stuck my arms out trying to find something, anything to hold onto. I blindly groped air until my hands rested on something soft and fleshy that I realized was a woman.

A male voice said, "Let's get out of here. He's a cop."

The female voice said, "He's tripping to Aldous just like us. I think it's groovy."

The male voice said, "We should leave him alone."

I squinted and made out the outline of a face in front of me. It was probably the face of a typical high school student, but it seemed to pulsate because of the atmosphere, and her lips kept turning into bulbous frog lips and then back into human lips.

I said, "It is true I am a cop. My name is Peter Donovan." Then, I paused. Was my name Peter Donovan? The name suddenly sounded foreign, as if it were the name of somebody else. Afraid I would forget my name, I repeated, for my own benefit, "My name is Peter Donovan. My name is Peter Donovan." Then I said to the girl, "But I am not here to arrest teenagers. I am looking for a murderer who may be hiding out on this planet. His name is Richard Morales."

The woman gasped. "A murderer! How dreadful."

I continued, "But the problem is, I can't see a thing."

"Hasn't your mind adjusted yet?" asked the male voice.

"No. Is it supposed to?"

"If you want to see, you have to look. Look around you."

I strained my eyes, but still all I could make out was a blur of motion trails. Frustration caused my chest to tighten.

"No. Not like that. You've got to relax. Relax, and just look. Don't try too hard. Just breathe."

After a few moments of deep breathing, the motion trails dissipated as the outlines of things became sharp and clear. My head was tilted downwards, facing the grass and flowers at my feet. The colors were flat. There was only one shade of red, one of orange, one of yellow, one of green, and one of blue.

Fascinated, I picked up a red flower and examined it. It was a solid shade of red, and because of the uniformity of color, the flower appeared flat, as if it lacked depth. As I stared, the red separated into a rainbow in front of my eyes. But it was a rainbow of red. Each stripe of the rainbow was a different shade of red, but each shade of red was also its own distinct, unique color. There was a painful harmony to the colors as the stripes of the red rainbow swirled around each other and the spectrum of red colors dispersed chaotically across the petals. A tear came to my eye. I said, "It's so beautiful."

"Yes! Yes! That's it. You're seeing."

I felt a strange kind of loving warmth towards my two companions. I don't know why I hugged them. I was suddenly so full of emotion, and hugging potential witnesses seemed like the most natural thing in the world. "But... how?" I asked.

"Color is in your mind. Your eyes see, and your brain interprets. The air of Aldous is loosening your mind, making your brain more flexible. More elastic. As you continue to look, the colors will become more vivid to you, and more distinct from each other, as they form into a new color scheme." The man paused, looked up at the sky, and added, more to himself than to me, "What if the universe is a giant machine?"

I remembered why I was on Aldous. I had an obligation I needed to fulfill. I had to arrest Richard Morales. I took a picture out of my pocket, showed it to my companions, and asked if they recognized the man. They said they had seen him.

More tears came to my eyes, and I said, "Thank you."

For reasons I don't understand, instead of following up with more questions, I turned and walked away, and jubilant but mysterious sounds I hadn't noticed before faded into the distance. Aldous was lush and beautiful. I played my fingers over a green leaf. But the leaf was more than green. It was a spectrum of green colors.

I spent some time contemplating a blue waterfall. But the waterfall was more than blue. It was a spectrum of blue colors.

If the leaf was more than green, and the waterfall more than blue, was the leaf more than a leaf, and the waterfall more than a waterfall? Perhaps these things were as different from leaves and waterfalls as rainbow shades of colors were from the colors of the rainbow, and my mind only interpreted them as leaves and waterfalls because that was what it was used to.

As I thought about leaves and waterfalls, my theory that there was a deeper reality hidden behind the veil of the visible world seemed to bear out. The leaf I had been playing with became many leaves on the tree, and the waterfall I had been contemplating became many small waterfalls, attached to tiny twigs at the ends of branches, spinning and revolving, multiplied. *I thought leaves instead of leaf, and the leaf became many, and I thought waterfalls instead of waterfall...*

A man whose body was broken up into prismatic diamonds that dispersed around its edges approached and finished my thought as if he had heard it, "...And the leaves and waterfalls became the same thing. It is as if the differences between things are as arbitrary as the words we name them."

I said, "I am looking for a murderer

named Richard Morales. Here is a picture. Have you seen this man?"

The man answered mysteriously, "What is a murderer?"

I backed away, suddenly frightened that the man meant me some sort of unspeakable harm. I said, "Who are you? Do you know Richard Morales?"

"I live on this island."

I recoiled with horror and shouted, "This isn't an island. It's a planet."

"It's a planet on an island."

I screamed, "Don't you mean we are on an island on a planet?"

The man opened his prismatic mouth wide and let out bellowing laughter. I turned to run, and the frightening sound echoed deeply behind me as it faded away.

Dense foliage tumbled past me in a blur of exploding colors and shapes that became other shapes in the corners of my eyes, which dispersed before I could clearly make them out. *Stupid,* I thought. *Stupid. Here was someone who may have had knowledge of Richard Morales, and instead of following up with more questions, I ran. I wonder if she knows where Richard Morales is.*

I didn't know when I had stopped running, or how long I had been staring at the woman with the long golden hair that went down her back, expanding like a curtain in a breeze, pulsating like a star, and down the side of the bleached coral stone she sat on. Her hair was part of the coral. The coral was alive. I climbed down the mossy hill towards the sand of the beach.

The woman with hair that beat like a heart rose and faced me. I felt guilty for some reason. The clear sea behind her shimmered in the tropical sun.

She smiled up at me as I approached and said in a whisper, "Who is Richard Morales?"

I was startled. Again someone had answered my thoughts as if they heard them. I panicked at the thought that all this time I had been thinking out loud. What if I had thought private thoughts I didn't want anybody to hear and had spoken those out loud? I wracked my brain to recall if I had thought any private thoughts recently, but my mind was so fragmented I couldn't recall the information, which made me concerned that what I had thought out loud was so shameful my mind was hiding it from me intentionally to spare me the humiliation.

Although I hadn't said anything all the time I stood there, the woman told me to be quiet. "You will scare away the giraffes."

I clenched my jaw to keep from speaking. But suddenly I had the uncontrollable urge to hear my voice out loud. I tried as hard as I could to keep my lips pursed but couldn't help myself and, trying to speak as quietly as possible, whispered, "What giraffes?"

She waved an arm across the clear, mirror-like water that reflected the transparent blue of the sky. "The giraffes of the sea."

I looked across the sea and saw it was dotted with yellow and brown spotted giraffes, their long necks sticking out of the water, their tiny brown antlers towering high in the air, their contented faces standing out against the blue horizon. "Listen to their moos," the woman said.

I listened and heard the deep-throated moos of the giraffes float from across the still sea. They were happy moos, so happy they brought tears to my eyes. Why should these giraffes be so happy to be standing in the salt water? Why should they be so content? I sobbed and sobbed. It was the most profound thought I had ever had in my life.

The woman squeezed my hand sympathetically and pointed up at the sky above the sea. I saw that just as the sea was a reflection of the blue of the sky, the sky was a reflection of the sea, and the same giraffes in the sea hung upside-down in the sky, mooing contentedly. This confused me. Normally when you have two mirrored surfaces facing each other, the images caught between them reflect back and forth, disappearing into infinity. But here, there were simply two identical sets of giraffes, one in the water, and one in the sky, their heads reaching towards each others'. It made me wonder which was the original image and which the reflection.

My gaze went higher, and I saw my image and that of the beautiful woman with the long pulsating hair were also reflected in the sky, along with the beach we were on.

I looked back at her and wondered if I was the original or the reflection. Did my conscious thoughts emanate from my body on the ground, or my body in the sky? Was my reflection mirroring my actions, or I mirroring its?

The woman answered, and I was sure I had been thinking out loud, "There is an infinite iteration of us reflected back and forth between the mirror ground and the mirror sky. Not only are our physical bodies reflected, but our minds and souls, so that each iteration thinks and acts the exact same way. Each one is technically of free will, but each thinks and does the same because it is the same, and its surroundings are the same, so it is living in identical circumstances and reacting to identical stimuli."

Then she gave me a mysterious look that pierced my soul and added, "But when you look at your reflections, it is important that you recognize the person you see."

I stepped back in horror and stumbled, and as I did, my position changed, but not my position in the three dimensions of space. Rather, I stumbled ever so slightly along a fourth dimension of space, and found myself looking at the three dimensions of my surroundings from a new angle that had been hitherto unknown to me. The woman's suggestion... Her suggestion that I was... it was horrible.

I looked up from this new angle and saw that reflections of myself, the woman, and our surroundings soared up in a curved line to the sky, and into space beyond, each image vivid, each image real, and each image alive like I was. Each image was independent of thought and movement, but each one thought and moved identically.

My mind reeled with the horrible, unthinkable possibility that I was... A lump formed in my throat. I fought to push it down as I fought to get rid of the unbearable guilt.

I turned to the woman and saw her for the first time from the new angle. She was more beautiful than before, and it made my heart throb in my breast. Her long hair blew all around her now, no longer part of the coral, rising above her head in a crown. I thought fearfully that she might know who I was.

I screamed, "Please, tell me I'm not... tell me I'm not..."

My heart pounded so hard I was afraid it would burst. I shoved the woman away, and reality snapped back like a rubber band as the trail of reflections disappeared. Through my tears, I said softly, "No. I can't be. I can't be. I can't!"

The woman looked at me strangely. I remembered I was here to arrest Richard Morales. But I was suddenly terrified that she thought I thought she thought I thought I was... It was too horrible.

I turned and ran. There was a loud crashing noise, and a crater appeared in the sky as if someone hit it with a sledgehammer, and ocean blue colored pieces broke off its dome and fell in violent pelts to the ground around me as cracks tore all the way to the edges of the sky. I fell to my knees, crying, because I could no longer distinguish between the shards of the shattered sky and the shards of my shattered mind.

Then, all was calm. I looked up at the sky. It was a whole mirror again, no longer broken into shards. I gazed with horror at my reflection in the sky. It was the reflection of the murderer Richard Morales.

I slowly regained my sanity over several days in a detox chamber and then was transferred to a hospital bed. A few days later, I was talking to the shrink assigned to me by the department and said, "It was horrible. I actually thought I was a different person. I thought I was a murderer, and the guilt was unbearable."

He said, "When your fellow officers found you merely a couple of feet from your IPV, you were huddled on the ground crying like a baby, and when you saw them, you were so far gone in your delusion that you actually tried to surrender.

"In a way you are lucky. Every year a number of people wander off and get lost on the planet, and the prolonged exposure can result in permanent psychosis, and in some cases, death.

"But just think. You are a grown man. The others you spoke with were just kids, and the reason they said such strange things was because they were tripping to Aldous too. If the atmosphere of that horrid planet reduced you to such a state, so that you will now require years of therapy, imagine what it does to them."

I shook my head and muttered, "Those poor kids."

And that is why when your peers pressure you to go tripping to Aldous this summer, no matter how persistent they are, just say no!

Tripping to Aldous is J. Manfred Weichsel's fifth appearance in Cirsova. He is the author of The Calydonian Boar Hunt, Not Far from Eden, Jungle Jitters, Five Maidens on the Pentagram, and Ebu Gogo. Visit his website to learn more: https://j-manfred-weichsel.mailchimpsites.com/

Cerulean

By J. THOMAS HOWARD

On the run and dying of thirst on a desert world, Roger Campbell-Thorn finds salvation in a flask of nourishing intoxicant that sends him to the world's distant past!

Ochre

The ochre desolation rarely knew winds. Whatever tempests had molded its shapes had long since died out. Yet, for some hateful reason, the man suffered a rare maelstrom of shrieking gusts. He was not a tall man, though his wide shoulders would have frightened most. He wore a covering of slick jet leather, at his side hung a khopesh, and his hair, now riddled with dust, was a shock of obsidian turning a wistful gray.

Since the dancing girl Ahnlia and her party of jackals had driven Roger Campbell-Thorn from the calcifying canal city, he had gone with little food and even less water. If the air of this world had been thick enough for a cognate of vultures, they would have circled him. Certainly the shade of Death stood on the horizon, awaiting his final victory over the man—as he always triumphed, save, perhaps, against his own mother, Time.

Roger stumbled. He cursed every god he had heard of in every trader patois he had ever learned. Was he really to survive the colony's collapse, and the bloody swath he had carved across an already-red world, to die here, murdered by howling winds?

Perhaps the storm did not truly wish him dead, for a lash of air revealed the skeletal outcroppings of a long-abandoned fort. Roger made the best pace he could for the opening. Even if it had just been unearthed, he took no chances and slunk in, blade at the ready. Who knew what creatures might have made their home in the vacant garrison?

Luckily, only moldering bones, long calcified by the dry air, greeted him. They were so ancient that the skeletons did not appear to have the wide chests of the dry-landers. This place must have been entombed since before the fleeing of the air. Roger wanted to recoil, for these ghosts had likely sat undisturbed since before his own forebears laid down their first harvests, but he needed shelter and food.

As if Roger summoned it out of the ether, he saw the body of what could only be a dry-lander. The man's ruddy skin had calcified, and the face still shrieked. Roger looked in the man's satchel. In it, he found the libation of the dry-landers in a hefty clay jug. It was the dust of some distilled fungus, and in small quantities it caused drunkenness, but in large volumes it caused hallucinations. Roger had only over-imbibed once, and it had given him horrid visions, but he had no choice. He drank the nutrient-rich intoxicant. Slowly at first, hoping to stave off some of the aftereffects, but the animal in him won out, and he gulped lustily until his starvation-worn belly felt it might burst. Then he slept, huddled amongst the chorus of the dead.

Ruby

Roger woke to the sensation of heat. It did not swelter, but it did burn. Without the slightest consideration, he stripped to the buff. He went for his sword but dropped it in a sudden crash. It had burned his hand to the touch. He wandered out into the ochre dunes. There he gazed up at a hateful ruby sun. It expanded across the firmament with a jeweled indifference. All around him the sands were melting into rivers of glass. Upon an island in the glassy wetlands he saw two figures. He had seen them once before. Neither seemed affected by the heat. One was a woman, more beautiful than the ruby sun was terrible. Half her form was a skeleton, the other the mold from which all femininity was imitated. With each exhale, the living wilted, but with each inhale a new beauty was born, as incomparable as the previous incarnation. Behind her stood a towering apparition, entombed in dark robes, and at his side was a great flint sword with no crossguard and a simple rope-wrapped handle. It seemed a piece of the great blade had been chipped away.

Roger went to speak but found no words escaped.

Roger woke amongst the dead. Their empty sockets looked indifferently past him, save the corpse whom Roger had robbed of its libations. The head had rolled down and the empty gaze was upon Roger. He was no superstitious man, but he recoiled all the same. He leapt up, khopesh in hand, at the sight of the dead man. Then the floor beneath him began to quake. Without warning, it gave way and down Roger fell. He did not scream, merely awaited the splat and the embrace of death, as he saw no end to the yawning abyss he had fallen in. As he fell, he thought he caught a familiar tellurian smell, but it could not have been true.

Cerulean

Roger woke once more, though this waking was unexpected. He felt wet, and his face was warm. He opened his eyes and beheld an unblemished sapphire sky. Roger stood. He was lying on a beach. Before him was the cerulean expanse of a sea. It was impossible! There were no more seas. His nostrils drank in the smell of salt. It was a sensation all but forgotten, although in this ocean's smell, there was a spice his telluric memories did not know. It was exotic and made his heart race with glee.

Roger stripped off his heavy leather coverings. They were all but suffocating him in the humid air. His buttery umber skin absorbed the warmth of the sun. He still kept his khopesh in hand, but Roger was beside himself with joy. Then, around the cove, he thought he heard singing.

No, Roger was sure it was a tune that carried on the wind. At first, he could not make out the language. After a time, the tune began to take on meaning. He had heard bits of this tongue in some of the trader patois, though this dialect was still almost utterly alien.

Roger, with only sword in hand and breechclout for clothing, made his way around the bend and saw the source of the song. She did not have the ochre skin, black stripes, or wide chest of the people he had met since fleeing the colony. Nor did she have their willowy height. Still, she had their elfin face with its Fae beauty. Her skin was aquamarine, and her eyes and hair were as cerulean as the waves. She wore little more than a tunic and a belt with a sword meant more for chopping than theatrics. Before her was a fire, and upon a spit roasted some cognate for fish.

Perhaps she was an outcast as Roger had been, lost too amongst a sea of strangers? Perhaps she was in as desperate need of ally as he was? He had long since pressed his luck and was in sore need of a tribe to fall in with. For now, even a solitary partner would do.

Roger had been a fool, for she already had a tribe. From every hidden vantage emerged men; they too sang a shanty, though this one was cruel and no doubt intended to frighten him. They looked the same as her, all with swords for chopping, all drawn and ready.

"Wait," Roger shouted. He realized how frightening he must have looked, turning the corner, all but nude, with sword in hand. Before he could continue, a man shot a rock at him from a leather slingshot. Rog-

er deflected it deftly with his blade. There was a crack. Another rock must have been cast from some hidden angle, but he would never know from where, and drunken blackness crept over his eyes.

A harsh slap woke Roger. He looked up at his aquamarine captors. Then he struggled a moment. His hands and legs were bound, so tight that he was losing feeling in them.

"Who are you?" the woman commanded. Her voice had lost all its musicality and all that remained were the notes of the lash.

"Roger Campbell-Thorn," he answered. "Where am I?"

"What do you mean by that?" the woman replied. Her pack of jackals was around her. They did not speak, though their leers said plenty enough.

"What country is this? There are no oceans anymore."

"Are you daft? No oceans…? Most of the world is oceans, if you take traders' words for it. I know little beyond the Sea of Kyna and these shores."

Roger's mind raced until it found what it sought, buried deep in the haze of memory. Kyna had been a name he had heard some traders call a region of dry-lands, but it was an old name, rarely spoken.

"What kingdom is this?" Roger asked, almost fearful of the answer. Understanding was budding, and it was more impossible than what the colonists had first found.

"Mine," the woman snapped. "No one claims these shores. Though I suppose the Empire of Ill Minya would like to reach this far south. Tell me, are you some kind of spy? I've never seen a man the color of mud."

"I've never seen a woman the color of the sea," he answered. She was as beautiful as the sea, and seemingly just as deadly.

The woman shook her head. "Just where in the hell are you from?"

Roger did not answer. It would do no good explaining, and he did not believe it either.

The woman clawed out, raking his features with her sharp nails. "Answer me," she demanded. Her jackals looked on. Their sea-colored eyes were thirsty for blood.

Roger strained, and his telluric muscles snapped his bindings. It seemed, in this new impossibility, this gift had not been lost.

The woman stepped back and drew her blade.

Roger looked around; he would die, but at least it would be on his feet. He would not give them the chance to torture him. For all his unearned strength, it would not avail him against so many swords, but at least he could hope for a clean death this way.

"Wait," the woman commanded. She extended a hand to warn off her encroaching killers.

"Roger Campbell-Thorn," she said like the words had an acrid flavor. "I am called Ell Mara. I wonder how a man could be so strong? I found no talismans on you. You are muscled, but no more than my Lith Luc here." She pointed to a burly cutthroat. The man was smiling at Roger.

"I like him," Lith Luc said. "None of our crew can beat me at any feats of strength.

No one will gamble with me anymore. Maybe we should take this umber man into our crew. At least then I can have someone to wrestle."

Roger smiled at the man. "I've yet to lose a bout. How about I fight you for my freedom? I win, you let me go."

"Silence," Ell Mara demanded. "I'll not have two men decide for me. This is my crew, and I am its sole captain."

"Apologies," Lith Luc demurred.

"Tell me truthfully, are you a demon? Will you put some curse on us, Roger Campbell-Thorn?"

"If I say yes, you'll free me?"

"A demon would not ask, I think," the woman temporized. "If you were some spirit, you would have punished us already. So you are a man, a strange one, but one nonetheless. Therefore, you should know the penalty for trespassing in my cove is death."

Roger looked around, his eyes devoured the scenery, and he thought of where to make his last stand.

"Yet, I may yet let you live," Ell Mara said.

"If?" Roger asked.

She smiled brightly.

They rowed against the wind, which sang in an eager gust above them. Roger had been set to the oars in chains; this time reinforced against his strength. Ell Mara and her lieutenants had been happy lashing him. All save Lith Luc, who seemed to begrudgingly admire him. The burly blue man sat beside Roger, for all men in the crew of Ell Mara took their turn at the oars.

"Do you know where we go, stranger?" the man asked.

Roger gave him an angry look for response.

"The Wailing Ship. She thinks you can snatch up its treasure for her. None who have entered have returned to tell the tale of what cries out from within. Ell Mara thinks your strength might match this nameless horror. You are stronger than any man I have ever seen. Not even the most renowned gladiator of Ill Satal could have snapped those bonds. I see now even the metal of your chains struggles against your might. We will soon replace it. I saw you test it last night, when all others thought you to be asleep."

Roger glowered.

"What devilry made you so strong? Would you share it with me?" He whispered in Roger's ear. "Even for your freedom?"

Roger shook his head. "If I could, I would, but this gift was never mine to take, nor mine to give," Roger answered truthfully, though he doubted the pirate could understand the explanation of why that was so.

"Alas, if only your gift did not have such a geas on it, you would be a free man." Lith Luc patted Roger on the back, but there would be no more conversation, only the escalation of the howling winds. Soon the din drowned out all else. The pirates had piloted a course alongside the shore. Roger could see it in the distance, a dark speck, and knew it for their destination.

It was a massive vessel unlike any Roger had ever seen. Unlike the pirate's galley, it bore no cognate to any memory Roger had. Nor did it seem to be made of wood. What it was made from, Roger could not say, but it reminded him of papyrus save that it was jet, and its atramentous sheen sent rivulets of fearful sweat down his brow.

The wreck kept true to its sobriquet, for the sound that emanated from it was a terrible lament, and Roger doubted it had natural origins. The men around him looked wary, but they followed their dread captain's orders. They came right up to an opening in the wreckage.

Suddenly, many swords pointed to Roger. He found himself forced to stand away from the oars. A plank was lowered. Its edge jutted into an opening. Roger saw his sword tossed into the yawning maw. The points of the tips jabbed until he was at the end of the plank. He strained with all his might against the chains; they bent more but would not break. Then the men parted, and Ell Mara advanced.

The captain had two daggers in hand. One she placed against Roger's throat, the other was against his thigh. Either cut would be fatal. She smiled, and Roger thought he glimpsed something in her teeth. She whispered in his ear. "We'll return in one day's time. Bring me whatever treasure there is, and you may live."

Ell Mara kissed him, and her lips were harsh and warm as the summer sun. Roger felt her push something cold into his mouth. Then with swiftness belied by her embrace, she kicked him into the wreckage.

Roger landed upon the alien substance.

He spat the key onto the floor. Then rolling, he grasped it with his hands and undid his chains. He searched for his khopesh and found it lying by a pool of water. He snatched it up. Already, the pirate ship was retreating. Roger wondered if he should swim for the shore. However, even when distracted on the plank by testing blades, he had been able to make out the great slithering shapes swimming in the sea. He did not want to be eaten, so he turned inwards, towards the dappled light that illuminated the ancient rubble.

Roger stalked as best he could. He leaped over pools of water and their shadowed depths. The relentless wailing smothered any warning sound that might come. His eyes darted around, drinking in their surroundings as deeply as they could, for they would have to do double the work.

Despite his trepidation, Roger made it to a vast main chamber unharmed. There the sleek hull of the ship vibrated from the rueful sound. Here the bottom of the hull had hollowed out. A great pool of stagnant water sat. It was still against the vibration and seemed congealed. The outlandish nature of the liquid gave Roger pause. His fingers tightened around the hilt of his sword.

Searching, he saw the littering of countless skeletons, most of which Roger recognized for their familiar contours, but some had foreign curves. The parallels were there, but he knew whatever flesh had once housed these moldering bones was not human. Perhaps they had been the original voyagers of this improbable sea?

At the end of the chamber was a great shattered window. Roger saw the analogues of a table and many chairs strewn carelessly about, in snapping ruination. The table still had a stained tablecloth about it with a pattern woven into it, and even beneath the dust and desolation of the sea, he could make out the patterns of scenes he could not understand.

Reclining carelessly atop a cathedra was the remains of one of the inhuman skeletons. His mouth was open wide, and in it, resting against shriveled lips, was a mighty horn. From this, the terrible sound wailed.

Roger had seen no sign of any treasure in his traversal through the ruined hull. Now, he watched this horrible artifice. He wondered if this would be enough to satisfy Ell Mara's greed?

Another thought occurred to Roger as he studied the blasting artifact. In trekking the ship, he had seen no bodies, until he came here. The pool was surely inhabited. Perhaps its strange stagnation came from whatever dwelled in it?

Roger scanned. His telluric muscles might make it to an outcropping in the wall, and then to the screaming prize, but what dwelled in the water? Should he cast in some debris to see if it would react? Was its denizen absent? Was it slumbering, and if so, could he simply leap to his goal and leave unmolested?

Fate decided for Roger. The water stirred. From it emerged spindling legs. They were not unlike that of a spider, though far more plentiful, and far larger. The legs ran across the desolation, their thick feelers sensing for him. Roger held perfectly still, though he feared the animal could feel his breathing and the thunder of his heart.

A leg careened for him. Roger jumped aside, saved only by his great leap. Another limb snapped, and Roger made to jump, but the many appendages were ready. He felt his body collide against the trunk of a leg. It was hard as steel and did not give. The air rushed from his lungs; the trajectory of the strike sent him for the listless water.

The torn wall of the ship cut into Roger's hand, as he grasped the wall above the pool. He yanked his body up just in time to miss the strike of another spindly leg. A twirling lash caught him and sent him flying into a wall. His khopesh was knocked from his hand.

Roger ran for his sword, clutched it up, and parried the strike of a limb, but there was not even a dent; even with all his preternatural strength, he was harmless against this beast.

The force of the blow crushed Roger's fingers. He dropped the blade. Another slap sent him once more towards the pool. He was being rolled towards the water. What course was left to him?

Roger shot up, ran as fast as he could, and leapt for a vantage in the wreckage. It was a bound a normal man could not make, but to Roger Campbell-Thorn it was within reach. He grasped the ruin, his fingers sweaty, and from it, he swung his body to the screaming skeleton.

Roger ducked under the carcass and snatched the horn from the doomed lips. He pointed the wailing horn at the pool. Everything the sound touched was shattered. The legs snapped and flew in the air as if they were stalks of grass, and they left behind them trails of gore.

The limbs retreated into their oily pool. Roger advanced, aiming the screaming weapon into the water. Even its thick form was forced to motion. It danced with the desolation of the sound. Soon the detritus of a spindling and twisting hulk rose to the surface. The horn had destroyed all that its lament had touched, even that which had endured both sea and time.

Roger studied the instrument. It was carved from an amber-colored ivory. The bone felt almost soft in his hands. He searched the lines of runes that ran across its wrapped handle. His fingers ran across a jewel of swimming violet. He touched it, and the sound ceased, but the ringing in his ears lingered on.

The sun had come and gone. Roger sat upon a shard of the boat awaiting his rescue. Around him swam eager slithering shadows, which occasionally snapped out of the cerulean calm, hoping to catch him up, but he was too high, and this sea knew only a slight tide, made by the two moons that were no more than crumbs on the firmament.

The pirate ship came into sight. Ell Mara stood atop its bow. They were close now and weighed anchor.

"What have you done? I heard the screaming end. It has never ended," she called out. Beside her was Lith Luc, and his hard features were restless.

"My freedom?" Roger asked.

"My treasure," Ell Mara demanded.

Roger took the horn from the loop in his breechcloth. Ell Mara stared on, puzzled. Her eyes swam with ambition.

"Is that it?" she asked unamused.

Roger pointed the horn at the sea adjacent to the pirate's ship. He twisted the jewel, and the lament began. It shot out in fury and parted the waves, slaughtering the life that swam in them. He touched the jewel once more, and it was quiet. Blood stained the waves, and carcasses blemished the surface.

"My freedom? Take me to some trader's port and let me be; otherwise, I'll sink your craft. You could not row to safety before I blasted you to hell." Roger said flatly.

"That is a terrible weapon; we should row out to the farthest depths and cast it in." Lith Luc interjected.

Ell Mara went to snap, but she halted. "If you give me the horn when I leave you at Cas'a'cal, I'll take you there. You'll find libations, work, and women there."

Roger nodded. "How far to this port?"

"Three days, at our fastest," Ell Mara answered.

Roger would have to stay awake the whole time, for they would likely slit his throat in his sleep.

"Agreed."

They lowered the plank, and Roger stepped onto the ship.

"I still think we should discard it," Lith

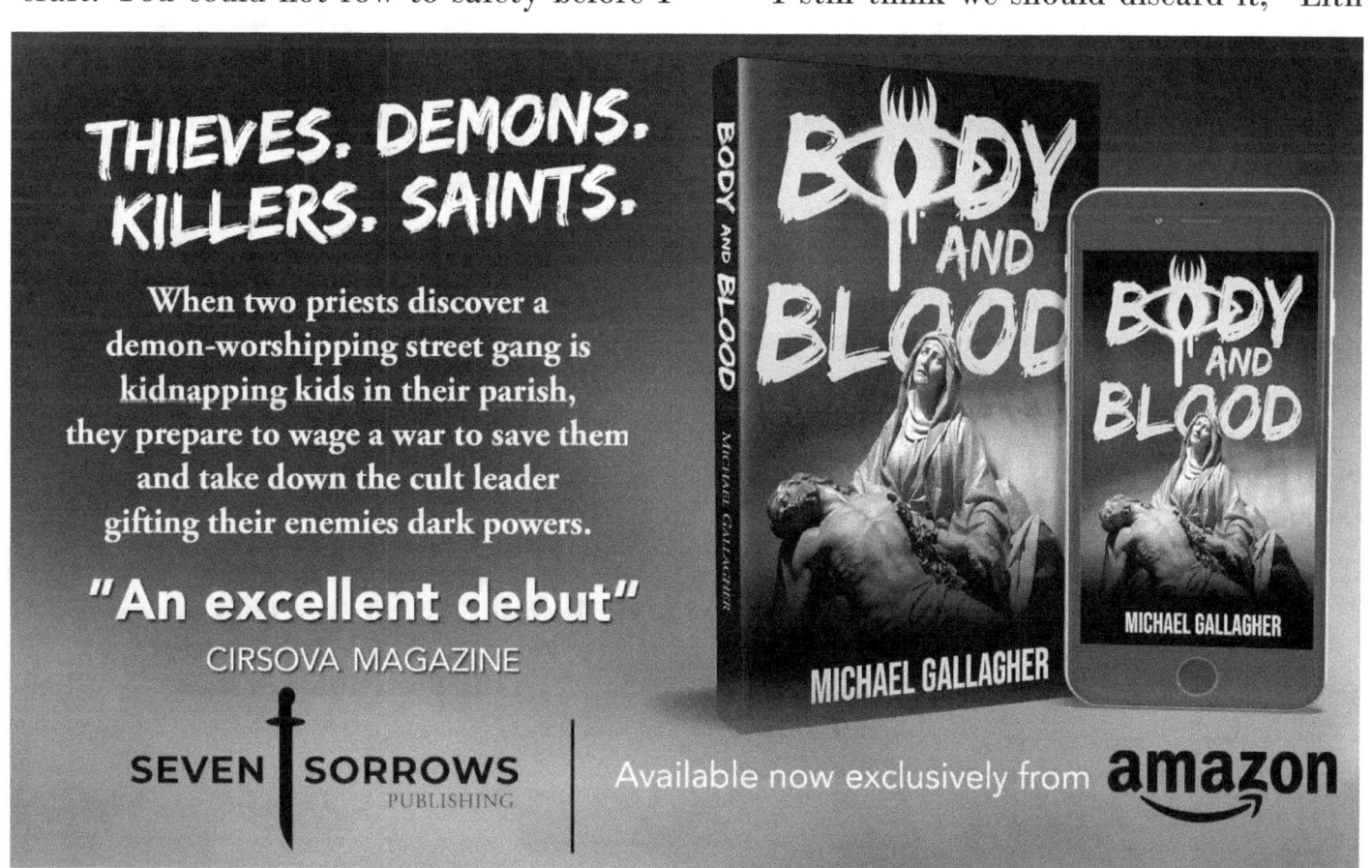

THIEVES. DEMONS. KILLERS. SAINTS.

When two priests discover a demon-worshipping street gang is kidnapping kids in their parish, they prepare to wage a war to save them and take down the cult leader gifting their enemies dark powers.

"An excellent debut"
CIRSOVA MAGAZINE

BODY AND BLOOD
MICHAEL GALLAGHER

SEVEN SORROWS
PUBLISHING

Available now exclusively from amazon

Luc grumbled. "Tell us of the Wailing Ship. I can wait no longer, I must know what was inside," the man pleaded.

So, Roger did, and all listened.

"You are a mighty man to have conquered such a beast, and to think to use the horn. I would have died having put faith only in my strength," Lith Luc said.

"Me as well," Ell Mara demurred. It was a strange admission for one who exuded such strength. With that, the crowd dispersed, and the pirate captain took to her post.

"Why not join us? You'd do well by our captain," Lith Luc whispered when the two were alone at the oars.

Roger thought on it. Would this crew take him in? By all odds, he would live longer in communion with them. He was a man, and a man was meant to be amongst men, not the lonely company of his nagging thoughts.

"I'm no brigand, I warn you. I've not the heart for cutting the throats of children or the embrace of unwilling women."

Lith Luc smiled so wide his pearly teeth seemed to burst from his mouth.

"A man to my liking. Perhaps with your aid, I can temper my beloved Ell Mara's failings."

"A mutinous lieutenant," Roger answered.

"No, just a loving one," Lith Luc answered.

"I would sleep on it, but you're liable to slit my throat for the horn. But I will consider your offer all the same."

With that, the umber man and the aq-uamarine man rowed in unison.

J. Thomas Howard is a fantasist from the receding woodlands of Southeastern PA. His works have been featured in Whetstone & DMR Books. For news about future releases follow his blog https://jthowardpulp.wordpress.com or his twitter @j_sklad

WILD STARS V:
The Artomique Paradigm
Collected Edition Out This Summer From Cirsova Publishing!
www.thewildstars.com

The Strickland Line

By ALEC CIZAK

The Strickland Line has a bug problem! Journalist Harv Wallender is accosted by a nasty critter... Quite the inconvenience! But then the critter starts to grow...!

If you wander south of Pawpaw Grove, past what civilized folks in Chicago call the boonies, don't blink and you'll catch sight of the Francis property. Until the 1970s, the Francis family survived off wheat and corn. Their crops grew around a stretch of rusted, abandoned railroad tracks. The Strickland Line. Used to stretch from Rock Island to South Carolina. Mostly industrial. The Milby family rented it for a small commuter train. Started in Gary and ended in Indianapolis. Back and forth, three times a day. That orange, flaking monstrosity you see in the middle of the weed-plagued Francis fields? That's the last Milby train ever to run its route. Logic dismisses the gaping hole in the ceiling of the second-class car as the result of decay. The truth, however, is much more interesting.

December 23, 1914. Folks from Lake County and Chicago headed to Indy for Christmas. Good cheer, as you might expect. A heavy snow started an hour before the second southbound departed. Engineers figured they'd chug along fast enough to beat the serious stuff.

One gentleman on board, a writer from the *Bee Ridge Tribune*, suggested they hold off, see how deep the snow'd gather. The engineer assured him the locomotive would decimate any obstacles. The journalist could best be described as a fragile noodle of a man ahead of his time with respect to his fear of germs and microbes. Harv Wallender. Carried spare handkerchiefs in his pockets. Placed them over his share of the bench he occupied in second class. His nose recoiled at the stench of dust and grime on the unwashed window allowing a view of the swelling storm outside.

As the train cleared Haggard and Lublin, the child of a couple seated across from Harv plopped next to him on the bench. Harv opened the morning edition of the *Tribune* and marveled at his editorial in which he predicted global tragedies would pollute the second half of the decade. While fussing over a comma the typesetter had failed to include in a crucial sentence near the end of the piece, he froze. A tick of some sort traversed the arc between his thumb and forefinger. He squinted, his mind skimming his bank of knowledge to identify the offensive beast. Two pincers long as the bug's diamond-shaped torso protruded from the top of its presumed head. An itch accompanied the insertion of these pincers into Harv's flesh. His research expedition de-

163

livered bad news: he did not recognize the insect.

"Conductor!" He snapped his fingers at the lone man tearing tickets near the rear of the car. Waiting for the man to heed his call, he flicked at the creature in an effort to remove its barbed extremities from his skin. The plump child beside him giggled. "You think this is funny?" he said to the boy. The boy's father glared at Harv.

"I'll thank you not to speak to my son in a parental manner," said the father, a dandy in a bowler hat and cheap, thin tie the color of fresh manure. Harv refrained from commenting on the father's performed baritone.

He thwacked the bug with his other hand. The pest somersaulted through the air and landed on the window. Crimson rivulets painted the smudged glass. His blood, or the bug's?

The boy giggled.

The boy's mother said, "Edward, mind yourself."

Her husband blushed. The woman tipped the brim of her hat, a floppy, sun-colored Easter bonnet, and stared out the window, her head bobbing to the rhythm of the wheels.

How Harv would have loved to witness their private arguments. Women setting their feet and taking command in the world thrilled him. His mother had been a balloon-sized, willful boar who drove his father to hang himself. Not that Harv minded. The old man's only shows of affection involved pointing to the woods outside their cabin, indicating Harv had erred and thus

required appointment with a switch.

The conductor arrived. A codger beset, as all codgers, by tell-tale gravity coloring his hair and bushy mustache the same shade as snowflakes tumbling around the train. "My good man," said Harv. "Your line is plagued." He pointed over his shoulder at the splotch on the window.

"Sir, I do not judge others for their private habits." The conductor's sandpaper voice hinted at a tobacco habit. "Seeing as how this is a public transport, could you be so kind as to refrain from whatever odd practice it is you engage in that demands you wipe fluids on public surfaces?"

Harv faced the window. Before he could question the family surrounding him as to where the pest had disappeared to, a deeper, more annoying itch announced itself. The bug had returned to its original feeding spot between his thumb and forefinger. "Heavens…" He held his left hand high. "What in creation is this?"

Upon extracting a silver-framed monocle from his breast pocket, the conductor leaned closer. "That is unusual, isn't it?" He nodded to the child and the child's parents. "I will require, at this point, your boarding papers." The mother nudged the father with her elbow. He produced three tickets which the conductor ripped in two, returning the upper halves to the father. "And you, sir?" He placed his monocle in his shirt pocket.

"Beg pardon." Harv raised his left hand once more. "I insist we tend to this first."

The valleys that time had carved into the conductor's face expanded and constricted with his unsure breathing. "It's an insect, sir. If need be, go into the washroom and run water over it until it disappears down the funnel in the center of the sink." He smiled at the child and said, "That's called a drain, young man. Did you know that?"

The boy stuck out his tongue. His father snapped his fingers. "Edward!" The father's attempt at discipline did not seem to affect the boy. The child slapped his knees and announced, "I want my Goo Goo. Now."

The father glanced at the mother. The woman shook her head. "You'll exhibit manners worthy of reward, or there will be no reward."

To this, the boy crossed his arms over his chest. His lower lip smothered his upper lip as he demonstrated the pouting disposition of a spoiled brat.

"With all due respect..." Harv's voice cracked in his attempts to best the surrounding chatter. "What are we going to do about this?" He stood and waved his contaminated hand.

"Sir..." The conductor grimaced and backed into the aisle. "If you must, use the facilities at the end of the car."

Harv plucked his tissues from his seat. No telling what the child might do with them in his absence. Noting the frayed edges of the ornate, Persian design on the strip of rug blanketing the aisle, he frowned. Did the Milby clan have no pride? He would write an editorial when he returned to Lake County and suggest the Milbys either sell the line or hire someone with aesthetic sense to update their passenger cars. He estimated no improvements had been made since the previous century. Perhaps the Milby

clan, like so many lessers, feared progress.

The bathroom confirmed his suspicions—upturned tiles on the floor revealed no one relevant cared about the finer details. He placed several squares of toilet tissue under the soles of his polished wingtips. Holding his infected hand above the basin by the toilet, he pulled the chain overhead and smiled as water doused the bug. It tumbled, along with a stream of blood, into the basin. Another tug on the chain and the damned thing spun down the drain. "Very well." Harv smacked his palms together. Blood oozed from puncture wounds. He dabbed them with fresh toilet tissue. A thin, round waste receptacle overflowed with refuse. He dropped the soiled paper into the toilet and stepped on the flusher.

Returning to his seat, he took a deep breath. The child now occupied Harv's place by the window. The conductor rushed over. "Sir, your ticket, or I will ask you to deboard at the next stop."

Harv reached into his jacket's inside pocket and produced his boarding pass. To the boy's father, he said, "My good man, would you tell your son to allow me to return to my rightful seat?"

Strained wrinkles in the man's forehead suggested he'd been tasked with disproving Newton's law of gravitation. "Many apologies." Sincerity evaded his tone. "I see nothing indicating assigned seats."

"Yes, true." Harv could not present a logical retort and, in times of lighter stress, he might have congratulated the man for conjuring such a simple, effective argument. "In the spirit of the holiday, perhaps we could amend that my having been in this seat before your family arrived grants me the right to claim it as my own."

The conductor shook his head. "There are no reserved seats in second class." He tore Harv's ticket and gave him the stub.

"Thank you." Harv offered a circus grin intended to burrow under the conductor's nerves. He turned to confront the father and stumbled forward as the train squealed to a halt. He lost his balance and collapsed, hitting his head on an armrest as his body crashed to the floor. The carpet stank. Urine. Dirt. Dust. A hint of dried feces. His editorial grew from one to two columns as he imagined the verbal flogging he'd administer to the Milby family. His father would have instructed them to explore the woods for a switch as thick as his wrist. He rolled over, expecting a ring of concerned faces peering down at him. He saw only the ornate, wood-carved ceiling, its worn lacquer, and spiderwebs filling the crevices. He grabbed a bench on each side of the aisle and pulled himself to a sitting position.

Objects wide as human fingers thrust into his ankle. He shot a glance in the direction of his feet, expecting to admonish a groping stranger. The door to the cabin swung open and the conductor returned. "We've run into a bit of a snowbank," he said. "We only have two shovels on board, so it will take some time to dig our way out."

Flakes big as playing cards crashed into all sides of the train. Beneath the passengers' panicked chatter, wind howled like a spree killer whistling in an alley. Harv gripped the unraveling fabric on the bench

to his right. Once standing, the pain in his ankle mimicked a woman's manicured nails driving into his flesh. Though he would never admit it to another human being, he'd once paid a professional at a bordello in Gary for *precisely* such an experience. "Pete's sake!" He bent over and lifted his pants leg. He tumbled to the floor again, unable to breathe.

Either the insect he'd drowned in the washroom had grown as broad as one of his wingtips and returned for a third course, or it had a much bigger cousin employed in revenge. The grotesque, barbed pincers each resembled a blacksmith's drawing knife. He drew a tissue from his pocket, covered his palm, and smacked the side of what he assumed was the creature's head. The pincers angled toward his knee and sliced below the joint.

Several passengers noticed the struggle. A few screamed. The father of the brat said, "Conductor!"

Harv yanked on the pincers until the bug released his kneecap and swung in the direction of his fingers. "Blast!" With the help of strangers, he stood, resting his weight on his unmolested foot. The conductor weaved through the crowd. His eyes traveled downward, no doubt prompted by the stares of everyone else.

"Good Lord." The conductor encouraged passengers to return to their seats. "We're clearing the tracks as fast as possible. Sit tight." He allowed Harv to put an arm over his shoulder and provided balance as he led him, Harv hopping on one foot, toward the gangway connection between second and first class. "One moment." He opened the wooden door leading outside. "We'll just dispose of the rascal right here." The conductor guided him onto the metal platform and encouraged him to lean against him as he forced Harv's foot over the side. He kicked the beast into the darkness. It twirled into a bank of snow walling in the train. The jolt to the creature separated it from its pincers, leaving them in Harv's shin. Without using gloves or even tissue to protect his hands, the conductor tore the orphaned pincers from Harv's flesh. More blood. Gashes round as silver dollars. Harv wanted to pass out. His eyes searched the snow for the bug. The conductor must have seen what he had at the very same time:

"My word..."

A slit near the tip of the creature's head opened and closed, drinking the snow. With each gulp, its body grew. Its mutilated pincers regenerated. The thing would be as large as a man in minutes. The conductor pushed Harv back into second class. "I must warn the men in front of the train." He locked the door to the car from the outside and disappeared into a throng of wealthier commuters.

Gritting his teeth, doing his best to look tough for his absent father, Harv limped to the window closest to where he'd last seen the bug. Shadows shifted as the creature, now the size of a Packard automobile, climbed to the top of the car. A hollow thud quieted the passengers, Harv included, as the creature penetrated the ceiling. The flimsy, unkempt material tumbled to the floor as the pincers, now javelins, poked in-

to the crowd of people, feeling their terrified faces and shoving them aside. Harv saw his father in the brisk air. The same age he always pictured the old man, plucking his thumbs at the straps on his faded overalls. He started for the door on the other side, the door leading to the caboose. He recalled the one time he'd opted to prank his father and bring home a twig thinner than the tooth on a fork. His father wrapped his fingers around his collar and dragged him through the forest until he found a switch a civil human being would call a log.

"If you don't own up to your foibles," his father said, "your foibles will own you." He beat Harv's backside until the exaggerated switch split. Harv did not walk upright for three weeks. As he struggled to turn the knob on the door, he heard the ceiling collapse and the other passengers scream in symphonic terror. He stopped fidgeting with the door and turned around.

That is where the story ended for Harv Wallender. Aside from myself, the fractured, four-car train on the old Francis farm remains the only witness. Scholars insist the incident never happened. The train simply stalled in the snow. The passengers were rescued, and the Milby family, destitute following lawsuits, never recovered their damaged property. No rationalization, however, accounts for the oval hole in the ceiling of the second-class car, or the pole-sized punctures in its floor.

Alec Cizak is a writer and filmmaker from Indiana. A collection of his weird fiction, Lake County Incidents, *is available from ABC Group Documentation. He is also the editor of the fiction and pop culture digest,* Pulp Modern.

My Name is John Carter (Part 13)

By JAMES HUTCHINGS

Though my reason suggests that my lesion was
    dressed
and my body brought in from the field,
I can't say I could sense these, or any, events
till I woke with my wound fully healed.

There was no one to ask how much time had gone
    past,
though for that I was pretty damn grateful.
When a man has been killed then his head should
    be still,
and the thought of my captors was hateful.

That those things must have touched me was al-
    most too much
to endure. My skin was acrawl
when that thought was deferred, for I suddenly
    heard
harsh commands coming out of the wall.

I was threatened with doom should I damage my
    room
or give credence to hopes of escape.
It was utterly plain that it felt a disdain
great as that of a man for an ape.

Were I docile, it said, I would find myself fed
And—this seemed its assumption—contented,
and I struggled to hide the red fury inside
till my rage could be gainfully vented.

Sleep would fill me with dread, for that foul, sev-
    ered head
laughed and bit me in dreams without number.
There was naught that was new. Hair and nails
    never grew.
I suppose they were cut as I slumbered.

I could sit. I could brood. Now and then, there was
    food.
Though I found not a trace of a portal,
still, it always appeared. I feared madness. I feared
that my captors had made me immortal.

Or perhaps I was wrong, and that gold-girded
    throng
had not taken me captive but killed me.
I believed I was damned and with that was un-
    manned,
and a frenzied hysteria filled me.

Yearning not to exist, I bit down on my wrist,
gnawing hard till the skin split and bled.
I was dragged into sleep, artificial and deep,
and woke healed, and all sanity fled.

So I howled like a bear who is caught in a snare—
with no hope and no purpose or plan.
I continued to shriek till my voice grew too weak,
and I drooled, more a beast than a man.

MY NAME IS JOHN CARTER

I forgot how to stand, put my face in my hands,
and I lay on the floor of my cell.
It was pleasantly cool—and I wiped off my drool,
for I knew I could not be in Hell.

\---

Seal him up in that room, and the dullest buffoon
would turn madman or studious learner.
My abductor, I found, could detect any sound
that I made, to the softest of murmurs.

For to whisper a threat of self-harm was to set
myself sinking in sickening slumber,
yet they seemed to be blind: the same purpose, if
    mimed
and not spoke, never carried me under.

So in silence sequestered, I carefully tested
each inch of the walls of my prison.
If a weakness existed, I guess that I missed it.
It seemed water-tight to my vision.

Bleak despair had retreated, but far from defeated,
it rallied anew with my failure.
Still I clung to a phrase that kept courage ablaze:
There are jails without flaw, but no jailors.

Thus I fixed my mind's eye on the question of why
I was held here, a thing unexplained,
for there seemed little sense in the time and expense
they had taken, with naught to be gained.

A policeman would question, a priest seek confes-
    sion,
a bully would batter me bloody,
but this hermitish Hell had a scholarly smell:
was I held as an object of study?

And if that were my job, then how easy to rob
my oppressors of what I provided:
if the actor says "No," that's an end to the show.
And with that, my approach was decided.

"End your silence," I said, counted down in my
    head
from a dozen, repeated my order
then began a fresh count of the selfsame amount
and again bid my unrevealed warder

end his silence—and so on, determined to go on
till death or my captor's reply,
either one an improvement on living entombment,
sealed off from the earth and the sky.

\---

Was it thousands or less? I will not try to guess
at how often I spoke, and no matter:
in a hundred or so, time refuses to flow,
and the past and the future are shattered.

When two mirrors oppose one another, each shows
naught but mirrors, in infinite number,
and who stands in between them will thereby have
    seen
themselves too made unending, and wondered—

if they looked for too long—if that light-painted
    throng
might not be something more than illusion.
Might they always be real and the mirror reveal,
not deceive, and the self be profusion?

Or at least that was my way of thinking when I,
as a child, found myself thus positioned.
I suppose Momma called or the novelty palled,
and forgetting my strange intuition,

I lived on till, marooned upon distant Barsoom,
seeking speech from a monstrous captor,
with a mind now unmoored, slowly drifting toward
what, perhaps, was my life's final chapter,

I remembered that sight, as a drowning man might
grab at aught of the wreckage around him.
If he finds naught but dross, then he suffers no loss:
disappointment adds nothing to drowning.

True or false, this, I think, was what kept me from
    sinking
in final defeat and despair,
for an infinite horde of John Carter seemed poured
in one vessel, my body, and there

all our vigor combined, so my body and mind
felt as keen as a new-sharpened saber,
and the wounds of my woes were as fast-melting
    snows
and repeating my order, no labor.

I felt ready to meet all Barsoom, and to beat 'em
and Phobos and Deimos beside.
I suppose it was plain that I wouldn't be tamed,
for the voice of my captors replied.

I could not help but hear that inhumanly clear—
that impossibly clarion tone—
yet my overwrought brain lacked the means to re-
    tain
any word, and like rain from a stone

they are gone. Yet a door opened up, where before
there was naught but a wall of my jail,
and the voice bid me go, and I heeded my foe,
all alert for some hidden betrayal.

It would make me a liar to claim a desire
to meet with more monstrous fighters,
but the way the voice sent me was, thank the Lord,
    empty,
which rendered my mood somewhat lighter.

I had always assumed that the voice in my room
had come out of some hidden device,
but the voice was still there, coming out of the air,
cold and clear as a dagger of ice,

and it served me as guide till my path led outside—
and what glory to stand in the Sun!
To again feel its heat was as wine strong and sweet
after ten thousand battles hard-won.

*James Hutchings lives in Melbourne, Aus-
tralia. The nostalgia of things unknown, of
lands forgotten or unfound, is upon him at
times.*

365 INFANTRY

SHARP-CLAWED
SCI-FI, RUNNING ON THE REDLINE
JOIN THE FORCE AT:
365INFANTRY.SUBSTACK.COM

Notes From the Nest

Wow, it has been a stupid busy summer for Cirsova Publishing! By the time you're reading this, we will have already finished our readings for 2023 [hopefully], but at the time I'm writing this, it's still looming on the horizon like a tsunami.

We've done three successful Kickstarters over the course of 2022 so far: Wild Stars V, Mongoose and Meerkat 2, and An Atlas of Bad Roads. Unless disaster struck, Wild Stars has completely fulfilled, and if future me (past me, by the time you're reading this) hasn't let us all down, Mongoose and Meerkat and An Atlas of Bad Roads are both in the process of being shipped out, maybe even already out the door! I *did* upload the files for M&M and Atlas the very night I wrote this column... So, you ought to be able to pre-order those if you missed the Kickstarters, and you ought to be able to actually buy Wild Stars V by now.

We've also started the process of getting the rest of Wild Stars back on Amazon for everyone who'd rather buy there instead of from Lulu (boo!), but the Omnibus is still Lulu-only.

As you may have noticed, we've brought on a guest artist for Mongoose and Meerkat, Raven Monroe, who did both the Fall 2021 cover and colors for the Wild Stars virgin variant. [Our main M&M artist is on a sabbatical.] You may have already seen some of her work in M&M volume 2!

Next issue will feature the return of Usanekorin doing both cover and interior illos for John Daker's Sister Winter and Mike Ray's Take the Sword.

Of course, it will also include the conclusions of Wild Stars VI: Orphan of the Shadowy Moons and Vran, the Chaos-Warped.

We've also entered the final arc of Jim Breyfogle's Mongoose and Meerkat—you may have noticed the story in this issue was a bit different: the typical picaresque adventuring is over, mysteries have been revealed, and fight for Alness will soon be underway!

I also promised to mention that David Skinner's story, The Impossible Footprint, takes place in Nictzin Dyalhis's science fiction universe—if you enjoyed it, DMR Books has an anthology of all of Nictzin Dyalhis's Hul Jok stories called The Sapphire Goddess. Check it out!

I don't know what else I'm supposed to tell you to buy... Support our advertisers, of course. Buy all of our playsets and toys!

Thanks for sticking with us through 25 issues! [Oh, right, this was our 25th issue! It's hard to tell because of our numbering, 10 issues in volume 1, 3 specials, and now 12 issues of volume 2.] Lucky 13 (26?!) is next!

P. Alexander

www.ingramcontent.com/pod-product-compliance
Lightning Source LLC
Chambersburg PA
CBHW080815250626
47159CB00010B/3391